New Orleans Confidential

O'Neil De Noux

Introduction by James Sallis

New Orleans Confidential

O'Neil De Noux

for Dana

Too Wise – 2009 DERRINGER Award for **BEST NOVELETTE**
> first published in *Ellery Queen Mystery Magazine*, Vol. 132, No. 5, November 2008

St. Expedite
> first published in *Hemispheres: In-flight Magazine of United Airlines*, September 2000

The Iberville Mistress
> first published in *Flesh & Blood: Guilty as Sin* Anthology, Mysterious Press, 2003

Erotophobia
> first published in *Kiss and Kill: Hot Blood 8* Anthology, Pocket Books, 1997

Friscoville
> first published as "The Problem on Friscoville Avenue" in *Hemispheres: In-flight Magazine of United Airlines*, April 1999

Lair of the Red Witch
> first published in *The Mammoth Book of Short Erotic Novels* Anthology, Carroll & Graf (U.S.) and Robinson Publishing (U.K.), January 2000

The Heart Has Reasons – 2007 SHAMUS Award for **BEST SHORT STORY**
> first published in *Alfred Hitchcock Mystery Magazine*, Vol. 51, No. 9, September 2006

Hard Rain
> first published in *Pontalba Press Presents: Short Stories, Vol. 1*, 1999

Expect Consequences
> first published in *Fedora 2* Anthology, Betancourt & Co., September 2003

Published by:
Big Kiss Productions
New Orleans and Covington, LA

Introduction

What we do as writers, paradoxically, is attempt at one and the same time to summon up the whole of experience, to limn the world at full tilt, and to render some small portion of this world with such specificity that, walking past, the reader feels the grit of it catching in the soles of shoes. It's impossible, of course; we know that. Just as it is impossible to make characters come alive on the page with only pale ghosts of words as tools. But we plod on, one eye crossed to the tip of our nose, other aimed to the stars, meanwhile falling, like Aristophanes's caricature of Socrates, into every pothole. And while it's true that we may be smarter when actually writing than at any other time, that's not saying a lot. We don't know any more of the world, its people and its ways than you do. We're just better at making up lies.

O'Neil De Noux tells marvelous, compelling lies adrench with the presence and personality of a very particular place. Even in the work he sets in contemporary time, there's a strong feel for the history of this unique, ever-surprising city; in *New Orleans Confidential*, with stories set in the late Forties, that sense of history becomes paramount.

When we moved to New Orleans some years back, Karyn looked up one day to say, "We've left the United States behind." I realized in a flash how right she was. We were on an island that had floated free of the mainland, a fourth-world republic that, having been re- leased on its own cognizance, kept to an intensely personal pace and style and remained, through all its massive changes – of colonization, ownership, character, upsurge and decay – oddly changeless. I have lived there five times. The accents shift, sounds get slurred or clipped, but the city still speaks the same language it did when I was seventeen.

So: New Orleans, forever a fascinating place, and the Forties, a particularly fascinating time.

America had begun in the past decade to transform itself from a rural to an urban society. During the war years, vast population shifts occurred as men departed for training camps and civilians moved to industrial-defense centers like Los Angeles, Baltimore and Chicago. Guys were coming back from the war with their first intimations of how huge and unmanageable the world might be – coming back to the northeast with a taste for hillbilly music learned from barracks mates, coming back to the hills and hollows of Virginia with the sound of swing in their heads. Driven by war- generated prosperity, bolstered by newspapers, movies and radio, the great homogenization had begun.

It's no mere circumstance that the American detective novel developed simultaneously with this transformation from rural to urban. Writers such as the Black Mask group, Hammett and Chandler – interestingly enough, those who relocated America's eternal frontier myth in the person of the detective – were the first to look closely at our cities: how we made them, and what they are making us. Crime fiction remains the urban fiction.

O'Neil De Noux pays homage here to that time of transition, and to those early, seminal stories. This is a bit like playing baroque music on period instruments, or re-creating the sound of Forties Hawaiian ensembles. Never mind the awesome skill it takes, or the difficulties encountered: one does it from sheer love.

No other city so enshrines the contradictions upon which our society is based as does New Orleans. The city is a stew of French, Spanish, Caribbean, Creole, Indian, African-American, Irish – and yet oddly, purely American. Proud of its rich intellectual heritage, it is vibrantly sensual, a place of strong appetites and strange appeasements. Great wealth and astonishing poverty exist side by side; driving to the opera, you pass through some of the city's worst areas, which for blocks at the time resemble bombed-out rubble. One can still stand and look across the river to Algiers, from whose pens slaves were brought to be sold on French Quarter auction blocks. When Karyn and I lived there, the city had become the nation's murder capital, averaging a homicide a day. Yet it was, and remains, the easiest, friendliest city we'd ever known. In many ways it feels like a small town circa 1950.

I admire O'Neil's work tremendously. No one writes New Orleans as well as he does. No one else ever gets the mix just right, the grime and glory, the shine and shame – as he, to all appearances effortlessly, does. André Gide once likened the detective's search for truth to a man hunting out a black hat in a pitch black room. As writers, we're the same. O'Neil finds that damned hat every time. Then he slaps it on his head and goes walking jauntily down Esplanade.

If we're much of anything as writers, we are witnesses. It's our job to save the reader from dailyness, from all the assumptions and inattentions that weigh us down, to say: This is how the world looks, this is what it seems to be. O'Neil De Noux takes that job seriously. He is a great witness and a fine writer. He can help us save ourselves.

James Sallis • Phoenix, 2005

New Orleans Confidential

Second Edition 2010

Come prowl the lonely, sometimes violent streets of American's most exotic city, the city that care forgot, New Orleans, with a lone-wolf private-eye named Lucien Caye.

Unlike most Forties P.I.s, Caye rarely drinks, doesn't smoke or wear a hat (it messes up his hair). He's six feet tall with wavy, dark brown hair and standard-issue Mediterranean-brown eyes, a sly smile and a clever mind that often gets him into trouble. Caye lives and works in the run-down New Orleans French

Quarter of the late 1940s.

He has a weakness for women, children and fellow World War II veterans, down on their luck. He knows how to make a decent living but often finds himself working pro-bono – in one case working to find a little girl's missing cat, in another searching for a boy's runaway father and in yet another, canvassing the Quarter for the child who wrote a note to Santa Claus, asking Santa to take him to live with the angels so his mother and father didn't have to buy food for him anymore. They don't have any money.

Born in New Orleans of French and Spanish descent, Caye attended Holy Cross High School before working as a copy boy, then cub reporter for *The New Orleans Item*. A stint as a crime reporter drew Caye to law enforcement and he joined the New Orleans Police Department in 1939 where he was a patrol officer working uptown until December 7, 1941.

Caye joined the U.S. Army serving in North Africa, Sicily and the subsequent Italian campaign at Anzio and Salerno. At the Battle of Monte Cassino, Caye met and befriended journalist Ernie Pyle during the bitter stalemate. Leading an assault on the infamous monastery, Caye was seriously wounded by a German sniper and sent home with a Purple Heart medal and a Silver Star for bravery.

After the war, he returned to the police department, working the French Quarter beat until deciding he preferred working alone and set up shop in 1947 in an apartment building at the corner of Barracks and Dauphine Streets, not far from the fictional residence of Tennessee Williams' Stanley Kowalski. Living upstairs, Caye's office faces Barracks Street and the small Cabrini Playground across the narrow street where he usually parks his pre-war, 1940 two-door DeSoto coach.

Women float in and out of Caye's life, like the alluring brunette who wants him to bodyguard her while she poses for sexy pictures and the long, tall blonde seeking to discover the secret of the 'red witch' living down the street from Caye, a woman calling herself a love sorceress. Murder is often the name of the game and Caye sometimes leaves town, usually aiding a pretty woman in need of help, in more ways than one. Unfortunately, the truth is often ugly, often dangerous and usually resides on the loneliest part of town.

Two of the stories in this collection have appeared in *Hemispheres: In-flight Magazine of United Airlines* (worldwide distribution). Others have appeared in *The Mammoth Book of Short Erotic Novels* (edited by Maxim Jakubowski, simultaneously published in England by Robinson Publishing and in the U.S. by Carroll and Graf); *Kiss and Kill* (Hot Blood 8 Anthology, Pocket Books); *Pontalba Press Presents Short Stories, Vol. 1* (Pontalba Press, New Orleans); *The Mammoth Book of New Erotica* (edited by Maxim Jakubowski, simultaneously published in England by Robinson Publishing and in the U.S. by Carroll and Graf) and *Flesh and Blood: Guilty as Sin* (Max Allan Collins and Jeff Gelb, Mysterious Press).

This Second Edition includes two award winning stories. "The Heart Has Reasons" won the Private Eye Writers of America's prestigious **SHAMUS AWARD** for BEST SHORT STORY. The **SHAMUS** is given annually to recognize outstanding achievement in private eye fiction. The Short Mystery Fiction Society awarded the **DERRINGER AWARD** for BEST NOVELETTE to another Lucien Caye story, "Too Wise." The **DERRINGER** is given annually to recognize excellence in the mystery short form.

Set between 1947 and 1950, the stories sometimes reflect the political incorrectness of that era. African-Americans were called "Negroes" then and women were often seen as dames. Some of the stories are properly hardboiled, while some are gentle enough for in-flight magazines.

Hope you enjoy this stroll along the wild side of New Orleans.

CONTENTS

Too Wise

Friday, February 14, 1947

It was a kiss with promise behind it, as much promise as a good girl would give, enough to make my heart race as we stood under the yellow bulb on her front gallery, Annette's lips pressed against mine for long, scintillating seconds before she pulled away. Her blue eyes seemed to shine as she smiled, disentangled herself from my arms and went inside. I glanced at my watch and she'd made it in by midnight, two minutes to spare.

I took in a deep breath of cool February air, shoved my hands into the pockets of my brown suit coat and backed down the steps to the sidewalk, which we call banquettes here in New Orleans. I watched lights go on in the narrow shotgun house where Annette Bayly lived with her parents. Turning to my left, I headed home. The faint echo of the band at the Knights of Columbus Hall echoed across Washington Square and I looked through the wrought iron fence toward the hall where I'd met Annette four hours ago at the Valentine's Dance.

She'd come with a friend, Annette in a dark blue sweater, tight black skirt, strawberry blonde hair hanging in long curls past her shoulders. I spotted her immediately but waited to ask her to dance. When she finished dancing with a stiff who danced like an awkward ostrich, I eased up and asked for the next dance. It was a slow one and she felt so nice in my arms. Except for a pushy blond guy with a familiar face I couldn't place, who cut in three times, we danced every dance.

While Annette politely put up with the pushy guy, I got us Cokes and ran into an old buddy. I hadn't seen Len Connelly, starting guard on our city champion Holy Cross Tigers football team, since before the war. He looked flushed, out of shape in a rumpled pre-war gray suit. He still stood a good two inches taller than my six feet, but had put on weight, well over two-fifty now. He had called me by my high school nickname, 'Rocket', before hurrying off to dance with a chesty brunette.

I crossed Frenchmen Street, heading for my new digs in the lower French Quarter. A couple cars eased along Dauphine but I was the only pedestrian, which suited me fine. I lifted my belt, felt the reassuring weight of my .38 Smith and Wesson, tucked neatly in its leather holster at the small of my back.

"What's this?" Annette had asked when she'd felt it.

I told her I was a private detective and she laughed. It took a few seconds for her to realize I was serious. "That's good, actually. Better than you carrying a gun because you were a hood."

She told me she was five-nine, stood over five-ten in those heels, her slim body pressed against mine. She wasn't top-heavy but I felt them up against me and she filled out her sweater very neatly. Annette said she was twenty-one and I guess the word 'vivacious' described her, full of personality beyond her good looks. I remember my twenty-first year, heading to the police academy then riding in a prowl car in that sweet NOPD uniform. That was all before Pearl Harbor, before I joined the rangers and saw the world, North Africa, Sicily, then Italy where a German sniper put an end to my military career.

A long, sad moan from a ship's horn echoed from the river, six blocks away. At Esplanade Avenue, I spotted two scummy-looking guys standing beneath one of the oaks on the neutral ground – a median in any other city. They eye-balled me but didn't make a move as I eye-balled them back. Maybe I still walked like a cop. I crossed into the Quarter, which was getting worse all the time. When I was a kid, few of the buildings were crumbling. Since the war, the lower Quarter was filled with day workers, Bourbon Street regulars, mobbed-up dock workers and guys like me – someone who needed inexpensive digs to start up a low-scale business.

No sense wasting time, I'd call Annette later today, ask her out. Why waste a Saturday night? Why be coy? We liked each other and Annette wasn't the kinda girl who played games. She looked me right in the eye, didn't flit around, playing flirty games or hard to get.

At Barracks Street I hung a right and dug the keys out of my pocket. My building's double-door faced Barracks and Cabrini Playground across the narrow street. I went in, making sure the door locked behind me, then opened my office door, flipped on the lights and just glanced inside. I'd been in business two weeks exactly, working on my first case – an insurance fraud case.

The hardwood floor still looked polished and my beat-up mahogany desk looked better in dim light. I locked the door and went upstairs to my apartment, directly above the office at 909 Barracks Street. I went in, crossed to the French doors which opened to the balcony wrapping around the building's corner and let in some brisk air before going to bed. I needed an early start in the morning.

I tried not to think of Annette's sleek legs and the faint outline of her brassiere against her sweater, tried not to think of those full lips and the lines of her pretty face, the sweet smell of her hair as we danced, cheek to cheek. I thought instead of those bright eyes and the way she talked with me, without a hint of pretension, without the typical man-woman banter, no beating around the bush. Annette was as bright as she was pretty and I liked that in a woman.

Like the way she explained her nickname – Too Wise. You see, her last name had two 'y's and not a single 'i' or 'e', as the standard spelling of Bailey. Calling her Two-Ys changed to Too Wise in school, as she was always a wise guy in class, too wise for her age, claimed the nuns. Hell, when I played wise guy in grammar school, the nuns took a ruler to my knuckles.

"Bayly's Scottish," she said.

I quipped, "And I thought you were Irish."

She put her hands behind her back and leaned forward, jaw jutting. "And what are you, Mr. Lucien Caye?"

"Half French, half Spanish. A real half-breed."

I felt a stirring in my loins as I rolled over in bed and switched to thinking about Len Connelly, replaying the city championship game against Jesuit. I remember the rain came just as the second half started, the score tied 7-7. I'd scored our touchdown on a five-yard scamper around the right side, Len leading the way, bowling over the outside linebacker. I darted into the end zone.

It seemed every time we got the ball, the rain increased. When the Blue Jays got it, it seemed to slacken, enough for Jesuit to boot a twenty yard field goal as the third quarter ended. It got real sloppy then. Both quarterbacks fumbled snaps from center, receivers dropped passes, punts were shanked. Len's knee was killing him. With a minute remaining we were backed up on our twenty yard line, rain pelting our helmets so hard we could barely hear the play calls in the huddle. The Blue Jays were bouncing in place, anticipating the championship. Our quarterback called two plays. A slant off right guard, Len's position. Then a fake off left tackle and a long pass.

We never got to the second play. I took the handoff deeper than usual and hit the crease, accelerating in the mud. Len trapped two linebackers with one block and I cut back, sending another linebacker sliding into the safety and the field was open in front of me. I hit the afterburners and used my 100-yard dash track speed all the way to the end zone, two Blue Jays right on my tail but never able to catch me.

Didn't hear the crowd noise until I turned around and suddenly the rain hammering my helmet faded with the roar of the Holy Cross fans, all drenched, all standing, all screaming. Holy Cross Tigers 14, Jesuit Blue Jays 10. Len Connelly lay flat on his back at our twenty-five yard line. He need two operations to be able to graduate without crutches.

•

Saturday, February 15, 1947

I left before six a.m., wanting to set up on my prey before anyone got up in his neighborhood. Herb Moity was forty-two, stood five-five, weighed close to three hundred pounds. Balding and unmarried, Moity lived on the left side of a shotgun double on Port Street, Bywater. His parents lived on the other side. He'd slipped and fell at work and was permanently disabled. Oxford Insurance Company had a problem with Mr. Moity. This was the third time he'd been 'permanently disabled', hitting up Farmers Insurance and Delta Insurance along the way. The man brought home an easy twelve thousand a year in settlement money, with more to come from Oxford.

I had two problems. The first I'd solved when I found an alley between an abandoned house and Nick's Barroom to be able to sit in my pre-war 1940 DeSoto Coach, ready to photograph Moity if he did anything physical around the house, ready to follow him if he left in his baby blue 1947 Chrysler 4-door sedan. Being gray, my DeSoto was better for surveillances. The second problem – Herb Moity was a fat, lazy slob, not likely to do anything physical.

I took Burgundy over to Esplanade then a left on Dauphine on my way to Bywater. Wanted to pass by Annette's, slowing as I crossed Frenchmen Street. It was getting light out and the streetlights still lit up the area well. I spotted someone with a flashlight in Washington Square, turned to look at Annette's house and realized the front door was wide open. I slowed, then looked back at the square again, spotting a man in a suit with flashlight in hand, a man with a cigarette dangling from his mouth. I pulled over and parked, took a couple deep breaths.

Whatever brought Lt. Frenchy Capdeville to Washington Square that early had to be bad. I got out and went through the gate at the Elysian Fields side of the park and approached Frenchy as he stood on the concrete walkway next to some thick bushes. Two uniformed coppers beyond Frenchy noticed me, one calling out, "You can't come in here."

Frenchy looked up, saw me and said, "It's OK." If he wore a cape and mask, Frenchy could pass for Zorro with his black curly hair and pencil-thin moustache. He wore a old dark brown suit, cigarette glowing in his mouth.

I looked back at Annette's open door, seeing a light on somewhere inside, feeling my heart pounding. I stepped up and asked Frenchy, "What happened?"

"Girl got murdered last night."

My knees felt week. *No. It couldn't be.*

"When?"

"Around one a.m. We came back to search the area in daylight. She lived across the street."

I stepped over to one of the black wrought iron benches to sit. I took in another breath and asked, "Her name? It wasn't Annette, was it?"

"Annette Bayly," Frenchy said, the words hitting me like a land mine. I couldn't move.

"What?" I heard Frenchy say as he moved closer. "You knew her?"

I couldn't see anything, as if I'd fallen into a black pit. I put my head down between my knees and tried to breathe. It couldn't be her. Couldn't be. But… if I'd learned anything as a cop, it was death was always possible.

Frenchy's black shoes moved into my line of vision. They needed a shine.

"You knew her?" he asked again.

I sat up and leaned back. "Met her last night at the K. of C. Dance." I pointed across the park. "Walked her home just before midnight." I looked up at Frenchy. "She have strawberry blonde hair?"

He nodded. "Wore a blue sweater, black skirt."

"What the hell happened?"

"Her paw says she was all excited when she got home, talking up a storm, realized she'd left her purse at the dance and went to get it just before one. They found her when she didn't come right back."

Two other detectives stepped up, Collins and Francona. I watched them search around the bushes. I could see now, in the morning light, branches were broken on the bushes.

"Three buttons were missing from her skirt," Frenchy said for my benefit. I remembered Annette's skirt had buttons down the front. "We found one up here on the walkway." Frenchy flipped off his flashlight. "See the dirt under the bushes? Red clay. Musta been put in by the parks department 'cause it ain't native to New Orleans, that's for sure."

I watched Francona collect some of the dirt into an envelope. Frenchy fired up a fresh cigarette just as a scream echoed from across the street. A girl I recognized as Annette's friend stood out on her gallery with her hand raised, finger pointing right at me. "That's him! That's him!" she screeched. "That's the one took her home last night!" She crossed the street to the fence. "He's the one smooching with her!"

A large man came out on the gallery, followed by a small woman with strawberry blonde hair. The man hurried across Dauphine to the fence. Frenchy went over and talked with him. The big man, who I took for Annette's father, shouted, "He was probably waiting outside for her!"

I got up and eased toward them, watched Frenchy flip away his cigarette and take out his note pad. He asked, "What about this other guy you mentioned?"

The girl stared at me with such anger in her eyes. "The masher?" she said. "He was pushy, but him… " She pointed at me again. "He's the one took her home."

New Orleans Confidential · O'Neil De Noux   **17**

Frenchy glanced back at me for a second before reading from his notebook. "This masher, you said he was about six feet, blond hair, small moustache, little white scar on his chin, right?"

"Yes." She still glared at me.

"He wore tan linen slacks with cuffs, white shirt, brown jacket and had a gold Bulova watch?"

"Yes."

French nodded back to me. "This the guy you said wore the brown suit?"

She described my clothes to a tee, the brown suit, white shirt, beige tie with geometric designs, down to my brown and white Florsheim shoes.

Annette's father reached a fist through the fence and snarled, "The killer always comes back to the scene of the crime!" The man read too many detective novels.

Frenchy fired up another cigarette, gave me the same look my old man used to give me when I'd disappointed him and said, "You need to come with us."

I nodded, lifted my coat and turned my .38 toward him. "You better take this."

"He's a cop!" said Annette's father.

"Private Eye," Frenchy said as he took my .38 and slipped it into his coat pocket. Francona tapped my shoulder and I went with him, across the park to Royal Street where their prowl cars were parked, directly across from the K. of C. Hall. As Francona unlocked one of the cars, I spotted Len Connelly standing beneath the awning of the hall. He lifted a hand and hesitantly waved to me.

"Who's that?" Francona asked.

"Guy I know. You need to talk with him. He was at the dance too."

•

I'd been in the tiny interrogation rooms in the Detective Bureau before, but for only brief intervals. I'd never been left inside one to fester for hours until that morning. Never realized it smelled that badly, reeking of stale cigarette smoke, body odor and ammonia, probably from urine. It looked clean, however. They must wipe it down, but the pungent scents remained. There was no window, only four blank walls painted light green, a small gray metal desk and two hardback chairs.

Right after they put me inside, Frenchy came in with a consent search form for me to sign. "Better get two," I said. "My car's parked next to Washington Square." I pulled out my keys for him. He knew my apartment and office. I wanted him to search it, search for the missing buttons, for branches broken from the bushes, for that odd red clay.

"Suit I wore last night is in the closet," I told Frenchy as I signed the consent search forms. "Lighter of the two brown ones. Tie's in there too, shoes on the floor. Only brown and whites ones I have. Shirt, undershirt and jockeys are in the dirty clothes hamper."

Passing him the forms and the keys, I asked, "You're not going to let Hays in there, are you?"

I'd spotted Jimmy Hays in the squad room. A squat man with stubby arms, hair cut like Moe Howard, Hays worked with me at the Third Precinct before the war. He'd shot a dog that had knocked over the garbage can outside the precinct house one night. I knocked him out with one punch to his glass jaw. He never liked me much after that.

"I'm taking Francona."

"Thanks."

I tried leaning one of the chairs against the wall, closed my eyes, trying to think of a beach or the Rocky Mountains, anything to escape, but I kept seeing Annette's face smiling at me after we'd kissed. The coffee I drank that morning churned in my belly and tried to work its way back up my esophagus. It didn't occur to me to worry that I was a suspect, not really. The fact that I'd never see Annette again was enough to fill my heart with a sharp pain, fill my brain with images from the dance. Obviously, the 'masher' was the pushy guy who'd cut in. I still couldn't place his face, but I'd seen it before. I started thinking like a detective, wondering who could have done this, instead of focusing on the loss of such beauty.

I'd just glanced at my watch again, seeing it was almost ten-thirty, when Frenchy came in and placed my gun on the tiny desk. "I had to go through the motions. You have an alibi witness, to boot."

"I do?"

"Sergeant V. M. Clortho."

"Clortho? He can't stand me." Another one of my fans, Clortho was the laziest cop I'd ever worked with. I told him that once at roll call, which got the whole platoon roaring as I gave Clortho his nickname – Slowdown. Like Hays, he never forgave me.

Frenchy lit up another cigarette and sat across from me. "Slowdown was outside your building just now, shooting off his mouth about you. He was on the beat last night. Saw you kiss the girl and walk home. He tagged behind you in his prowl car, said you were all moonstruck. Waited for you to fall off the curb, but you weren't drunk enough. Saw you go in your building. He parked next to Cabrini Playground and caught up on his reports. I asked how long he was there. He said a good hour, hour and a half and you didn't come back out. That's an alibi witness, best when it's someone who don't like you."

I picked up my keys, tucked the .38 back in its holster and stood up. "So what now?"

Frenchy said they were going back to the K. of C. Hall, see if they could locate this 'masher' and anyone else who was there, see if any neighbors saw anything in the park last night.

"You." He tapped my chest with an index finger. "Don't go anywhere near there. We already drove you car home."

I spotted Francona in the squad room and asked him what Len Connelly had said.

"Said he saw you leave with the girl. I asked about the 'masher' and he saw the guy leave too, about the same time and none of y'all came back inside."

Frenchy gave me a wary look. "Don't go back around there. Let us handle this."

I told him OK, but we both knew better.

·

I thought about trying my luck with the wonderful Mr. Herb Moity that afternoon, anything to get my mind off the fact Annette was lying in the parish morgue. But the rain came in just as I was about to leave, and if I didn't know better, it looked like a hurricane. The huge branches of the live oaks in Cabrini Playground bounced in the wind as rain hammered my building. The thick black branches of the magnolias seemed to bend precariously in the storm.

I watched through my office windows, spotting a man running along the banquette and stopping outside my building then ringing my office doorbell. I hit the buzzer and went to see who I'd let in. Len Connelly pulled the coat off his soaked head and smiled weakly at me. "You got something to drink, Rocket?"

I'd picked up a coat rack at a used furniture store and draped the soaking coat over it as Len went and plopped in one the chairs in front of my beat-up mahogany desk. I went over to the kitchen area, calling back, "Scotch, Bourbon or Irish?

Len opted for Bourbon, neat. I reached into the small refrigerator for a beer, not wanting to get loaded. My office was once an upholstery shop, so most of the interior walls had been removed, leaving the kitchen and bathroom and enough room to play a little touch football without knocking anything over.

I put the bottle of Bourbon and a glass in front of Len and went around to sit in the captain's chair, Len wiping his face with a handkerchief, saying, "Got your number from the operator. You're not in the book."

Not yet. I took a hit of beer as he poured himself a triple.

"Falstaff? They use Mississippi river water with that, don't they?"

"No," I said. "Been to the brewery. They truck in spring water from Abita Springs." When I was a rookie there was a burglary at the Falstaff brewery on So. Broad. Everyone figured it had to be cops, being across the street from police headquarters, only Jefferson Parish deputies caught the perpetrators when their getaway truck broke down on Airline Highway. College students on their way back to LSU. It was a fraternity prank. Morons. Being charged with Revised Statute 14:62, Simple Burglary, wasn't a prank.

Len took a hit of bourbon, let it settle a moment before he focused his dark eyes at me and said, "Why'd you sick the cops on me?" His voice wasn't as friendly.

"You were at the dance."

He nodded, looked at the row of windows facing Barracks Street. "Yeah. I just don't like coppers."

"I used to be one. You've had cop trouble?"

"Naw. I never liked bullies and the dicks, they're just bullies with badges. Like to slap people around."

I couldn't imagine anyone trying to slap Len Connelly around. He took another drink, this one not as heavy, pointed his chin at me and asked, "Why'd they pick you up?"

"I was one of the last people to see her alive."

Len leaned back and looked up at the ceiling. "Man-o-man. She was pretty. I watched y'all dancing and damn, what a tragedy."

It came flooding back, I could almost feel Annette in my arms again. Funny how that worked. I took another hit of icy beer.

New Orleans Confidential • O'Neil De Noux   **22**

"There was a guy there, blond hair, little moustache, about your size. Real pushy with the girls. You see him?"

"Yeah. He cut in a couple times. Annette's friend called him a masher."

"Man, he looked familiar." Len focused his eyes on mine. "And he left the same time as y'all and didn't come back."

"The cops will track him down."

He gave me a pained look. "You're a detective. Find him."

Thunder rolled in over the Quarter, sounding like distant cannon. A bright streak of lightning lit up the dark sky.

"How's the knee?" I asked.

"Goes out now and again." Len refilled his glass. "Kept me out of the army."

Guess he could see that bothered me.

"Hey, I did my duty. Worked for Higgins building landing craft."

Higgins Boat Yard, right over there on the Industrial Canal, built the boats that took the troops ashore at Normandy, Saipan, Iwo Jima, brought me ashore with my fellow rangers in Algeria, Sicily and Anzio.

"Saw in the paper how you came back a hero and all." Len said between hits of Bourbon. "Almost lost an arm, as I recall. Cassino, right?"

I nodded.

"They don't give medals like you got unless you earn them. If I was you, I'd have 'em up on the wall."

My silver star and purple heart were tucked away in a drawer upstairs, next to my police marksman pin and football MVP plaque from Holy Cross.

"Maybe I could help you track down this masher."

Talk about bad ideas. Then I remembered Frenchy's warning and said, "OK, why don't you snoop around the K. of C. and I'll try to figure why the guy looked so familiar."

Len raised his glass just as a bolt of lightning lit up the sky and thunder hit the building like a concussion.

"Damn," said Len.

"Exactly." I drained the beer and went for another.

•

Sunday, February 16, 1947

Herb Moity was even too lazy to go to the Mardi Gras parades. Setting up early, I watched his neighbors pack up their kids and ladders and head for the parade routes. I spotted Moity once around two p.m., when he peeked out his front door. He was shirtless. When it got dark, I drove home, avoiding Washington Square completely.

On the radio that evening they replayed the Mercury Theater production of H. G. Well's *The War of The Worlds* and I turned off all the lights, sat back in my easy chair facing the French doors and my balcony overlooking the playground and let Orson Welles and company take me away from everything for a while.

I'd never heard the broadcast before, didn't even know it had caused a panic across the country back in '38. It hadn't panicked many people in New Orleans. Remember hearing about it after, people saying, "Hell, if the Martians wanted New Jersey, they could have it."

The deep voice of Orson Welles echoed, "We know now that in the early years of the twentieth century this world was being watched closely by intelligences greater than man's, and yet as mortal as his own… "

I closed my eyes and remembered reading that same opening in the book when I was a kid. Can't improve on good writing.

"… across an immense ethereal gulf, minds that are to our minds as ours are to the beasts in the jungle, intellects vast, cool and unsympathetic, regarded this earth with envious eyes and slowly and surely drew their plans against us… "

•

Monday, February 17, 1947

A detective will take luck in any form, whenever it comes.

At eleven-ten a.m., a Sears & Roebuck truck pulled up in front of Herb Moity's shotgun. Two men got out, one knocking on Moity's door, the other opening the back of the truck. I focused my Leica on the door as Moity came out to hold open the screen door for the two men, now wrestling with a huge refrigerator. I figured they'd take it around back because the kitchen in a shotgun house was always at the rear, but these geniuses decided on a frontal attack and promptly got stuck going up the front stoop.

They tried wiggling the refrigerator on the dolly, tried going back down the steps, tried tipping it, almost losing it, before they stopped and scratched their heads. Moity had been shouting instructions, getting red-faced in the process, then let go of the screen door and went to show them how to do it. I got a good shot of him plopping his big butt on the edge of the stoop, bouncing to the ground, a better shot as he went around to put a shoulder against the fridge as the man above pulled on the dolly and the other used his shoulder next to Moity.

They got it up two of the three steps before the man next to Moity jumped up on the porch to hold open the screen door. I got a series of pictures of Herb Moity shouldering the fridge up the final step. The growl of a dog caught my attention as I photographed Moity shoving the appliance through the front door. I looked down and a black mutt was snarling up at me.

I'd brought ham sandwiches, so I unwrapped one and dropped it for the dog who wolfed it down. After, he sat waiting for another. I trained the Leica on the house and waited. When the dog started growling again, I gave him my last sandwich. Fifteen minutes later, the three men lead a rusty fridge back out, back down the front stoop, back into the truck, ole Herb Moity helping all the time. He waved to the men as they pulled away. I waited until Moity went back inside to slip out of the alley, making sure I didn't run over the dog.

I was feeling pretty good for a few minutes, until I approached Elysian Fields and it hit me again – Annette Bayly and that smile, that Too Wise gleam in those blue eyes. The sinking feeling gripped my heart again. OK, I'd just met her, barely knew her, but she was alive, so damn sparkling.

Just as I pulled up in front of my building, Frenchy Capdeville arrived in his prowl car. Flipping his cigarette into the street, he joined me on the banquette and said, "Got something to show you." He wore another rumpled suit, this one dark green, and had his black tie loosened, his dark hair looking disheveled.

I led the way into my office, called back over my shoulder, "Want a 'smile'?"

Frenchy called a beer, a 'smile'. He shook his head and plopped down in the chair Len had used. Funny how most of my visitors sat in the right chair in front my desk, rather than the other. I sat in my captain's chair.

From an inside coat pocket, Frenchy pulled out his notepad and said, "Listen to this. Came in a letter today addressed to the detective in charge of the murder at Washington Square." He cleared his throat before reading, "The girl was a sacrifice. No need to worry until next February 15th." Frenchy looked up at me. "Signed, Brother of the Wolf. There was a return address on the envelope that read, 'Cave of Lupercal'. It was postmarked New Orleans, with today's date."

"Since when you get mail the same day?"

"Somebody at the post office must be trying to impress one of their big shots, I guess." Frenchy put his notebook away.

I shrugged. "What do you make of it?"

"I checked. Whoever wrote it's got education. Lupercalia was a Roman festival celebrated on February 15th, a pagan fertility festival. The Christians countered it with Valentine's Day on February 14th, sort of to trump them a day early."

"Lupercalia? They sacrificed girls?"

"Not according to Doctor Walker, professor over at Loyola. They sacrificed goats and dogs." Frenchy looked at his watch. "Maybe a 'smile' would be all right."

I brought us two Falstaffs and Frenchy went, "Jesus, you gotta start getting Schlitz or Budweiser. They make this stuff with river water."

I didn't correct him. I just sat there thinking about Annette as a *sacrifice.*

●

A detective will take luck in any form, whenever it comes.

Ten minutes after Frenchy pulled away, I went down the block to my cleaners to drop off my blue suit and felt the hair stand up on the back of my neck when the masher from the K. of C. Dance hurried into the cleaners right in front of me. I went in behind him to make sure, the little moustache was neatly trimmed and there was the light scar on his chin. Annette's friend said he wore a gold Bulova and there it was on his left wrist.

When he plopped his bundle of clothes on the counter, I saw the tan linen slacks with cuffs, white shirt, brown jacket he'd worn to the dance. I watched Mr. Juan, owner and operator of Praca's Cleaners, corner Barracks and Burgundy, stuff the masher's clothes in two separate bags, attach tickets to the bags and hand the man his receipts.

I put my blue suit up on the counter and followed the masher outside. No way I could just follow him without being spotted and since he didn't get in a car, he lived nearby like me. What I hadn't expected was for him to wheel about and say, "What's your problem fella?"

"Whaddya mean?"

"Ogling me like you're about to pull a stick up."

I smiled. "Weren't you at the K. of C. Dance Friday night?"

He hesitated a half-second and said, "No. What's it to you, anyway?"

"I saw you there."

He took a step closer. He was about an inch shorter than me, but more solid, a pretty boy with his hands in fists now, set and ready for me and I figured there was only one reason for him to lie about the dance. I slowly raised my left arm to glance at my watch and threw a right cross at his jaw, stepping into it, catching him square, sending him straight down.

I landed with both knees on his chest and he gave out a whoosh of air and whatever fight was left in him went gone with the wind. Yanking him up by the front of his yellow dress shirt, a couple buttons popped off and his receipts went into the gutter. I shoved him against the wall and waited for his eyes to clear. When they did, a minute later, they'd lost their fight.

It wasn't easy lugging him all the way down the street and into my office, plopping him in the popular right chair in front of my desk while I called Frenchy, who stammered, "You did what?"

"You wanna come get him or do I drag him to headquarters?"

I frisked my prisoner, who just sat there with drool running down his chin. Driver's license in the name of Maurice Bullock, he lived at 1212 Dauphine Street, a half block up Dauphine from my corner building. He also had a Tulane University ID card, listing his job as assistant professor and two hundred dollars cash.

Wait a minute – Maurice Bullock? Mo Bullock? No wonder he looked familiar. I stuffed the card and money back into his wallet and shoved it back in his pocket. I went around to my chair to take a long gander at New Orleans's Most Valuable High School Athlete of 1935, the man I'd just cold-cocked. Mo Bullock was the best baseball player to come out of Jesuit, maybe forever. He also played right halfback and safety for the Blue Jays my senior year. He was one of the guys I outran on my eighty yard scamper in the rain. Last I heard of him he signed with the Detroit Tigers farm club.

"You're in big trouble," he told me as I saw Frenchy's prowl car park in front of my DeSoto. "My family's got enough money to bury you in lawsuits."

He told Frenchy the same thing, but after hearing my side of the story, the lieutenant took Mo to the detective bureau, me trailing behind in my DeSoto. I had to wait out in the squad room, sitting at one of the desks while the dicks ignored me. The room smelled of cigarette butts and stale coffee and the windows had a yellow tint on the inside. I sat there massaging my right hand. Should have kicked the sucker.

After about an hour, Jimmy Hays brought two men in fancy suits into the room, had them wait outside Frenchy's glass-enclosed office while he went to the interview room where Frenchy was questioning Mo. Hays gave me his meanest look, which looked so much like an angry Moe Howard, I almost laughed.

Frenchy guided Mo Bullock by the elbow out of the interview room and into his office with the two fancy-suited men, leaving Hays outside. On his way to the coffee pot, Hays shot me a evil grin. "You're in big trouble now."

"How's Larry and Curly?"

He growled.

Ten minutes later Mo and the suits left without looking my way. Frenchy waved me into his office and said, "Close the door." He fired up a fresh cigarette and I didn't know why, the room was cloudy with cigarette smoke.

"Those were the Bullock family lawyers. Did you know your boy's father is a millionaire? Some kinda shipping magnet."

"Nope."

"Well, prepare yourself for a lawsuit."

"What about the dance? He lied about it. He was the masher."

Frenchy kicked his feet up on his gray metal desk. His shoes soles were almost worn through. Flatfoot, right? "Said he saw you at the dance. Claimed you were all over the Annette girl. Claimed he didn't even know about the killing. Doesn't read the papers. It ain't against the law to lie to a PI."

I sank back in the uncomfortable metal folding chair. "I've been thinking. He's a professor at Tulane, right?"

"Teaches European History."

I perked up. "Then he'd know about this Lupercalia."

Frenchy nodded. "So would anyone who could read an encyclopedia." He tapped ashes into an overflowing ashtray on his desk. "I don't think he did it. Wrong shoe size."

"Shoe size?"

Frenchy shook his head. "You know, Sherlock, we don't tell civilians everything we know. We found two good footprints in the dirt. Our killer wore a size fourteen shoe with a worn left heel. We got close-up pictures and casts of the prints."

My chin dipped slowly to my chest.

"Bullock wears a size ten. Like you," Frenchy added. "You need a good lawyer, let me know."

"I have one."

On my way home I wondered if the attorney who hired me to catch Herb Moity would represent me. There went any money I'd make on Moity. Then I remembered Praca's Cleaners and gunned the DeSoto. Why hadn't I thought of it earlier?

I found both receipts in the street.

"I wait this for you," said Mr. Juan, handing me a receipt for my blue suit.

I handed him Bullock's receipts, along with a sawbuck to look inside the bags with Bullock's clothes. Holding my breath didn't help as I searched the white shirt, brown jacket and linen pants, even the cuffs. No branches, no red clay, no missing button from Annette's dress.

•

Tuesday, February 18, 1947

When I was little I loved Mardi Gras, going to the parades with my parents, dressing up in costume, yelling 'throw me something, mister', catching beads. But when my parents died, well, how did St. Paul put it? Something like, "When I was a child, I spoke as a child, thought as a child: but when I became a man, I put away childish things." I think it was St. Paul who said that. One of those apostles. Wait, he wasn't an apostle. He a disciple or something like that. Good Catholic would know. I wasn't much of a Catholic.

Frenchy had called me a 'civilian'. Don't know why it bothered me. I guess because I thought I was a detective. The din from the parade two blocks away up on Rampart Street sounded like a distant riot as I sat out on my balcony, feet up on the wrought iron railing. I watched a pair of mockingbirds run off a blue jay and two crows in quick succession. Smaller than the crows, the mockingbirds looked like P-51s hounding Heinkel 111 German bombers. They must have a nest in the one of oaks in Cabrini Playground.

A ship's whistle echoed dolefully from the river to my left. I thought it changed tune when I realized, the second tone was my doorbell. I hit the buzzer, went into the hall to look downstairs to see who I'd admitted. Len Connelly stood unsteadily at the bottom of the stairs.

"Up here," I called down. He spotted me, raised the bottle of Bourbon in his left hand to me and started up. Needless to say, he was more than half-looped and I wondered if he'd make it all the way up. He did, smiling at me and saying something profane about the crowds outside and the dumb parade.

"Can't understand the attraction," he said as he came in to drop heavily on my sofa. Focusing bleary eyes at me, he said, "Got any ice?"

I went for a Falstaff and dropped ice-cubes in a glass for him. He managed to pour himself a triple without spilling any on my coffee table. He raised the glass to me and said, "City Champs!"

I sat in the love seat, both of us kicking our heels up on either end of the coffee table.

"Funny you should mention that," I said. "Remember the masher at the dance, the guy who looked so familiar?"

"Yeah. Blond guy."

"Mo Bullock."

"Huh?" It took a second and his eyes lit up. "Oh, yeah. No wonder he looked familiar. Howdja' remember him?"

"Ran into him. Dragged him to headquarters. He's not the killer."

Len took another belt. "You sure?"

I took a hit of beer and spotted something that made my throat tighten. I had to wait for the swallow of beer to go down.

"What size you wear?" I tried making it sound light, friendly, nodding at his shoes.

"Fourteen." He chuckled but all I could see was the worn spot on the left heel.

I tried to control my breathing as my mind put the pieces together. "Wasn't your father a professor?"

Len grinned drunkenly. "Ancient History at St. Mary's Dominican College." He didn't sound as drunk as he looked. "First Catholic women's college in the south. Taught all those girls but it didn't help me get any." He took another long drink, raised his glass and added, "Bet that jerk off Mo Bullock gets lotsa women at Tulane with them Newcomb college co-eds runnin' around in tight sweaters."

The word 'sweater' almost set me off. The pieces just kept coming and my neck burned, my hands opening and closing into fists. Tulane. I never mentioned Mo was at Tulane.

"Did you find anything for me around Washington Square?" I asked in a controlled voice.

"Huh? Oh, uh, no."

I'd bet he didn't even go there. And for a long moment I saw it all played out like a horror movie. Len following us through the park, watching us kiss, watching me walk off. Len waiting, watching the lights in her house, then seeing her come out in that sweater, come right for him and then…

"You know," my voice came out deeper now, "cops don't need to know why. Don't need to prove motive at all. They just have to prove how it happened, when it happened, who was killed and then who did the killing. Why isn't important to the police."

He gave me a shrug.

"But I'm a civilian detective and I want to know why."

Len stared back at me, as if frozen in time.

"I knew her. I kissed her. We were going to be something, man." My voice quivered in anger.

"Why you yelling at me?"

"Because I want to know why you did it."

He sobered immediately and I could see the guilt in his eyes. "You're crazy man."

"Lupercalia," I said and he wouldn't look me in the eye. "Got it from your old man, didn't you? All those years him giving the family tid-bits from history. Any prof would do that. You knew about Lupercalia and the Cave of Lupercal from your old man."

"Bullock teaches it," Len snarled.

I got up, went to the phone and tried calling Frenchy on Mardi Gras day. It took three calls to get someone at the detective bureau to answer. Thankfully it wasn't Hays. Hanging up, I stood there waiting for Frenchy to call back. Len stared straight ahead, as if in a trance, not looking at me as the minutes ticked by. When the phone rang it startled both of us. I snatched it up, my eyes still staring at my old friend.

"You better get over to my place," I told Frenchy. "I'm looking at the killer right now. No, I haven't been drinking. It's Len Connelly. Yeah, my friend."

Len stood as I hung up and turned toward the door, glaring at me. "You gonna try and stop me?"

I pulled out my revolver, raised and cocked it, pointed it at his head.

"You gonna shoot me?" Len opened the door.

I hesitated, then lowered the gun slowly.

He left quickly and I felt better, thinking like a detective now. I wanted him back at his house. When Frenchy arrived, I would talk him into getting a search warrant. We'd find something from the bushes, maybe some red clay, maybe even one of Annette's buttons at Len's.

When Frenchy arrived, I told him and he went, "Man, that's kinda weak."

"Not weak enough for a search warrant. He's wearing shoes with a worn heel. Size fourteen."

Frenchy shook his head. "You're in luck it's Mardi Gras. I'll do about anything to get away from parade duty."

•

Len Connelly lived in an apartment at the rear of a crumbling Creole cottage on Burgundy Street, on the far side of Elysian Fields, not three blocks from Washington Square. I waited outside with a rookie patrolman while the detectives searched inside. It didn't take a half hour before Frenchy came out with a handcuffed Len, his head down. They put him in a prowl car and Frenchy came over to show me a button from Annette Bayly's skirt.

"It was up on the mantle, like a damn trophy."

On my way to the detective bureau, I remembered that Edgar Allan Poe story "The Purloined Letter" where the letter sat in plain view for any visitor to spot. It also occurred to me that Annette's father was right after all. The killer *had* returned to the scene of the crime. I could just envision Len watching the detective in the square.

I sat out in the squad room again. At least the hand I'd hurt punching Bullock felt better. An hour after Frenchy took Len into an interrogation room, the other detectives who'd searched Len's house came in. Hays wouldn't look at me. Francona came over to show me Len's grass-stained pants, red clay embedded around the knees. He also showed me twigs from the bushes found in the bottom of my friend's dirty clothes hamper.

Frenchy came out a while later carrying Len's shoes, which he passed to Francona as evidence. "Check out the left heel." He turned to me and said, "He copped out. Crying in there like a baby."

"He tell you why?"

"Made a pass at her and she slapped him. Said he was drunk and he lost it."

Before I left, Frenchy asked me to write up something for him. "Put what he told you on paper for me, will ya'?"

"Sure."

·

Wednesday, February 19, 1947

Mo Bullock's place was a bright yellow, two-story Greek Revival wooden house with three bay windows in front. A three step stoop led up to a front gallery with four wooden posts and fancy gingerbread trim painted pale blue. I rang the doorbell and retreated to the steps so he wouldn't think I was gonna pounce on him.

He answered wearing a maroon dinner jacket over off-white pants, a brandy snifter in his left hand. His pretty-boy face sported a purple bruise on his left jaw.

"I came to apologize. I was dead wrong." I held out one of my business cards for him. "Here. You can spell my name right on the lawsuit."

His squeezed his left eye partially shut. "You're a peculiar bastard."

"I also came to tell you they caught the killer. It was a friend of mine. Played ball with me at Holy Cross." I figured he'd read it in the paper.

His eyes widened. "Son-of-a-bitch. I recognize you now. You're the speed demon from the championship game. I knew I knew that face."

I stepped closer so he could take the card. He did and then asked, "Want a drink?"

"Sure."

He opened the door wide and I stepped into a small foyer, following him into a formal living room with thick Persian carpets, walls filled with books and copies of impressionist paintings. Hell, maybe they weren't all copies.

"What's your poison?" Mo headed for a wet bar at the back of the room.

"Beer."

He brought me an imported brew, something called Stella Artois. It was icy cold with a light taste. We sat across from one another in thick recliners. Mo gently touched the bruise on his chin and said, "You were always fast, but I didn't think you were that fast."

"It was a sucker punch."

"Well, it worked. Never been decked like that."

I took another hit of Stella Artois and he started talking about the game. I didn't remember him scoring Jesuit's only touchdown. I didn't play both ways like he did. My coach kept me fresh that way.

"Man, I'll never forget that run," he said. "I was right on your butt only you kept accelerating and I couldn't close."

"My friend Len Connelly was the one who bowled over two of your linebackers with one block. He sprung me."

"And he's the reason we're here right now."

I nodded, then asked, "I thought you went with the Detroit Tigers."

His turn to nod. "I made it to the big show for one season. Then the damn Japs hit Pearl Harbor and I went into the Corps." He took a drink from the snifter. "Shoulda died on Iwo Jima but they saved me only I was shot in the back and never made it to the show again."

He'd framed his Navy Cross and had it on a wall between paintings.

"You in the war?" he asked.

Didn't mind talking about my Silver Star, since his Navy Cross trumped me.

"Cassino, huh? Couldn't have been as bad as Iwo Jima," he said, "but I heard it was bad enough. How'd they catch your friend?"

I told him about the footprints and the other evidence.

"So you're the one who figured it, right?"

"Yeah, just like I figured you."

"Batting five-hundred ain't bad."

"Maybe in baseball. Not when it comes to murder," I said, finishing off the beer. I thanked him and didn't want to overstay my welcome.

Mo took my business card out of his pocket and said, "Caye. French isn't it?"

I nodded and he slipped the card back into his pocket. "I'm not suing you. But you owe me one. I might need a private investigator someday." He stood up. "And it takes a big man to admit a mistake and face up to it."

"Helluva mistake."

We shook hands and I headed back home. It was getting dark already and for a moment I thought about how it was different all over again. It was so different before the war, different again when I got out of the army, different after VJ Day, different after kissing Annette.

I drifted back to that night, seeing her for the first time, waiting to dance with her, how she felt pressed against me, the clean scent of her hair. I'd never forget those eyes. And as I walked, I let myself feel the loss all over again, let my heart stammer and ache. I wanted to feel something other that the rage to strangle my old friend to death.

Her name was Annette Bayly, of Scottish descent, nicknamed Too Wise for the two 'y's in her name.

It was a kiss with promise behind it.

If only.

Life was full of 'if onlys'.

END of TOO WISE

St. Expedite

He was leaning against my car, his little elbow propped up on the right front fender of my gray pre-war DeSoto. I watched him from the doorway of my apartment house – which is also the doorway to my office.

Looking at his feet, he rubbed the soles of his black canvass high-top sneakers against the top of the cast iron storm drain that supposed to keep the street from flooding. In New Orleans the streets became canals with the slightest rain and it rained all the time, especially during late summer. He looked about six, maybe seven years old. With a mop of dark brown hair cut like one of the Three Stooges, the one named Moe, he was a cute kid with a delicate frame and nice sculptured features. Of course, I immediately wondered what his mother looked like, if she had that nice chiseled nose, olive complexion and the dark hair. That's the kinda guy I am – see a good-lookin' kid and wonder what the mother's like and if she's available, if you get my drift.

The kid turned his face up to the morning sun, closed his eyes and scrunched up his little face. Besides sneakers, he wore a gray tee-shirt and coarse-looking blue jeans rolled up at the ankles.

I stepped out on the sidewalk – actually we call them banquettes in New Orleans because they serve as banks when the streets turn into canals. OK, I stepped out on the banquette and fanned myself with my tan fedora. The summer of '47 was setting heat and humidity records daily.

Looking spiffy, I had on my new blue suit, a powder-blue tie adorned with a green Hawaiian palm tree, and a tan belt which matched my tan-and-white wing tips. My own dark brown hair was slicked back, my face still tingled from my morning shave. I felt the full wrath of the heat-and-humidity immediately, even under the overhang of the balcony that ran the length of my building.

I leaned my hand against one of the balcony's black wrought iron support posts, waited until he looked up at me and said, "How's it goin', son?"

He pulled his arm off the DeSoto and shoved both hands into his pockets. Blinking a pair of the darkest brown eyes I've ever seen at me, he said, "Are you a detective?"

There was a sadness in those brown eyes that made me pause before answering.

"There's a rumor to that effect," I said.

"Huh?"

That's what I get for a bad joke.

I extended my right hand and said, "Lucien Caye, private-eye."

He took my hand reluctantly, looking down as he shook it. He shoved his hand back into his pocket as soon as we finished.

I waited. Back when I was a real copper we learned that if you wait, the other person usually restarts the conversation. It's the polite thing to do. It worked well in confessions. It didn't work well with the kid, so I asked him his name.

"Sam," he said. Rubbing the sole of his left sneaker against the storm drain again, he added in a softer voice, "Can you find my Daddy?"

It was my turn to look at my feet. I rubbed the sole of my left shoe against the banquette and asked him how old he was.

"Seven," he said, his voice catching.

I looked up over his head at the black wrought iron fence surrounding Cabrini Playground across the street, at the dark magnolia trees and wide oaks. Usually kids played there, but not this morning – too hot already. A cloud moved and the sun shined even brighter, illuminating the lower French Quarter, and especially Barracks Street, in a super-nova spotlight.

"You live around here?" I heard myself ask. I wasn't sure, but I think I'd seen him playing in Cabrini Playground. I like to watch the kids from my office window on the first floor.

"I live on Kel-a-reck." Of course he meant Kerlerec Street, but in New Orleans, we have these secret pronunciations of street names so we know you're a tourist if you pronounce it correctly. He pointed to his left.

I nodded slowly, felt sweat on my temples now and along the small of my back. I pulled off my suit coat and folded it across my left arm.

Sam stared at my snub-nosed .38 Smith and Wesson in its tan leather holster on my right hip. I was about to tell him not to worry about the gun, I never use it, when he told me something that made my stomach bottom out.

He said, "My Daddy's gun is just like that, only bigger."

"What does your daddy do?"

"He's a policeman."

He put his hand up over his eyes to shield them from the sun and smiled weakly, his little lips shaking.

"Come on," I said. "Let's go see your mother."

He looked down again and told me his mother didn't know where his daddy was either. I sucked in a deep breath of hot air and told him if he wanted me to take the case, I had to talk with his mother. It's the law, I lied.

He batted those big brown eyes and me and shrugged an O.K. and I wasn't thinking about what his mother looked like anymore. It didn't matter. A cop – even an ex-cop like me – never saddled up to another cop's wife. At least I never would.

I started slowly up Barracks Street and he followed. I asked him where he lived on Kerlerec, figuring he'd walked so it must be close, not way the hell up by Claiborne, I hoped. He told me at the corner of Kel-a-reck and Dauphine, and took the lead down Barracks to Dauphine. We took Dauphine out of the Quarter and into the second oldest neighborhood in New Orleans – the Faubourg Marigny. The ironwork Spanish balconies of the Quarter gave way to smaller houses, Creole cottages with front dormers and roofs slanted toward the street. They even had small front yards in Marigny.

Slowing as we approached Kerlerec Street, Sam said, "I've been praying to St. Expedite." He pointed over his shoulder. "Back at Guadeloupe Church. But he hasn't found my Daddy either."

The morning's coffee-and-chicory felt sour in my belly. St. Expedite rang a bell, but it wasn't a nice one. I remembered something about the saint, but couldn't put my finger on it.

Sam led me to a narrow shotgun house painted white with pale green trim around its front door, windows and gingerbread trim on the overhang. He took the three wooden steps up to the small front gallery and went through the screen door, letting it bang behind him. I heard voices in the back of the house; and through the screen door I saw the figure of a woman moving toward me.

She hesitated just inside the door, then opened the screen and stepped out on the porch, her left fist on her hip. She blew a strand of her long brown hair away from her face and narrowed a pair of bright blue eyes at me. I took a step down off the gallery.

Damn, she was a looker, even in a full umbrella skirt and loose-fitting blouse. In all white, her olive complexion looked extra dark; and there was a hint of crimson lipstick on her full lips. She looked about five or six years younger than me, somewhere in her mid-twenties.

"So, what's your game, mister?" she said in a deep voice.

I took another step down and heard a screen door slam across the street and another door creak open on the house to my right. She looked around at her neighbors, let out a resigned sigh and asked me in. She held the screen door open for me and waited.

The front room was much cooler with two fans blowing. I could hear a attic fan overhead in the next room where Sam sat on a child's bed, his arms and legs folded as he looked past me at this mother.

We call them shotgun houses because the rooms are built one behind the other in a straight line; and if you open all the doors you could fire a shotgun from the front yard to the back yard without hitting anything. I never knew anyone who tried it, though.

"What's your name, mister?" the mother asked, her arms folded now.

I pulled a business card from my coat pocket and showed it to her before putting it on the coffee table in the center of the small front room.

"Lucien Caye," I said. "I'm an ex-cop and a private detective now and I wouldn't be here if your son hadn't asked me."

She brushed the hair from her face again and looked past me at Sam with genuine surprise.

"I don't want any trouble, ma'am," I said. "It's just... "

"Just what?!"

"Sam asked me to help."

"And that's what you do? Go around helping children?"

"But mommie," Sam's voice was high-pitched and urgent.

She looked at him again. Then her shoulders sank slowly and she moved to the sofa and sat and told me to take a seat.

The front room had tan walls, a beige sofa with matching chair, a wooden rocker, a coffee table with end tables that matched. It smelled faintly of pine oil. Black and white French Quarter scenes hung in gold wooden frames on the walls and a light brown rug covered most of the hardwood floor.

I sat in the rocker across from her. She waved her son to her. He bounded over and curled up next to her; and she wrapped her right arm around him.

I waited.

She cleared her throat, looked out the front window and said, "Al left me. It's no big mystery. He left me for the bottle." Her voice caught on the word 'bottle'.

She patted her son's head and said, "Unfortunately, he also left Sam and that's... well, that's a different story."

I asked myself, *again*, how in the hell do I get myself into messes like this.

"We have no money to pay you," she said, as if that mattered. I wanted to tell her I didn't need money right now, not with the wad sitting in my bank from the Choppel Case, but I kept my mouth shut, which I think she preferred anyway.

She looked down at her son's wide eyes and said that if I could get a message to Sam's father from Sam, she would appreciate it. She didn't sound like she would, but I took her at her word, figuring the faster I got out of there the better. I waited until she looked at me to ask her husband's full name.

"Ever work the Third Precinct?"

I nodded.

"Al Mokeo."

She waited for my eyes to react before she said, "Figured you knew him. Good ole Al." She looked at the front window again. "Everybody's pal Al. Buy a round for everyone, Al."

I hoped my eyes didn't tell her everything I was thinking – like how in the hell did a slob like Al Mokeo get a fine woman like this and such a good lookin' kid?

Sam pressed his head against his mother's side and blinked his big eyes at me and I could see they were wet.

"I'll do what I can," I said, standing up. "You have any idea where he hangs out?"

"I'm sure the boys at the precinct know."

Before I could make a clean getaway, Sam called out, "Find my Daddy. Please."

What could I say, except, "Sure kid. I'll find him."

•

I used my fedora as a fan all the way back to my office. The air smelled like rain and I could see dark clouds floating over the Quarter, moving in from the north. She was probably right, this was not much of a mystery. Somebody at the precinct would know where Al hung out.

I thought about Sam kneeling in church, praying to a saint to find his daddy. St. Expedite, the name rattled around my brain as my feet began to feel the heat from the banquette. There was something about St. Expedite, but I couldn't remember.

I started breathing heavily and wiped my sweaty brow with my hand. What the hell was happening to me? I'm only thirty, I thought, and I can't walk eight blocks in the sunshine without sweating to death.

Was it the heat? Was it the humidity? Or was it the mother, standing in the doorway, her fist on her hip? Was it the way she blew that strand of hair out of her eyes? Or was it those cool blue eyes?

You know, I didn't even get her name.

Or was it the boy?

My chest felt so tight, I loosened my tie. Turning on Barracks Street, I pulled out my handkerchief and wiped my face. Closing my eyes momentarily gave my mind time to dig up a memory I didn't want to relive. I saw myself sitting on the back porch of our shotgun house, my elbows propped up on my knees, my face buried in my hands. A man in a black car had just come by to tell my mother we'd never see my dad again.

At nine, I felt the weight of the world crush me. My father was killed in a car wreck outside a little village called Golden Meadow. He died in a ditch next to a bayou named Lafourche in a part of Louisiana I will never visit. Ever.

Then I saw Sam's wet eyes, saw him kneeling in church. And I suddenly remembered what it was rattling in my brain about St. Expedite; and my stomach bottomed out again.

•

After three quick phone calls from my office, I climbed behind the ceramic steering wheel of my '40 DeSoto two-door and drove up to Rampart. Seven years old and her engine still hummed quietly. I took a left all the way to Conti Street where I took a quick u-turn and parked on the street just across from Our Lady of Guadeloupe Church.

I looked over at the gray church, at the four rounded archways of the Spanish building and the tall steeple that looked a little like the steeple of St. Louis Cathedral, now that I thought about it. I pulled on my coat and walked down Conti to Burgundy and then left a half block to the Maggie The Cat Bar, which occupied the bottom floor of what once was a three-story Creole townhouse.

The only customer, a heavy-set bar fly with carrot-red hair, sat at a corner table. The bartender, a bald man with an out-of-style handlebar moustache said he knew Al Mokeo all right, officer, but Al only came in on weekends.

Officer? – I still have the look, I guess.

The air smelled heavy with rain as I retraced my steps back to Rampart. I stopped and dug my umbrella from the trunk of my DeSoto and crossed Rampart. Along the neutral ground I spotted a brass historical plaque that explained how Our Lady of Guadeloupe Church is the oldest surviving church in New Orleans. Once the old mortuary chapel, where victims of the Yellow Fever epidemic of 1826 were blessed before burial, it was now the official chapel of the New Orleans police and fire departments.

Crossing to the other side of Rampart, I paused in front of the church, took the two brick steps up to the entrance and went in. It felt cooler in the church, even with the smell of burning candles. I dipped my hand in the marble cistern of holy water just inside the doorway, genuflected and crossed myself with the holy water, then looked at the statues at the back of the church.

I found St. Expedite half-hidden in a rear corner of the church. Elevated on the back wall, he looked like a pretty nice Medieval fella, maybe twenty years old with wavy brown hair. He wore a serf-looking outfit, a baggy green shirt with a brown leather vest, brown pants and brown high-top sandals. He also wore a plum colored cape. Too young to grow a beard, his smooth face looked delicate and handsome in the way a child's face is handsome.

St. Expedite held up a wooden cross in his right hand.

Beneath the statue was a plaque that read, "St. Expedite. Pray for us." And I remembered how this saint came to be and shook my head and left.

I walked up Conti to Basin Street, hung a left for a block and a half until I reached the open front door of the Storyville Bar. Al Mokeo sat perched on a bar stool just inside the doorway. Leaning forward, his arms were up on the bar. In a white undershirt and baggy black pants, he was unshaven and looked half-looped.

There were two other customers at a rear table. I could barely make them out in the darkness. The walls were painted black and the only light in the place was a lamp behind the bar and whatever light could sneak in through the narrow front door. The place reeked of stale beer. I moved around Al and the skinny bartender asked if he could help me.

"Jax," I said as I took the stool next to Al.

The bartender popped open a Jax beer longneck and put it on the bar in front of me without bothering with a coaster. I took a swing and tasted ice shards in the beer. Nice and cold, it nipped me all the way to my belly. I put my Jax down and tapped Al on the shoulder.

He looked at me with bloodshot eyes.

"How's it going Al?"

He looked hard at me. His mouth opened, but nothing came out. So I told him my name and reminded him how I used to work the other shift at the Third.

"Yeah. I remember you." He picked up his Dixie beer and took a deep drink. He wiped his mouth with his free hand and asked what brought me to such a fine establishment in the middle of the day.

"I do private detective work now."

"Yeah. I heard." Al turned to the bar and took another drink. "I've got a message for you."

The bartender, who was washing glasses, was listening big time. I shot him a hard glint; but he didn't take the hint.

Al put his Dixie down and stared at it.

"I've got a message for you from a little boy about this high." I stuck my left hand out at about Sam's height.

Al didn't look.

"He's got the biggest brown eyes I've ever seen."

Al didn't even blink.

"Lives with his mother on Kerlerec Street." I took another hit of Jax. "You remember them don't you?"

Sitting back, Al raised his Dixie and said, "They should be happy I'm gone. I'm a drunk, don't you know?" He downed the rest of the Dixie, wiped his mouth again and told the bartender, "Another."

I took another swig.

"His mama's got nothin' to complain. I give her my whole check. I live off my disability check from Uncle Sam." He pointed to the Marine Corps emblem tattooed on his right shoulder, belched and said, "Guadalcanal."

I could have rolled up my left sleeve and pointed to my scar and say, "Monte Cassino," but what would that prove?

At that point we both took a drink and I remembered a scene played out one rainy night at the end of Esplanade Avenue. I remembered helping to surround a house where a cop killer was hiding and how we all prepared to rush the place when Al Mokeo came out dragging the cop killer's body behind him. Al was leaner then; and I remember the grim look on a tough Marine face.

The face that looked at me now was flaccid and puffy. He blinked his bleary eyes and said, "Why'd she send you? She ain't got no use for me."

"She didn't. Sam sent me."

"Yeah. Yeah." He went back to his beer and I wanted to punch him so bad it hurt.

I waited until he put his Dixie down before I said, "Your son's been praying for you to come see him?"

"Huh?"

"He's been getting down on his knees, in front of a saint that never even existed, and prays for his daddy to come see him."

Al gave me a drunken I-don't-know-what-the-hell-you're-talking-about look.

I grabbed the front of his undershirt and twisted and he almost fell off the stool.

"You ever hear of St. Expedite?"

His eyes were wide now and his face twisted in anger.

"Sam's been praying to St. Expedite for his daddy to come see him?"

Al tried to slap my hand away, but I held on too tightly. He glared at me and spit out a, "So?"

I wanted to punch him until he came to his senses, but I knew I'd could punch him to death and he'd never come to his senses. Instead, I let him go, tossed a buck on the bar and stormed out.

I walked back to my car in the drizzle, my hands in my coat pockets, my umbrella back at the Storyville Bar. I walked past Our Lady of Guadeloupe, but didn't even look at it. I just kept thinking about the story – how, long ago, church workers opened several crates that had arrived from European statue makers.

They found one marked 'St. Joseph', one marked 'Jesus' and one marked with the word 'Expedite' and New Orleanians have been praying to him ever since.

My DeSoto knew the way home. My mind was far away, re-fighting the dusty Battle of Monte Cassino – May, 1944, shooting it out with crack Nazi troops dug in so snugly we had to blow the whole monastery to bits to get the bastards out. Which did no good actually. It only gave them more rocks to hide behind.

Just as I walked into my office, the big rain hit. It came in sheets across the Quarter and turned the streets into canals. I sat behind my beat-up mahogany desk and watched the water creep up on my DeSoto. It covered half the tires, but never got any higher, never reached the running board. Soon, the rain slackened.

I closed my eyes and remembered – Cassino. Not the Nazi bastards, not getting shot and nearly bleeding to death, but the children. I remembered the children sticking out their little hands, begging the GI's for food. Their faces were dirty, their lips quivered, their dark hair matted, some caked with mud. I gave them everything I had to eat, went in and raided the supply room, gave it all to them; and they scampered away like mice. But it wasn't enough.

I've seen dead Germans, dead Italians, dead Americans. As a cop after the war, I saw my share of dead New Orleanians, the good and the bad, but I've never seen anything as sad as those hungry children. I'll never forget their vacant, haunting eyes – dark brown eyes.

The clouds moved away from the Quarter and the sun returned with a vengeance. After a while I saw the heat shimmering off the hood of my car. I waited a little longer for the water to go down in the streets before going upstairs to my apartment to change. I slipped on a Yankees baseball shirt, jeans and climbed into a pair of white tennis shoes. On my way out, I grabbed my football and black sunglasses.

It was steamier after the rain. I could almost see the water vapor rising back up into the sky. The old Creole townhouses along Barracks Street smelled moldy after a good rain. They smelled of wet wood.

The streets of Faubourg Marigny were also drying quickly. I climbed up the front steps and knocked on the screen door. I stepped back away from the door and decided I'd give any neighbor who peeked out a hard stare. I heard her footfalls behind me and waited until the screen door creaked before turning around to face her.

"You were right. It wasn't much of a mystery."

She stepped out on the gallery and put her right hand over her eyes to shield them from the sun. She let out a long sigh.

"So, what did he say?"

I looked around to make sure Sam wasn't hovering behind the screen door.

"I told him Sam wanted to see him, told him Sam prayed in church for his daddy to come see him. He said, 'So.' That's all he had to say."

She said, "Bastard," half under her breath.

Looking at my football, she said, "You slummin' or something?"

"No. I thought maybe Sam would like to play some catch."

Her head fell to one side, the way a woman's does when a man says something really stupid. She let out another sigh. Then she asked me something I hadn't expected, like women often do. "What do you mean, pray in church?"

I told her about Sam praying to St. Expedite for his daddy to come see him.

"Saint who?"

"At Our Lady of Guadeloupe."

"Oh." She closed her eyes.

I was about to tell her more when her head fell slowly forward and her shoulders began to shake. I felt hollow inside, and pretty damn helpless as she cried next to me. I looked around again, ready to leer at the neighbors. But no one even looked out.

Then she looked up at me with wet eyes, grabbed the door and opened it, then stopped. She wiped her eyes with her free hand and through shaking lips said, "Sam doesn't need... another father."

"I know."

She stepped in and started to close the door. I grabbed it and said, "But maybe he could use a big brother."

"Yeah. Right!"

She started to move away, but paused a moment and gave me a long stare before letting go of the door and disappearing into the house.

I closed the screen door and waited on the gallery.

A minute later I heard running footsteps. I turned just as Sam bounded out the door. He looked past me and then up at me and said, "Did you find my Daddy?"

I nodded and sat on the top step, my football in both hands.

"Yeah," I said. "I found your daddy."

"Where is he?" Sam looked around.

What was I supposed to say? The truth? His daddy was a drunk. His daddy wouldn't be coming home. Or was I supposed to lie, tell him his daddy would be coming soon, just wait.

"Is he coming?"

"I don't know."

Sam looked up and then down the street; and I could see him, kneeling in front of that statue and praying to a saint that never existed for a father who might as well not exist and it broke me up inside.

"Come on," I said, standing up and moving out to the banquette. "Let's play some catch."

Sam sat on the top step and shook his head. He didn't look at me. He looked up and down the street again.

I tossed the ball in the air and caught it with one hand.

"Come on," I said. "Just throw me one. Just one."

He shook his head again.

"Hey, I did you a favor. I delivered your message. Now you do me a favor. Throw me one."

Sam batted his big brown eyes at me and stood slowly and came down the steps. I pretended I was a quarterback and just got the ball snapped to me. Sam pulled his hands out of his pockets and backed away from me.

He caught it and threw it back like a pro.

"Good arm," I said.

The next one bounced off his arms. He picked it up and tossed it back to me and I had to reach to catch it.

"You've got a good arm, boy."

When he missed the next one I told him to use his hands and his arms, not just his arms, even if the ball was big. He caught the next one perfectly and almost smiled.

I backed up and he nearly threw it over my head. I had to bat it back with one hand to catch it.

We moved out into the street and Sam started running to make catches, darting like a halfback before he threw the ball. I missed the next one, bent down to pick it up and saw her watching from behind the screen door.

I threw the next one a little farther and Sam caught it over his shoulder, smooth as silk.

"Wow," I said. "Way to go." And meant it.

Sam grinned at me and let one fly that I had to run down.

She came out on the gallery and sat on the top step, wrapping her skirt around her legs.

"Mom, watch," Sam said as I threw it back and he caught it with his hands and arms, like he'd been doing it for years. He threw the ball back to me, making me reach again.

He smiled at his mother and she half-smiled back. She looked tired and sad. But she sure was pretty sitting there in the sunshine; and it occurred to me that I still didn't know her name.

Already I was working up quite a sweat and it felt good. The next one bounced off Sam's head and he laughed and flashed a wide smile my way and it made me feel good to hear him laugh.

It really did.

St. Expedite is for Vincent

END of ST. EXPEDITE

The Iberville Mistress

"My husband is seeing another woman." Catherine LaVanchy's bright green eyes stare intently at me and I can't help thinking – *what kind of man runs around on a beautiful woman like this*? I know the old saying – *if you have steak every night, you want hamburger once in a while*, but we're talking filet mignon here. Catherine is prime cut female.

Sitting across my old mahogany desk in her trim, tan skirt-suit, dark brown hair curled on her shoulders, she looks so much like Hedy Lamar, even down to the dark red lipstick, it sends a chill through me. I catch a whiff of her perfume, sweet and expensive-smelling, probably Chanel, and nervously run my fingers through my dark brown hair.

"Mr. Caye, I think he's keeping a mistress." Catherine's voice is soft and near cracking as she breathes between quick sentences. "On Iberville Street. In a Creole townhouse. Upstairs apartment." She passes a paper to me with the address 813B Iberville. I put it next to my notepad and pick up my fountain pen.

"Please call me Lucien. What's your husband's name?"

"Martin LaVanchy, IV. He's with Skinner, North, and Wagner. A partner."

I focus my Mediterranean brown eyes on hers and try not to show I'm liking this more and more. When she'd called me earlier, I hated the thought of one of my first cases as a private investigator being a divorce case, but seeing her and the promise of nailing a lawyer sends another shiver through me.

"Martin is a wealthy man and can easily afford keeping a mistress." Catherine sits more erect, her ample chest rising. She's nicely endowed, for a petite woman, very nicely. "He comes from old money."

That partially explains it. The old New Orleans tradition, from the quadroon days when wealthy men kept their African mistresses in neat homes in Treme, while their wives stayed with the children. Back in the Nineteenth Century, it was common, but this is 1947.

"How long have you been married?"

"Two years. No children." She lets out a long breath. "Thankfully."

Being a southern boy, I'm too polite to ask her age, but she has to be a couple years younger than me, probably twenty-five or six. Her eyes become wet as she keeps staring at me and the look on her lovely face tells me she's facing up to a great failure in her life. I do want to nail this bastard. Almost as much as I want to comfort his wife. The Spaniard in me wants his ass. The Frenchman in me wants hers. It's a nice combination, being half and half, fiery Spanish and seductive French. Keeps life interesting.

Catherine opens her purse and pulls out a handkerchief and wipes her eyes. She withdraws a white envelope and places it on the desk. "I doubled what you told me you needed as a retainer. There's a picture of Martin inside too and a sheet with our address and telephone number." She takes in a deep breath, firming up her chin. "Can you start today? He meets her at lunch time."

"Sure." I play out my last hunch. "If you don't mind me asking. What is your maiden name?"

"Cortez. But my mother was French, a Landry," she tells me and I feel yet another chill.

•

Shortly before eleven, I step out of my building here in the low-rent, lower end of the French Quarter and put on my sunglasses. It's a bright autumn day in the mid-eighties and the neighborhood boys are playing football in Cabrini Playground, across narrow Barracks Street.

My office, on the first floor of 909 Barracks, is directly below my apartment, in a gray two-story building with a black, lacework balcony wrapping around the corner to Dauphine Street. Climbing into my gray, pre-war 1940 DeSoto coach, I lay my camera on the seat. I'd thought about changing out of my best suit, the navy blue Hart, Schaffner and Marx I'd put on after hearing Catherine's soft voice on the phone, but figured I look less like a crook in a nice suit while sitting in a car on surveillance.

It takes me less than ten minutes to set up on Iberville Street, just down from the two-story double Creole townhouse, which is sandwiched among seven other townhouses. Typically, the houses are up against the sidewalk with narrow passages between them to their rear patios. The townhouses at either end of the line are businesses now, one a stationery shop, the other selling leather goods. I'm parked across the street, at the rear of D. H. Holmes Department Store. This part of the upper French Quarter is evolving into a business section, only a block away from the CBD and busy Canal Street.

Pulling out Martin's picture, I catch a hint of Catherine's perfume again. He has a strong chin, deep set eyes and salt-and-pepper hair. He's pushing forty. Smiling confidently at the camera I can tell he's so full of himself.

He's also punctual. At noon he parks his silver Cadillac directly across from the townhouse. He's in a tailored brown suit and carries a matching attaché case. He's tall, about my height, six feet even. I pull up my Leica 35mm camera and focus on the townhouse. The door on the right side opens before he reaches it and a pretty brunette lets him in with a kiss on his cheek. I snap a picture. Exactly one hour later, I get another picture as old Martin leaves, still with his attaché case. I spot a movement on the second floor balcony of the townhouse and train my camera as the woman steps into the open French doors. She stands in the doorway in a white bra and panties. I focus and snap another picture and another as she leans forward to watch the Cadillac drive away.

She's also petite with a heavy chest. Skin as pale as Catherine's, she looks a little taller and maybe a little younger from this distance. She goes back inside, closing the door and I can't help wondering why a man cheats on his wife with a woman who looks like her. Why not a blonde or a redhead?

Sitting back, I wait for her to leave. Need to prove they were alone. Hope this isn't an all nighter. I should have eaten something. Lucky for me, the woman comes out two hours later. She wears a smart, blue dress and walks away from me, pocket book tucked beneath her arm. I step over to the townhouse and ring the bell twice, knock on the door once, then leave.

•

There's a note under my office door that reads: Call me! C.L.

I dial Catherine's number and she answers in the middle of the first ring.

As I tell her what happened, I hear her breathing on the other end of the line. She's upset, so I put it as delicately as I can, giving only the pertinent details.

"In her underclothes?" Her voice falls away and I listen to her breathing for half a minute before she tells me she wants to catch them again. Tomorrow.

"I want more than enough evidence when we go to court."

Sounds logical to me.

"And Lucien," her voice rises, "you've been a great help." And she hangs up and I realize there was more in the tone of her voice than what she said. The attraction I felt when staring across my desk at those green eyes wasn't my male imagination.

Leaning back in my high-back chair, I wonder why she didn't ask what the other woman looks like. Maybe she knows. Maybe she's seen her. Or maybe, she doesn't want to know.

•

Shaving the next morning, I realize I need a better plan, than sitting in my car down the street, two days in a row. So put my camera, telephoto lens and extra film in my attaché case, go to Iberville Street early and park two blocks away. Yesterday, I noticed a *For Rent* sign in a townhouse next to D. H. Holmes, near the end of the block. I talk the landlady into renting the room to me for the rest of the week. The rent doesn't even put a dent in Catherine's advance.

By ten a.m., I'm set-up across the street, the French doors of my balcony partially open, me sitting in an easy chair ten feet inside the dark apartment, Leica at the ready. Shoulda brought a book or the newspaper to read. Leaning back, I make myself comfortable.

At ten thirty, the mistress arrives in a maroon dress, lets herself in and goes upstairs, opening the French doors. I focus on them and wait. When she returns a half hour later, she's in bra and panties again and I squeeze off two pictures before she closes the door.

At noon, the Cadillac pulls up downstairs and Martin exits, carrying his attaché case again. He wears a silver suit today. The mistress, back in her maroon frock, lets him in with a peck on the cheek. I get pictures.

At one o'clock, Martin leaves, taking an extra minute to put his case in the trunk. I snap pictures of him climbing in and driving off.

Looking back up at her balcony, I wait. She doesn't disappoint me, opening her French doors. I train my Leica on the doors and she steps in the doorway, stark naked, turning her face up to the sun. I take a picture before she moves back inside.

She leaves the doors open, so I change rolls quickly, snapping on my telephone lens. I re-focus just as she does it again, stepping naked into the doorway, face turned toward the sun. Her full breasts are nicely oversized for such a petite woman and her dark pubic bush shines in the bright sunlight, just like her dark hair flowing past her shoulders. I carefully snap five pictures before she goes back inside.

•

"She left two hours later," I tell my friend, Eddie Billiot, as he puts the rolls of film in the dryer at the New Orleans Police Photo Lab. Short and stocky with black hair and moustache, my old partner from the Third Precinct grins at me. "I'm making a set for me, you know."

I'd expected as much when I told him I wanted two sets of prints, one for my client and one for me. I follow him into the darkroom and watch the images float up in the developing trays. He makes neat five-by-seven prints.

He make a yummy sound as we both stare at the naked image of the mistress.

"Aren't you glad you followed my advice and bought high speed film?"

I tell him yes. Don't mention I'm also glad he transferred to the lab. Easiest place in the world for an ex-cop to get nude pictures developed.

•

In my office at five o'clock, Catherine wears another skirt-suit, this one a deep purple. Standing next to me, she looks down at the pictures I've laid out on my desk and I catch the scent of her perfume again.

"She likes to pose in her panties, doesn't she?" Her voice is even, with no hint of anger.

"Actually." I pull one of the nudes from my coat pocket. "She stood in her balcony door with nothing on."

The green eyes look up at me and blink.

"You want to see the picture?"

She nods and I hand it to her and she holds it for a moment before letting it drop on the desk.

"I think," she says, "this'll be enough for my lawyer."

Catherine opens her purse and asks how much does she owes me.

"Nothing."

She starts scooping up the pictures and tells me she needs the negatives too as I move around to my chair.

"I usually keep the negatives. To keep the chain of evidence secure."

She gives me a wide-eyed look. "My lawyer told me to get the negatives."

"What's his name?"

She brushes her hair from her face. "I can't tell you that right now."

Tucking the photos into her purse she reaches her hand out. So I open the side drawer of my desk and dig out the envelope with the negatives. It doesn't contain the negatives from the second roll, those last five, carefully focused nudes. Those negatives are with my set of prints, upstairs in my apartment.

•

The rain starts around seven p.m., just as I'm cleaning up from my home-made dinner, a BLT sandwich and fries. I open the French doors of my balcony and watch the ran pelt the tile roofs of the quarter. It comes in waves, big fat rain, so I close the door, pour myself a Scotch and turn on the radio, just in time for NBC's Short Story Theater. A baritone voice announces tonight's feature is Edgar Allan Poe's *The Fall of the House of Usher.* Two Scotches later, just as the House of Usher sinks into the "deep and dank tarn" my phone rings.

It's Catherine and she's crying. It takes a while for me to get it out of her. She confronted Martin and left him. She's at the Roosevelt Hotel and wants me to come over. "I don't want to be alone tonight."

Neither do I. Taking in a deep breath, I have to say it. "Your lawyer should have told you to kick him out. Change the locks when he goes to work."

Her lawyer's a real douche-bag.

"It's Martin's house." She lets out a sob and I'm hooked. I'll be right there. Before leaving, I re-heat what's left in my coffee pot from this morning and down a strong cup of Joe to clear the Scotch away.

·

I gently tap on the door of Room 202. I have to rap twice before Catherine opens the door and stands there in a shape-hugging, dark green dress with her eye make-up running and her mocha lipstick streaked.

"I know," she cries. "I look like a raccoon." She turns and hurries back through the room into the bathroom.

I close the door on my way in. The room is bigger than most hotel rooms with a double bed, two oak end tables, matching dresser and chest-of-drawers and what's probably a closet across the room. It smells of her perfume.

"Can I get you a drink?" Catherine comes out with her face made-up and steps to the bottle of Bourbon on the dresser. She grabs ice-cubes from the bucket next to the bottle and drops them in her drink, which is half-filled.

"No thanks."

Catherine sits on the bed and kicks off her black high heels.

"I realize you don't want to tell me your lawyer's name. But has he talked to you about alimony?"

She nods as she drinks, finishing half her Bourbon in one swallow. She shivers and tells me Martin won't even miss the alimony. Her voice is angry. "Won't miss me or the money."

She finishes her Bourbon and puts the glass on the end table, steps back to me and says, "Can you help me with my dress?"

Can I help you? Jesus!

She turns her back to me and holds up her hair. I unzip her dress down to the top of her white, half-slip. She steps out of her dress and slip, tossing them on the bed.

"Can you get my bra?"

Usually I'm on the other side, with the woman in a wrestling hold. Unfastening a bra from the rear is much easier. Catherine tosses the bra atop her dress, turns and looks me in the eyes.

Those big green eyes are looking for something in mine and I hope it's there. She smiles slightly and closes her eyes, raising her hands behind her head, as if she's posing.

My gaze moves down to her chest, to those full breasts, those light pink aureoles and those pointed nipples. Her chest rises with her breathing. So does mine. Up close, her perfume is nearly intoxicating.

With her eyes still closed, Catherine unfastens her garter belt and lets it fall, with her stockings to the carpet. She pushes her white panties off and kicks them away and stands there, letting me gaze at her. She does a slow turn and climbs on the bed, shoving her dress and bra to the floor. She lies on her back, those green eyes searing into mine.

Jesus! I'm only human.

I undress quickly, but not too quickly. Don't want to seem over-anxious, although I'm more than ready. I make love to this beautiful, lonely wife. Frenzied at first, she gasps and cries out and I grunt and kiss her lips over and over.

Then we do it again to make sure we got it right. The second time is softer and deeper and more loving. The affection in her eyes is startling and we kiss more than I've ever kissed another woman.

After, as I roll on my back and she curls up against my side, I can't help saying it aloud.

"You're husband's a moron."

I can't be sure, but I think she's crying softly.

•

The moron bursts into my office the following morning, his face contorted, a brown envelope in his left hand that he waves menacingly at me as he storms to my desk. He's in another brown suit, blue tie loosened.

I pull my feet off my desk as he shouts, "Where is she?"

I just stare at him, my jaw fixed, my fists ready.

"Where is she?" He slams the envelope on my desk.

"I heard you the first time, counselor." My voice is low and emotionless.

He pulls pictures from the envelope and shoves them across the desk. I glance down and feel my stomach bottom out. They aren't the clearest pictures. Whoever took them must have been in the closet last night, but you can tell it's Catherine and me.

"You unmitigated bastard!" Martin starts around my desk. "You send this pornography to me!" He stops just out of punching range. "Where is my wife?"

I turn my left shoulder to him and snarl. "Step closer and you'll need bridgework." My fists are clenched and ready.

He raises a shaky right index finger. "You think you're getting money from me, you're nuts. I'll go to the police first."

"Money? Are you completely insane?"

Martin backs away. "You can try to blackmail me, but you won't get any money." He reaches over and snatches the pictures.

I put my hands on my desk as he backs away.

"I didn't send those pictures to you and I don't blackmail anyone, Jackass!"

He points his chin at me. "Stay away from my wife!"

"Go to Hell!"

He leaves, kicking the door and I don't know why the glass doesn't shatter.

I immediately dig my leather holster from my desk drawer and thread it through my belt, leaving it at the small of my back. I shove my .38 Smith and Wesson snub-nose into it. Throwing on my light-weight, blue blazer, I step outside just as the Martin's Cadillac runs the stop sign up at Rampart Street. He's moving fast, so I jump in my DeSoto and head after him.

He makes a left on Rampart and may be heading to the Roosevelt or back to Skinner, North, and Wagner in the Hibernia Bank Building. He crosses Canal and then Gravier Street and keeps going. I turn left on Gravier and work my way down to

Baronne Street and the Roosevelt Hotel. Catherine checked out this morning. Can't believe she used her maiden name, like her husband couldn't figure that out.

Thinking she might call, I head back to my office. On Rampart, I turn left on Iberville to pass the mistress's on my way home and Martin's Cadillac is parked out front. He sure got here fast.

I set up down the street and wait. A half hour later, I walk to the corner of Dauphine and use the pay phone, in case Catherine went home for clothes or something. No answer. It isn't long before Martin leaves the apartment in a big hurry. Don't see the mistress, but I have to follow him. If he finds Catherine, she's gonna be in big trouble.

He drives quickly, taking Royal to Canal up to Claiborne, heading uptown. Twenty minutes later, I catch the red light at Napoleon Avenue. He ran the yellow light, hanging a right. Figuring he's heading to their house on Fontainebleau, I drive straight there find his car parked in the circular drive of a white, three story Greek Revival semi-mansion with galleries along the first and second floors. I pull out the note with Catherine's phone number and it's their address all right.

Driving past, I set up across the neutral ground (that's what we call medians in New Orleans) beneath a towering oak. The narrow neutral ground is dotted with camellia bushes and small palm trees, but I have a perfect line of view to the front of the house.

Just before eleven, a light blue Cadillac parks behind Martin's Caddy. Catherine climbs out the driver's side and another woman exits the passenger side. It's the mistress, in an appropriate red dress. Catherine's in a white dress. She leads the way to the front door and starts to open it with a key, when Martin yanks it open. Both women take a step back.

I'm out of my car, crossing the neutral ground.

Martin's in his shirt sleeves, no tie. I hear loud voices. The mistress moves forward, kisses Martin on the cheek and stands between him and Catherine, who slips into the house. The door closes as I reach their side of the street. I stop behind another oak and peek at the house.

What the hell do I do?

What the hell's going on?

My heart thunders in my chest as I stand here wondering.

There's a sharp crack, unmistakably a gunshot, followed by five more in quick succession. I pull out my .38, and race for the door. I try the knob and it's unlocked. I slip into a marble foyer, and cock my revolver. There's a wide staircase straight ahead, what looks like a dining room to my right and a study to my left where I hear a sob.

I peek in and Catherine's just inside, a snub-nosed, nickel-plated .38 Colt in her right hand, her face streaked with blood. Martin lies on the carpet ten feet in front of her. The mistress is sprawled across a sofa, to Catherine's right. I slip up to Catherine and take the gun from her.

She blinks at me and says, "He hit me again."

The room stinks of cordite and blood. I slip her gun into my pants pocket and check out the mistress. No visible gunshot wound. She's breathing OK. She's even prettier up close.

"Did you shoot her?"

"No." Catherine starts sobbing. "She fainted."

I check Martin. He's not breathing. I hold my fingers against his carotid artery. Dead. She put all six shots in his chest. Looking up at Catherine, I ask, "Whose gun?"

She has her hands in front of her face. I guide her to the other sofa in the study and sit her. I have to pull her hands away from her face.

"Whose gun?" I repeat.

She answers between sobs. "It's... his... gun. I took... it... from... nightstand... when I left."

I step over to a nearby desk, pick up the phone and call the

New Orleans Confidential · O'Neil De Noux **66**

police. I manage to get Catherine to stop sobbing before the police arrive, just as the mistress starts coming to.

Don't know the two uniforms who arrive first, but they know enough to separate us, one leading me outside to wait for the detectives. Not ten minutes later, a black prowl car parks in front of the house and two men exit.

Lieutenant Frenchy Capdeville, in a baggy, blue suit, heads for me, his head shaking. He's a good five inches shorter than me with curly, black hair and a matching, pencil-thin Zorro moustache. If they remake 'The Mark of Zorro' and need a stunt double, Frenchy's the man. He pulls the cigarette from his mouth and flicks it to the driveway, sparks flying.

The other detective has a regrettably familiar face. Jimmy Hays, built like a fire-plug with stubby arms and a pug-ugly face, bounds up and reaches out to grab my coat. Frenchy cuts him off.

"Go inside," Frenchy tells him.

Hays narrows his dull, gray eyes, and spits next to my feet before going in.

Frenchy fires up another Camel. "What's it between you two?"

"I knocked him out once for shooting a dog." That was back when we were rookies at the Third Precinct.

Frenchy blows out a cloud of smoke and says, "Talk to me."

I tell him how it went down, leaving nothing out, not even the part in the Roosevelt. He's the best homicide detective in the city. He'll find out.

"Give me the gun."

I pull it out carefully, by the muzzle and hand it to Frenchy.

"Gimme your roscoe too."

I hand him my gun. He opens the cylinder, checks the rounds, sniffs the barrel.

Another prowl car pulls up and another familiar face, Detective Willie Spade, climbs out. Frenchy waves him forward and tells him to take me to the Detective Bureau. About an inch smaller than me with short carrot-red hair and too many freckles to count, Spade has deep-set brown eyes. I move to him and ask if it's all right if I follow him, not leave my car behind.

"Drive both of us." Spade waves his partner over, a tall dick I've never seen, and tells him what's up.

•

After running a paraffin test on me, to see if I fired a gun lately, Spade calls for the crime lab to come fetch and analyze the test. For the next two hours, Spade and I sit in the Detective Squad room, on the second floor of the concrete Criminal Courts Building, Tulane and Broad Street. We reminisce about old times, working the Third Precinct before the war, especially the night shift. Mostly we talk about women. Spade is partial to whores. The trampier the woman, the more Spade likes her.

As I'm finishing my third cup of coffee, Spade tells me about a gang bang he and three other cops lucked into. Jimmy Hays enters and Spade's story fades.

"What's he doing out here?" Hays kicks a chair as he passes. "Put him in an interview room!"

I don't need Spade to lead me. I go on my own into one of the tiny rooms with its square folding table and two chairs. Hays kicks the door closed on me. I don't have to wait long for the door to open and Frenchy nods me out. Hays, fuming as he stands behind Frenchy, glares at me as I pass. Spade pulls a chair out for me at the conference table near the coffee pot, which reeks of stale Java.

Frenchy pulls up a chair next to me and lays out the pictures from the Roosevelt. "Not only do you make more money than we do, you get fringe benefits, too."

Spade scoops up the pictures and stammers, "Damn!"

Frenchy Zippos another cigarette. Hays moves to the far side of the table, giving me the big, bad stare.

"The shooting looks justifiable," Frenchy declares. "Precinct boys tell me they've been out there before. Seems the respectable attorney was a well-practiced wife-beater." He lets out a long stream of smoke. "We ran a paraffin test on the wife. Confirms she fired the weapon, as you said." He shoves a hand-written crime lab report in front of me. "You, however, didn't fire a weapon. And her sister confirms the whole story."

It takes a second. "Sister?!"

"The other woman in the house." Frenchy stands and stretches. "The wife's sister."

"Whoa!" Spade howls as he looks at another view of Catherine and me.

I sit back and try to wipe the surprise from my face. Frenchy puts my gun on the table.

"Damn!" Spade snaps up another picture.

"Where are you going with those pictures?" Frenchy calls out.

Spade turns and says, "Bathroom. I'll only be a minute."

Frenchy snatches the pictures from Spade. He nods at me and tells Spade, "Take his statement."

Turning back to me, Frenchy adds, "You can go after. Just don't go near the wife. She doesn't want to see you again." He takes a step and tells me, over his shoulder, "We have men outside her house, Capiche?"

•

On my way home, I stop on Iberville Street and knock on the mistress's door. I ring the bell and knock again. As I turn to leave, the door of 813A, the other half of the townhouse, opens and a gray-haired woman peers out.

"You here about the apartment?"

"Uh, sure."

The woman steps out with a key in her hand. She's not five feet tall and wears a pink housecoat. "Tenant moved out yesterday."

Stepping back, I notice a small sign in her window:

Apartment for Rent. She lets me into the mistress's apartment, into a modestly furnished living room, then to the rear kitchen.

"There are two bedrooms upstairs," she says, leading me up the stairs. "Young people nowadays," she adds.

"What about them?"

"They don't believe in responsibility, suddenly moving out. At least the place is clean."

The master bedroom is in front with the French doors and balcony. There's a bathroom between the two bedrooms. There's a odd smell in it, like acid.

"That's strange." The woman stops and points to the only window in the bathroom, which is painted black. I look around and spot weather stripping on the bathroom door. It was a *darkroom*. I feel the pieces falling in place. They sure played me, didn't they?

•

In my apartment, I pull out my extra set of the pictures from Iberville Street, grab one of the mistress kissing Martin and one of the naked mistress-sister on her balcony. I slip them into an envelope, put Catherine's address on the outside and a note inside that reads: Call me!

I walk to the taxi stand up on Rampart and pick out the biggest cabbie, a huge man with a tattoo of a parachute with wings on his arm. He's an airborne veteran. I pull him aside and tell him I was a Ranger in Italy, mentioning Monte Cassino. He nods and tells me he was with the 82nd Airborne at St. Mere Eglise. Damn!

I offer him a ten spot to put the envelope in Catherine LaVanchy's hand.

He says no problem.

"Watch out for cops outside her house."

He says no problem.

•

Sitting in my easy chair, facing the door to my apartment, I sip my Scotch-rocks and wait for her. I close my eyes and can almost feel her moving beneath me. I can see the affection in those green eyes when we made love, how her pretty face glowed with the passion.

Maybe she'll call, but I've a gut feeling she'll come – for the pictures.

When the doorbell rings at nine o'clock I'm on my third Scotch. Cracking open my apartment door, I push the downstairs buzzer and hear the door open and shut. I look down at the top of her head as she starts up the stairs. I step back in and freshen my Scotch.

The door swings open and the sister-mistress stares at me from the doorway. She's in a form-fitting black dress with blue piping, black heels and matching gloves. Her pouty lips are painted a deep crimson, her eyes even more intensely green than her sister's. She's prettier too, if that's possible. Younger. That's probably it.

I step up to her and take her purse from her arm, open it and look through it.

"What are you looking for?" She has a silvery, seductive voice.

"Another gun. Where's Catherine?"

She slips into my living room and turns back to me. "The pictures are of me." She wears the same perfume and suddenly I wish I hadn't drank so much. "Lucien, isn't it?" Her voice deepens. "I'm Connie."

Crossing to the sofa, she peels off her gloves and drops them on my coffee table. I close the door and move toward her, watching as she looks up at me and says, "How much money do you want?"

"None." I lift my glass. "Can I get you a drink?"

"You don't want money?"

"That's what you and your sister were after. Alimony wouldn't be enough, but *all* his money would, right?"

Connie puts a hand on her hip, as I go for my bottle of Johnny Walker Red Label. "He was too good a lawyer for my sister to get much alimony." Her voice has that teacher-nun patronizing tone, as if I'm a child. "He was too well connected to every judge in town."

I put the bottle and my empty glass down. It's coffee I need right now.

"You know how it is," she says.

"I know he wasn't screwing you. Not with the way you kissed him on the cheek every time you saw him, like he was a cousin or brother-in-law, not a lover. Y'all set me up and used me to get him angry enough to beat her so she could kill him."

Her eyes don't react.

"The only weak link in your plan is me." I point to the rest of the pictures from Iberville piled on my coffee table. "I can put you on Iberville Street, can put it all together for the D.A."

I have to admit, she remains cool, those green eyes showing not a hint of worry.

"If you don't want money, then what do you want?"

I'm suddenly on her, scooping her up and holding her close. "She used me and I'm going to use her."

There's no fear in her eyes, just a searching look, a probing. I let her go and take a step back. "She comes to me, she gets the pictures, negatives, everything."

I sit on the sofa. She stands there for a long minute, still staring at me.

"You won't turn us in?"

"Without these pictures, I've got nothing. Man beats his wife and gets what he deserved. I just want you and Catherine to know I know what you did. *And* I want her." I raise my index finger. "For one more night, like it was at the Roosevelt." Maybe it's the liquor talking, but I mean it. A subtle change comes over her face. It's less confident, less intense. Her eyes become wider as she kicks off her heels and reaches around to unzip her dress.

"They're my pictures," she says in a husky tone. "Keep 'em. I didn't come for the pictures, anyway."

She climbs out of her dress, and stands for a moment in her white bra and panties. No stockings tonight.

"You were never a weak link in our plan," she says. "You, we can handle."

She unfastens her bra and lets it drop, freeing those full, luscious breasts.

"I watched you from the closet," she says as she climbs out of her panties and stands naked in front of me.

"No, I didn't come for the pictures at all." She moves to me, languidly, like a cat. She presses her hands against my shoulders and moves her face close to mine.

"I came for this."

And I'm suddenly sober and ready to be used again.

END of THE IBERVILLE MISTRESS

Christmas Weather

I find another letter, this one stuck in the lacework of the wrought iron balcony that wraps around my building. It's the ninth letter I've found since the hit-and-run driver destroyed the mail box at the corner, littering mail all the way up to Rampart Street. No surprise, really, finding a letter up on my second floor balcony. Cabrini Playground across the street was littered with letters.

This letter is wet from last night's rain and as I pull it out of the lacework, the envelope falls apart. There's no stamp on the envelope and the writing is in pencil, printed in large, block letters, addressed to *Santa Claus, North Pole*.

Shielding my eyes from the bright, December sun, I look out at the tile roofs of the lower French Quarter. Two days before Christmas and it's eighty degrees with matching humidity. The winter of '47 is the warmest I can remember. The radio warns of a cold front drifting down from Canada, but it's sure taking its time. I take another sip of strong coffee-and-chicory as I step back into my apartment. Placing the damp letter on my Formica kitchen table, I blot it with a dish towel, then lay it on the towel.

Stretching, I run my hands across my chin, rubbing the morning stubble. The fridge beckons and I go to it, pulling out bacon and eggs. Refilling my coffee mug, I look back at the letter, at the printed letters. I'm drawn to it and sit next to it, blotting it again with the towel.

The letters are block and all capitals:

DEAR SANTA PLEASE HELP MOMMIE AND DADDY THIS CHRISTMASS. DADDY DON'T HAVE A JOB. WE DON'T HAVE MUCH FOOD AND DADDY GIVES HIS FOOD TO MOMMIE AND ME. PLEASE HELP

MY MOMMIE AND DADDY AND
LITTLE JIMMIE. HE'S HUNGRY TOO.
I WANT YOU TO TAKE ME TO
HEAVEN TO BE WITH THE ANGELS.
MY MOMMIE AND DADDY WON'T
HAVE TO BUY FOOD FOR ME NO
MORE. I LIVE IN THE SAME HOUSE
WITHOUT THE PAINT. WE DON'T
HAVE LIGHTS. WE GOT CANDELS. I
WILL WAIT UP FOR YOU TO COME
IN MY ROOM AND YOU CAN BRING
ME TO THE ANGELS. I WILL NOT
SLEEP. WHEN YOU COME CAN YOU
BRING SOME FOOD FOR MOMMIE
AND DADDY.
LOVE, JASON

My hands tremble as they lay on either side of the letter. My throat is tight and my breathing shallow. I feel my heart beating in my ears as I read the letter again, slowly, swallowing painfully when I finish.

I walk through my living room, back out the French doors to the balcony and look around. Taking in a deep breath, I try to think. I'm a detective, after all. He lives around here, within walking distance.

The playground is still empty this morning. The kids, out of school for the holidays, haven't collected there yet. I wonder if he's one. I head inside for the razor and shower and my light-weight, tan suit. People are more likely to talk to a man in a suit. Learned that right out of the box, soon as I hung up my detective shingle earlier this year.

As I tie my black tie, with its brown geometric designs, I look at my light brown eyes in the mirror. They're red. Six feet tall and twenty-nine years old, I'm in pretty damn good shape, regardless of the scar on my left arm from that German sniper at

Monte Cassino, yet my eyes are red. I hear the words in a high-pitched, child's voice.

BRING SOME FOOD FOR MOMMIE
AND DADDY
TAKE ME TO HEAVEN.
MOMMIE AND DADDY WON'T HAVE
TO BUY FOOD FOR ME NO MORE.

I close my eyes and see the hollow faces of the children outside Cassino begging for food from GIs, like me. Their brown eyes were so – hurt. I've seen hunger up close and can't handle it. I raided the mess hall to feed those kids. Would have been court-martialed if I hadn't got shot the next day.

Leaving my building, I slip on dark sunglasses. Two boys are tossing a football in Cabrini Playground. I cross narrow Barracks Street and circle around to the gate in the brick-and-iron-lace fence. The boys are around ten or eleven. Neither knows anyone named Jason or a boy with a little brother named Jimmie.

I walk back to the corner of Barracks and Dauphine and lean my hand against the new mailbox. Glad I'm wearing my older, comfortable Florsheims. I move down to Esplanade and start working my way up Dauphine, all the way to Ursulines.

Here, along the low-rent end of the Quarter, there are plenty of unpainted houses. As I move from door to door, from Creole cottages with their front-slanting roofs and attic dormers, to the narrow shotgun houses with their rooms lined up back-to-back, I keep hearing the boy's voice –

DADDY GIVES HIS FOOD TO
MOMMIE AND ME.
PLEASE HELP MY MOMMIE AND
DADDY AND LITTLE JIMMIE.
HE'S HUNGRY TOO.

I move back to Barracks along Burgundy Street and approach a little girl with red hair sitting on her front stoop. She's playing with a line of dolls, talking to each in a different voice. When she notices me, she looks up, shielding her eyes from the sun with both hands.

"Do you know a boy named Jason, lives around here?"

"I'm not supposed to talk to strangers," she says and reaches down for her dolls as if I'm about to snatch them and run off.

I back away, off the banquette – we call sidewalks by their original French name *banquettes* because they serve as banks when a hard rain comes and fills our low streets – and stand in the street, hands behind my back so she'll see I can't grab anything quickly.

"Is your mother home?"

"She won't want to talk with you either."

I wipe the perspiration from my brow as I ask, "Jason has a little brother named Jimmie. Lives in a house with no paint on it and no electricity."

She points down the block without looking up, , "My Daddy says they're going to have to tear down the house down there before it falls down. They don't have any lights."

I spot a unpainted shotgun four houses down the line. I thank the little girl and walk away. As I approach the house, I can see how it leans to its left. The boards of its small front stoop are worn and sag in the middle. The screen door is patched in places.

I climb up the stoop and knock on the door frame, tucking my sunglasses into my pocket.

"Huh?" The voice is high-pitched.

I cup my hands against the screen and it takes a few seconds for my eyes to adjust to the dimness; and I see him sitting on the living room floor, surrounded by toy soldiers. Dark hair nearly covering his eyes, he wears a gray tee-shirt and faded gray dungarees. He stares at me with ovaled eyes.

"Jason?"

"Uh, huh," he answers hesitatingly. He's about seven, maybe eight. Small for his age, he's a looks delicate, almost fragile.

"Is your Mommy or Daddy home?"

"Mommie!" His high voice echoes off the hardwood floor. I can make out a dark colored sofa and a tired-looking armchair. The lamps are dark.

WE DON'T HAVE LIGHTS.

WE GOT CANDLES.

A figure moves into the living room from the back of the house, a slim woman in a long faded-gray dress. She carries an infant on her hip as she moves silently toward the door. She stops next to Jason and stares at me.

"Is your husband in?"

She shakes her head. Her long, dark hair hangs straight around her face. The baby waves his arms excitedly and she bounces him on her hip. Jason's mother is young, in her early twenties.

"You looking for Bill for any special reason?" Her voice is deep as she pronounces every syllable carefully.

"Not exactly, Mrs..."

"Speeling."

"I'm Lucien Caye. I pull a business card from my coat pocket and press it against the screen but she's not looking at it. She stares at my eyes.

"I understand Bill is looking for work," I say, putting my card back in the pocket.

"That's what he's out doing now." She shifts Jimmie to her other side. "Do you know my husband?"

"No, Ma'am. I'd just like to talk with him, if I may."

"What about?"

"A job."

She takes in a deep breath and lets it out slowly.

"I'll wait out here." I back down to the bottom step and sit on the edge of the stoop, a time-worn New Orleans tradition, the way to pass the evening, sitting out on the front stoop. I take off my coat and drape it over my arm.

Eventually, I hear breathing behind me and turn around to see Jason's face pressed against the screen. He's on his knees. His eyes are blue, the only color I've seen at the Speeling house, besides gray. He leans back, away from the screen and I get my first good look at his face. It's not a child's face at all. It doesn't have that spark, that curiosity, that gleam in the eyes. It looks like those kids in Italy.

Behind him, from the darkness of the living room, his mother calls out to me. "I can offer coffee, but we're out of sugar."

"No thanks." I stand quickly. "I'm uh, going over to the bakery. Can I get you something?"

"No," she says and I look into Jason's eyes, which stare intently as me. It's hard to pull away.

She offered me coffee. They still have gas. I hurry down to Esplanade and hook a left up to Carini's Bakery to wait impatiently for a dozen fresh glaze donuts and two loaves of bread. Across the avenue, I go into Jeanfreau's Grocery and fill two bags with cans of soup, cheese, sliced ham, a slab of bacon, ground meat, eggs, butter, a jar of mayonnaise, mustard, milk, coffee-and-chicory, two heads of lettuce, fresh Creole tomatoes, potatoes. I have to slow down. Can't carry the entire store in one trip. At the counter, I snatch up a few Milky Way and Baby Ruth candy bars, then rush back for a bag of sugar.

Jason still sits just inside the screen door when I return with the three brown bags, placing them on the top step of the stoop. The donuts are still warm. I dig one out and offer it to Jason, who blinks twice.

"Mommie, can I have one?"

"One what?"

I hear her light footsteps, then a long sigh before she tells her son sure, go ahead.

Jason pushes the screen door open and I hand him two donuts.

"One for your Mom."

Jason gives one to his mom and takes a huge bite out of his as he sits again. His mother, not holding Jimmie now, holds the donut down by her side as she moves toward the door. She stops just behind Jason, who's against the door, carefully eating his donut. I pull one out and take a bite, although my stomach's still jittery.

Mrs. Speeling stares down at me, raises her donut, then lowers it and says, "Why are you here?"

"I want to talk with your husband."

"What do you do for a living?" She has her fists on her hips now, donut dangling in her right hand.

"I'm a detective. No, not a cop, a private detective." Her face changes from instant alarm to an uncertain expression.

"I used to be a cop," I explain, "but I'm on my own now." No way I can explain my newly-bloated bank account, thanks to the Degas Inheritance Case, I was fortunate enough to solve just last week.

"How about another?" I ask an eager-looking Jason. He opens the door again and I pass him two more donuts. He gives another to his mother before sitting on the floor again.

His mother lets out another long breath and retreats slowly into the dimness inside.

"How old are you?" I ask Jason.

"Eight and a half. How old are you?"

"Twenty-nine." I smile. "Pretty old, huh?"

He nods as he eats his donut.

Moving to the top step, I lean close to the screen door and keep my voice low. "Jason, you can't go live with the angels right now. It would make your Mommy and Daddy so sad. It would be the worst suffering in the world."

Suddenly, he's frightened and looks down at the floor.

"Don't be afraid," I whisper softer. "Santa read your letter and sent me to help."

"You're not an angel," His voice is scratchy.

"Course not. You can't *see* angels."

Jason's lower lip quivers.

"That's why Santa sent me. He gave me the money for this food." I want to end that desperation.

TAKE ME TO HEAVEN.

MOMMIE AND DADDY WON'T HAVE

TO BUY FOOD FOR ME NO MORE.

I hear someone walking up behind me and turn as a lean fella in a white shirt and black slacks stops a few feet away. His dark hair is cut short, extra short around the ears, and his eyes narrow as he gives me the once over. His face is drawn into tight, sunken cheeks.

I step down to the banquette. "Bill Speeling?"

He nods. He's about a half foot shorter than me, about five-seven, and much thinner.

"Lucien Caye." I stick out my hand and he slowly moves his to mine. His grip is strong, but not overpowering.

"I hear you're looking for work."

"Just came from the V.A. Got nothing." He folds his arms. "What are you doing here?"

"I know some people looking for workers."

"Where? Mars?"

He quits squinting and I see his eyes are also blue.

"Just who the hell are you?" he asks in a low, even voice.

I search for an intelligent answer, something that won't offend and spot the Marine Corps emblem tattooed on his forearm. I nod toward it.

"The Pacific, huh?" Not a hard guess.

"Couple small islands." He unfolds his arms. "Saipan. Pelelieu. Iwo Jima."

Jesus! Just a couple of small islands!

"Where were you?" His voice has a mid-western twang. His wife is from here, with her typical New Orleans flat *As.*

"North Africa. Italy."

Speeling looks at the box of donuts, then at the bags of groceries. He slips his hands into his back pockets.

I look down at my shoes and notice he's wearing combat boots. The pause lingers until I finally say, "Look. One vet to anyone. Let's go look together."

"You don't look like you need a job."

I look up into his weary eyes.

"Let's just do it."

"Daddy, can I have another donut?" There's a high-pitched quiver to Jason's voice.

I pick up the box and hand it to Speeling, who takes his time taking it. He pulls a donut for himself as he climbs the stoop, opens the door and passes the box to his son.

I scoop up the bags and pass them to Speeling without comment. He takes them into the house while I wait outside.

"Mister?" Jason whispers. "Did Santa really send you?"

"Of course."

He almost smiles but he's not sure of me yet and moves aside as his father comes out with a donut in hand.

"I'm obliged," he says as I lead the way to Barracks Street and down to my 1940 DeSoto, parked against the curb in front of my apartment house. Two dozen boys are playing tackle football in the playground now, their excited voices bouncing across the narrow street.

We drive straight to the Industrial Canal and work our way along the companies. Have to admit, Speeling doesn't seem discouraged as we go from place to place along the canal connecting the Mississippi to Lake Pontchartrain. He reminds me of those guys back in combat, the ones who keep getting the bad jobs, taking point or hunting for snipers, just gritting their teeth and doing it, no complaints, just resignation to a job that has to be done.

Three hours after we start, when he climbs back into the DeSoto outside Billiot's Steel and Lumber Yard, he says, "No need to go to the next place. I start in the mornin'."

I smile but he doesn't seem like he has the energy. As we drive back up St. Claude, he thanks me in a low, serious voice that's nearly drowned out by the rattle of a passing streetcar.

I just nod.

Several blocks later, he asks, "How'd you know they were hirin' out by the canal?"

"Didn't. Just figured the law of averages." All those companies.

The tautness of his face seems to lessen as he leans back and closes his eyes.

Parking outside their shotgun, I don't plan to get out. They've seen enough of me today. Jason's out on the front stoop with his toy soldiers. He jumps up when he realizes who's in the car. As his father climbs out of the other side, Jason stepped up to my door.

"Mommie wants you to come in," he says and for the first time there's a hint of a smile on his little face.

I smell bacon cooking as I follow Jason and his father into the shotgun, through the living room, the master bedroom where little Jimmie sleeps in the center of the Speeling's double bed. We pass through Jason's room with its small bed and toy box made from a Roemer's milk carton. I see a silver airplane and a train engine.

Mrs. Speeling, a white apron around the front of her dress, points to their small kitchen table as I enter.

"Might as well eat some of the groceries you brought."

She serves us bacon and omelets made with potatoes and ground beef. They eat slowly, even Jason, without much conversation. Bill Speeling tells his wife he found a job. She nods and I wish I could just leave them alone to hash this out.

"I can get a half day's hours working tomorrow," he says.

Christmas Eve.

"That's good."

"Can we get lights?" Jason's voice is hesitant.

After a pause, his father explains how he gets paid at the end of every week and soon as he gets his first paycheck, he'll get the electricity back on. His voice has an edge to it, as if all this could go away any time.

I finish quickly and ask to be excused.

"Certainly," Mrs. Speeling says, putting her fork down.

All three thank me again. Before I'm through Jason's room, he's right behind me with those big eyes. He waves me down and cups his hand against his mouth.

"Did Santa really send you?"

I whisper back. "Yes. And I'm not finished yet."

"Really?" He leans back.

"Really."

He almost smiles.

Hurrying to my DeSoto, I hope I have time to make it to power company before they close at five. A lady with dyed hair that supposed to be red, but is more orange, takes my cash and promises the electricity will be turned on in the morning.

"Any way we can get it turned on tonight?"

"Hey, you should be grateful to we can get a man out on Christmas Eve!"

I ask to speak to her supervisor. Two supervisors later, they find a man just knocking off who'll follow me to Burgundy Street and the shotgun house. I wait around at the corner and watch the house light up.

Meeting the man from the power company after, I try to give him a tip, but he won't take it.

"Merry Christmas," he tells me as he drives off in his yellow truck.

Suddenly I get that sick feeling again in my stomach and my throat tightens just by his saying that – Merry Christmas.

•

Out on my balcony, I look across Cabrini Playground in the direction of the Speeling house up Burgundy Street. Can't see it. I finish off my third Scotch and swirl the ice around in the glass. My tongue is thick and my belly warn. I've a good buzz going, but it isn't enough.

> I WANT YOU TO TAKE ME TO HEAVEN TO BE WITH THE ANGELS. MY MOMMIE AND DADDY WON'T HAVE TO BUY FOOD FOR ME NO MORE.

Did I do a good thing today?

It wasn't enough, not enough to keep me from hearing Jason's desperate voice.

Why didn't I slip some cash into the grocery bag?

Why can't I stop hearing that desperate voice?

Who am I kidding?

I don't want to stop hearing it. I'm keeping his letter so I can read it every time I'm cocky enough to think I'm on top of the world. I want to remember the faces of those hungry kids in Italy. I want to remember Jason's desperation. I don't want to ever forget –

> I WANT YOU TO TAKE ME TO HEAVEN TO BE WITH THE ANGELS. MY MOMMIE AND DADDY WON'T HAVE TO BUY FOOD FOR ME NO MORE.

Don't know if I'll feel better tomorrow, but I've got something else to do. I toss the ice down to the street and go inside. Eventually, I'll fall asleep. Eventually.

•

The promised cold front comes through during the night. As I shave, I can't help thinking that's how it goes in New Orleans. One day it's a steamy autumn day in the eighties, the next it's a damp winter day in the low forties.

Christmas Eve. I've a lot to do today, so I start early.

Later – Jason is out on the front stoop, his elbows up on his knees, chin propped in his hands as I park my DeSoto in front of his house. His face is flushed in the nippy air. He looks at me excitedly but loses it immediately.

"Daddy's not with you?"

"I think he's still at work."

"Oh." Jason sits back down. I open my trunk and start pulling out the presents. I didn't think Jason's eyes could get wider. I start stacking the presents on the stoop.

Jason watches me, his hands now in the pockets of the same gray dungarees he had on yesterday. He won't even touch the gold and silver wrappings. He wears a thick sweater with worn spots at the elbows. As I step up with the last of the gifts, I see Mrs. Speeling inside the screen door with Jimmie on her hip. She's in a yellow dress today and doesn't say anything as she stares at me.

Jason reaches a shaky hand to the closest gift.

"Santa sent these," I say, loud enough for his mother to hear.

I sit on the bottom step and watch Mrs. Speeling disappear back into the house.

"Really?" Jason asks.

I lean close to Jason. "Really. Didn't Santa have your lights turned on last night?"

His brow relaxes and he looks as if he's finally believing me.

"Can I open my present now?"

"That's up to your Mom and Dad."

Jason runs inside, his footsteps hammering on the hardwood floors. I hear his high-pitched voice pleading. I spot Bill

Speeling coming up Burgundy from Esplanade. I stand as Jason slams open the screen door.

"Daddy! Daddy! Look what Santa sent."

Speeling gives me a long, tired look, which I have a hard time returning.

"Can I open mine now? Please!"

Speeling sits on the edge of the stoop and nods, pulling Jason close for a moment for a hug before letting his son go.

"Which one's mine?" Jason asks me.

"Check the names." I back away to the front fender of my DeSoto.

Jason passes the first gift to his father, then calls out for Jimmie, then runs inside with Jimmie's gift – a glow worm that wiggles when you wind it up.

I bought a gift certificate for Mrs. Speeling at D. H. Holmes Department Store and picked up a couple work shirts and pants for Speeling, who thanks me when Jason opens his present for him.

Surprisingly, Jason isn't disappointed in his first gift, a pair of U.S. Keds high top tennis shoes. He's really excited by the second, digging into the gift box to pull out the men and the sailing ship.

"Pirates?" he asks.

I pick up a rubber figure with blonde hair. "This is Jason and the Argonauts." I stand the Argonauts up, along with the Cyclopes, the multi-headed hydras and skeletons with swords.

"Jason and the Argonauts went on a great adventure to find the golden fleece." I pull out the golden fleece and show it to Jason who puts it on the sailing ship and starts playing immediately.

Speeling moves to my car and leans against it. Catching my eye, he nods me over.

He looks me straight in the eye. "Why are you doing this? You don't have any family for Christmas?"

"Actually, I don't. But that's not why I'm doing this."

"Then why?"

I want to tell him about the kids in Italy. I want to tell him I'm doing it to make _me_ feel better, to ease the ache in my chest. I open my mouth to respond when I see tears welling in the man's eyes as he looks at his son playing on the stoop.

"I did it because of the war," I tell him.

"What?"

"Because when we were over there, we went together and now that we're back, we're still together."

I look into his eyes and it looks like he's buying it.

END of CHRISTMAS WEATHER

Christmas Weather is for my Uncle Earl De Noux, U.S. Army

combat engineer –

from the beaches of Normandy to the Bridge at Remagen

Erotophobia

She shook out her long brown hair, turned her cobalt blue eyes toward me and winked as the slim Negro named Sammy began to unbutton her blouse. She was trying her best not to act nervous. Sammy's fingers shook as he moved from the top button of her green silk blouse to the second button.

I leaned my left shoulder against the brick wall of the make-shift photo studio and watched. The second floor of a defunct shoe factory, the studio was little more than an open room with a hardwood floor, worn brick walls lined with windows overlooking Claiborne Avenue and two large glass skylights above. It smelled musty and faintly of varnish.

The photographer, Sammy's older cousin Joe Cairo, snapped a picture with his 35mm Leica. Joe was thin and light skinned and about twenty-five. Shirtless, he wore blue jeans and no shoes. His skin was already shiny with sweat. Sammy was also shirtless and shoeless, wearing only a pair of baggy white shorts. His skin was so black it looked like varnished mahogany against Brigid's pale flesh.

Yeah, her name was Brigid. Brigid de Loup, white female, twenty-seven, five feet-three inches with pouty lips and a gorgeous face. Gorgeous. With her green blouse, she wore a tight black skirt and a pair of open-toe black high heels.

She bit her lower lip as Sammy's fingers moved to the third button, the one between her breasts. She looked at him and raised her arms and put her hands behind her head. Sammy let out a high-pitched noise and moved his fingers down to the fourth button.

My name? Lucien Caye, white male, thirty, six feet even, with brown eyes and wavy brown hair in need of a haircut. I stood there with my arms folded and watched, my snub-nosed

.38 Smith and Wesson in a leather holster on my right hip. I'm a private-eye.

"You're going to have to pull my blouse out," Brigid told Sammy.

Sammy nodded, his gaze focused on her chest as he pulled her blouse out of her skirt and unbuttoned the final two buttons. He pushed the blouse off her shoulders and dropped it to the floor.

I loosened my black and gold tie and unbuttoned the top button of my white, dress shirt, then stuck my hands in the pockets of my pleated black suit pants to straighten out my rising dick.

Brigid looked at me as she turned her back to Sammy, who fumbled with the button at the back of her skirt. Her white bra was lacy and low cut. Jesus, her breasts looked luscious.

I moved to one of the windows and opened it and flapped my shirt as the air filtered through the high branches of the oaks lining Claiborne. The spring of '48 was already a scorcher, yet the air was surprisingly cool and smelled of rain. A typical afternoon New Orleans rainstorm was coming. I could feel it.

Brigid had come to me two weeks earlier, in a Cadillac, with diamonds on her fingers and pearls around her neck, and told me she needed a bodyguard.

Yeah. Right.

"I suffer from erotophobia," she said, crossing her leg as she sat in the soft-back chair next to my desk.

"What?"

"It's the fear of erotic experiences."

Yeah. Right.

If someone had told me back when I was a cop that a stunning dish would tell me *that* one day, I'd have looked at them as if they were retarded.

She told me her doctor prescribed 'shock therapy', and she needed a bodyguard.

"I want to feel erotic. But I also want to be safe."

She told me she was married and her husband approved of what she had in mind.

"What's that?" I asked.

"Sexy pictures."

Sammy finally got the button undone and unzipped her skirt.

"Go down on your knees," Joe the photographer told Sammy, repositioning himself to their side. I kept behind Joe, to keep out of the pictures.

"Now," Joe said. "Pull her skirt down."

Brigid looked back at Sammy and wiggled her ass. Sammy's hands grabbed the sides of the skirt and pulled it down over her hips, his face about four inches from the white panties covering her ass. Brigid turned, put her left hand on his shoulder and stepped out of her skirt.

"Take her stockings off next," Joe said.

Brigid lifted her left leg and told Sammy he'd need to take her shoes off first. He did, then reached up to unsnap her stockings from her lacy garter belt.

He rolled each stocking down, his sinewy fingers roaming down her legs. Brigid put her arms behind her head again and spread her feet wide for him. She bit her lower lip again.

Sammy, on his haunches now, wiped sweat from his forehead and looked back at his cousin who told him the bra was next. I felt perspiration working its way down my back. My temples were already damp with sweat.

Brigid started to turn and Joe told her to do it face-to-face. He switched to his second Leica. Brigid gave Joe a look, a knowing look and something passed between them. I was sure.

"If you don't mind," Joe added in a shaky voice. "It'll be sexier."

Brigid smiled shyly. "That's what I want." Her voice was husky.

Her chest rose as she took in a deep breath. Sammy stood up and reached around her. It only took him a second to unhook the bra and pull it off, freeing Brigid's nice round breasts.

Oh, God –

Her small nipples were pointed. Her breasts rose with her breathing. Sammy stared at them from less than a foot away. He blinked and said, "Wow."

Brigid looked at me and smiled and I could see a nervous tick in her cheek. She took in another deep breath, her breasts rising again.

Joe stepped up and tapped Sammy on the shoulder and told him to go down on his knees again. "Now," Joe said, "take her panties off."

Joe hurriedly set up for more shots.

Sammy tucked his fingers into the top of her panties. Brigid leaned her head back to face the skylights and closed her eyes. Joe snapped away and my dick was a diamond-cutter now. Sammy pulled her panties down, his nose right in front of her bush. She stepped out of them, and he leaned back and stared at her thick pubic hair, a shade darker than the long hair on her pretty head. Brigid turned slowly and pointed her ass at Sammy who reached up and unhooked her garter belt and pulled it away.

"OK. Stop," Joe said, sitting on the floor. He pulled his camera bag to him and unloaded both Leicas before loading them again.

Brigid slowly turned to face me. Her face was serious now and flushed. I moved my gaze down her body and almost came just looking at her. She winked at me when I looked back at her face, she rolled her shoulders slightly, her breasts swaying with her movement.

Joe told Sammy to stand up when the cameras were loaded. He took several pictures of them standing face to face, looking at one another and then asked them to stand side by side.

"No touching," Brigid said, reminding Joe of the ground rules. He nodded and had them sit next, side by side with their legs straight out. Brigid leaned back on her hands and Sammy leered at her bush.

Then Joe had them sit cross-legged facing one another. I felt my dick stir again when she leaned back and shook out her hair and the light from the skylight seemed to illuminate her body. God, she looked so sexy with her breasts pointing and her legs open and all her bush exposed.

Joe asked Brigid to stand and put her hands on her hips and move her feet apart as Sammy remained sitting, staring at her pussy, which was at eye-level now. Brigid looked at Joe when he moved her, his hand on her hip. They exchanged brief, warm smiles as he moved her.

Sammy let out a deep breath and Brigid laughed. I was breathing pretty heavy myself. Jesus, what a scene. Joe moved them around in different positions and snapped furiously and switched cameras again.

He had them sit again and entwined their legs. Sammy's dark skin was in stark contrast with Brigid's fair skin. Joe moved in for close-ups of Brigid's chest and moved down to snap her bush. She looked at him and moved her knees apart as she sat.

"Yeah. Yeah," Joe said snapping away. "Don't stop."

Joe pulled Brigid up by the hand and had her stand over Sammy, straddling his outstretched legs as he sat. Then Joe had her sit on Sammy's legs, her legs open as she faced Sammy.

"Now lean back on your hands," Joe said.

Brigid leaned back, her legs open, her pussy wide open to Sammy and Joe behind him snapping away, and me peeking at her pink slit. She was hairy. I like that in a woman. I especially liked the delicate hairs just outside her pussy.

Jesus. What a sight –

She looked at Joe for a long seconds, staring at him the way a woman does when she's getting screwed. She wasn't looking at the camera, and Sammy was just a prop. She looked at Joe. The look on her face was for him. It was a subtle move, but I caught it. Joe snapped at a furious pace.

Brigid finally climbed off Sammy, turned and walked to the bathroom and closed the door behind her. She walked purposefully, as if she had trouble moving her legs.

Sammy lay all the way down and panted, his chest slick with sweat now. Joe picked up his cameras and hurriedly reloaded both. I opened another window. The air was misty now and felt damp and cool on my face. I looked down on the avenue at the tops of the passing cars and then looked straight out at the dark branches and green leaves of the oaks. I wondered what the passers-by would think if they knew what was going on up here.

The bathroom door opened and Brigid came out, walking more steadily. She stepped over to her purse and took out her compact, touching up her face with powder, re-applying dark red lipstick.

She smiled at Joe and said, "No pictures right now. OK?"

He nodded.

Brigid moved over to Sammy and said, "Stand up and put your hands on your head."

"Huh?"

She bent over and grabbed his right hand and pulled him up. Then she lifted his hands and put them on his head, the way we did the Krauts we took prisoner outside Rome. She yanked Sammy's shorts down, pulled them off his feet and tossed them aside. He wore no underwear. His long thin dick stood straight up like a flag pole. Brigid smiled and looked Sammy in the eyes.

She reached down and grabbed Sammy's dick. He jumped. Slowly, she worked her hand up and down his long dick. Sammy moaned.

Brigid looked at me and said, "I don't want y'all to think I'm just a tease."

Jesus, a white woman giving a Negro a hand job. Unbefuckinlievable. I figured she knew it wouldn't bother me in the way it would bother most white boys. She had me pegged from day one, I guess, from the way I treated Joe and the Negroes we'd come across during her posing sessions.

Brigid looked at Joe and it was there again, that come-hither sexy look, but only for a moment. She bent over, her legs stiff, her ass straight up, and leaned over and kissed the tip of Sammy's cock. He rocked on his feet and she increased her jerking motion until he came. She caught it with her free hand and wiped Sammy's cum on his chest when he finished. Then she turned to Joe and asked if he wanted a hand job. He shook his head.

She looked at me and said, "Need some help with those blue balls?"

I shook my head slowly and watched her go back into the bathroom. She left the door open this time and washed her hands. She toweled off, left the towel and walked straight back to me. She put her hands on my chest, leaned up and gave me a fluttery kiss on my lips.

Then she went over to Joe and gave him the same fluttery kiss. I could see him squirm and then close his eyes. He smiled warmly at her when she pulled away.

"Come on," she said. "Let's finish these rolls."

Joe told Sammy to go wash off. When he returned, Joe posed them together naked. The climax of the shooting had Brigid straddling Sammy's legs again as they sat, her pussy wide open and Sammy's dick up and hard again.

When Joe ran out of film again, Brigid got up and told me, "Time to get the film, big boy. I hope you counted the rolls."

I had.

Joe unloaded both cameras and gave me the six rolls of film. We watched Brigid dress. Sammy went into the bathroom. He was still there when Brigid and I left.

•

Sitting in my pre-war 1940 DeSoto, her legs crossed and her skirt riding high on her naked thighs, Brigid smiled at me and said, "Next time we'll shoot in a cemetery."

"Yeah?" I could smell her perfume again in the confines of the car.

"Joe knows some gravediggers at Cypress Grove. Posing naked among the crypts, in front of a captive audience... alive and dead, will be so delicious."

It didn't take a fuckin' genius to figure the one thing this woman didn't have — was erotophobia. I still hadn't figured her angle.

"When did Joe tell you about the gravediggers?"

She winked at me. "When I called him yesterday. That was when he told me he had his cousin lined up for today's session."

The rain came down hard now and the windshield was fogging as I tooled the DeSoto up Claiborne, away from the Negro section called Treme toward uptown where the rich lily-whites lived in their Victorian and Neo-Classical and Greek Revival homes. I cracked my window and felt the rain flutter my hair.

Brigid leaned against the passenger door and watched me. Her dress was so high I could almost see her ass the way she rolled her hips. She eye-fucked me all the way home, ogling me every time I looked her way.

Jesus, she was so fuckin' pretty and so fuckin' sexy and so fuckin' nasty. She hired me to make sure no one raped her. That was the last thing a man would do with a woman like her. At least, that was the last thing I'd do. I'd want her to come to me, wrap those legs around me and fuck me back.

"Want to come in and meet my husband?" she asked when I pulled up in front of her white Greek Revival home on Audubon Boulevard.

"No, that's OK."

"He's waiting for me to tell him what it was like." She raised her purse and added, "And to develop the film." Her husband had a built-in darkroom.

She pulled a white envelope from her purse and handed it to me. Cash. She always paid me in small bills. I actually got paid to watch her get naked and pose with her legs open. Tell me America isn't a great country.

Brigid opened the door, stopped, moved across the seat and kissed me. I felt her tongue as she French kissed me in front of her big house and I thought I would come right there. I watched her hips as she walked away, barefoot up her front walk to the large front gallery with its nine white columns. Her high-heel dangling from her left hand, she turned back and waved at me and went in the front cut-glass door of her big house.

•

The rain came down in torrents that evening. I stood inside the French doors of my apartment balcony and watched it roll in sheets across Cabrini Playground here on Barracks Street. The oak branches waved in the torrent. The wind shook the thick rubbery leaves and white petals of the large magnolias. I looked beyond the playground at the slick, tilted roofs and red brick chimneys of the French Quarter. The old part of town always looked older in the rain.

I leaned against the glass door and looked down at my DeSoto parked against the curb. The glass felt cool against my cheek. The street wasn't flooded yet at least. I took a sip of scotch, felt it burn its way down to my empty belly, and closed the drapes.

I sat back on my sofa, in front of the revolving fan, and closed my eyes and remembered the first time we'd gone out to shoot pictures. It was in Cabrini Playground. It was a real turn-on watching Brigid sit in a tight red skirt, sit so Joe could see up her dress and take pictures of her white panties.

The second time was in City Park where she stripped down to her bra and panties to pose beneath an umbrella of oak branches. Two workers came across us and Brigid liked that. She liked an audience. Joe moved us to the back lagoon for some topless pictures, only some fishermen saw us and got pissed at the half-naked white girl with the black boy, so we had to bail out. My dick was a diamond cutter again as I sat on my sofa. I finished my scotch, readjusted my hard-on, knowing the only relief I could feel would be in a hot wash rag.

I closed my eyes and remembered the two brunette whores we came across just outside Rome, the day before I was wounded, Monte Cassino, 1944. The girls were about twenty, a little on the plump side with pale white skin. They fucked the entire platoon and got up to wave good-bye to us early the next morning, when we moved out.

My doorbell rang. I stood slowly and walked down the stairs to the door. Through the transom above the louvered front door, I saw the top of a yellow cab. I peeked out the door and Brigid was there, her hair dripping in the rain. I opened the door and she turned and waved to the cabby who drove off up Barracks.

Brigid stepped past me and stood dripping in the foyer. Wearing the same clothes she had for the photo session, she shivered and cupped her hands against her chest, her head bent forward. I closed the door. I put my hand under her chin and lifted her face and she blinked those cobalt eyes at me. They were red now with a blue semi-circle bruise under her left eye.

"Pipi hit me," she said, her lower lip quivering. "Can I come up?"

I took her right hand and brought her up and straight into my bathroom. I grabbed the box of kitchen matches from the medicine cabinet and lit the gas wall heater. Standing, I turned as Brigid dropped her bra.

"Don't leave," she said, bending over to run a bath. "You've seen it all."

I put the lid down on the commode and sat and watched her take her clothes off. She smiled weakly at me, her lips still shaking as she climbed into the tub. The water continued running as she sank back.

"How about some coffee?"

"You have any Scotch?"

I stood and looked down at her. Her eyes were closed and the water moved dreamily over her naked body and she looked so damn sexy. I poured us each a double Johnnie Walker Red and went back in.

A silent hour and two drinks later, as well as two hard-ons, she stood up in the tub and asked me to pass her a towel. In the bright light of the bathroom, her skin looked white-pink. She dried herself and wrapped a fresh towel around her chest just above her breasts, and took my hand and led me out to the sofa where we sat.

She poured us both another Scotch, left hers on the coffee table next to the bottle and turned her back to me to lie across my lap as I sat straight up. I had to adjust my dick again and she knew and smiled at me.

"I'll take care of that," she said softly and closed her eyes.

With no make-up, with her hair still damp and getting frizzy, with the mouse under her eye – she was still gorgeous. Some women are like that, plain-knockdown-gorgeous.

After a while she told me that Pipi, that's her husband, couldn't get it up when she came in and told him about what she'd done. She even dug out the previous pictures and went down on him, but he was as limp as a Republican's brain.

Then he hit her, punched her actually and kicked her out, shoved her into the rain.

"At least he called a cab for me." She opened her cobalt blues and blinked up at me. "Guess you figured he's the one with erotophobia. Pipi's the one afraid of erotic experiences."

No shit.

She sat up, reached over and grabbed her drink and downed it with one gulp. I got up a second and moved to the balcony doors. I didn't hear the rain anymore, so I cracked them. It was still drizzling so I left them open and went back to the sofa. I felt the coolness immediately. It was nice.

She settled her head back in my lap and closed her eyes again. The towel had risen and I could see a hint of her bush now. I reached over and picked up my drink and finished it, then put the glass back on the coffee table. A while later, she sighed and turned her face toward me and I could see by her even breathing she was asleep. The towel opened when she turned and I looked at her body again.

I wanted to fuck her so badly. I climbed out from under her head, stood and stretched. I reached down and scooped Brigid into my arms. I took her into my bedroom and laid her on the bed. She sighed again and I leaned over and kissed her lips gently. I grabbed the second pillow and went back out to the sofa and poured myself another stiff one. I was feeling kinda woozy by then anyway so I lay back on the sofa and tried some deep breathing with my eyes closed.

There was a movie I saw where a private-eye turned Veronica Lake down because it ain't good business to sleep with clients. Fuck that shit. Brigid wouldn't have to ask me again. I pulled off my socks and gulped down the rest of my drink and lay back on the pillow and closed my eyes. I tried deep breathing and letting my mind float. And just as I was drifting I realized it wasn't Veronica Lake. It was Ann Sheridan. Or was it Barbara Stanwyck in a blonde wig?

•

The banging of the French doors woke me. I sat up too quickly and felt dizzy and had to lean back on the sofa. It was pitch outside and nearly as dark inside. Lightning flashed and the rainy wind raised the drapes like floating ghosts. A roll of thunder made the old building shiver.

The wind felt cool on my face. I started to rise and saw her standing next to the sofa. I sank back as lightning flashed again, illuminating her naked body in white light. I felt her move up to me and felt her arms on my shoulders as she climbed on me. She said something, but the thunder drowned it.

I felt the weight of her body on my lap as she ripped at my shirt. I tried to help, but she tore it and we both pulled it off. She grabbed my belt and slapped my hand when I tried to help. Rising, she shoved my pants and underwear down and then sank back on me. I felt her bush up against my dick, her mouth searching my face for my lips. Our tongues worked against each other as I raised my hands for those breasts.

She moved her hips up and down slowly as we kissed. I felt the wetness between her legs. She rose high and reached down to guide my dick into her. She sank on it and shivered and then fucked me like I've never been fucked before.

And she talked nasty.

"Oh, fuck me. Come on. Fuck me. Oh, God I love your dick. I love it. Fuck me. Yes. Yes. Oh, God."

I like it when women call me God, even if its just for a little while.

She bounced on me. "More," she said. "More!"

Hell, there was no more. She had it all.

She screamed and I came in her in long spurts and she cried out and held on to my neck. Then she collapsed on me and it took a while for our breathing to return to normal.

I looked over her shoulder as lightning flashed again and saw the wet floor next to the open balcony doors. The wind whipped up again and felt so damn good on our hot bodies. The thunder rolled once more and sounded further away. When I could gather enough strength, I kicked off my pants and shorts. I lifted her and carried her back into the bedroom. I climbed on her and fucked her nice and long the way second-fucks should be, deep and time consuming.

She wrapped her legs around my waist and her arms around my neck and kissed me and kissed me. She was one great, loving kisser. She made noises, sexy noises, but didn't talk nasty. She just fucked me back in long hip-grinding pumps.

After I came I stayed in her until her gyrating hips slipped my dick out. I rolled on my back and pulled her to me and she snuggled her face in the crook of my neck, her hot body pressed against me.

Every once in a while I felt the breeze come in and try to cool us.

•

She was still pressed against me when the daylight woke me. I slipped out of bed, relieved myself and pulled on a fresh pair of boxers before brushing my teeth. She lay on her stomach, the sheet wrapped around her right leg, her long hair covering her face.

I went to the kitchen and started up a pot of coffee-and-chicory, bacon and eggs. She came in just as I was putting the bacon next to the eggs on the two plates on my small white Formica table. Naked, she walked up and planted a wet one on my lips. She leaned back and brushed her hair out of her face and said, "I used your toothbrush."

"Sit down."

I went back and put the bacon pan in the sink and poured us two cups of strong coffee.

"You don't have a barrette, do you?" She moved around the table and sat.

"Huh?"

"Left over from a previous fuck?"

"Yeah. Right." I put her coffee in front of her and sat across the table and ate my bacon and eggs and watched her breasts as she lifted her fork to eat. OK, I looked at her face too and stared into those turquoise eyes that glittered back at me as she ate. But mostly I looked at her tits. Round and perfectly symmetrical, they were so fuckin' pretty. I can't explain it. Tits have a power over men. Women will never understand. We have no fuckin' idea ourselves.

The eggs and bacon weren't bad. The coffee was nice and strong. After, we took a bath together. Soaping each other and rinsing off, we stayed in the tub until the water cooled and that felt even better than the warm water.

•

"Will you take me home? I don't want to go alone."

Brigid stood in the bathroom, her belly against the sink as she applied make-up to her face. In her bra and panties, she had her butt out. I told her I'd bring her home.

"I want to pick up some things. Will you take me to my mother's after?"

"Sure."

I finished my coffee, put the cup on the night stand and then dressed myself. She came out and ran her hand across my shoulders as she passed behind me to pick up her skirt.

I finished tying my sky blue tie, the one with the palm tree on it, and ran my fingers down the crease of my pleated blue suit pants.

"Nice shoes," she said when I slipped on my two-tone black and white wing tips. Women always noticed shoes.

I finished in time to watch Brigid finish. I liked watching women dress, nearly as much as watching them undress. I grabbed my suit coat on the way out.

"You're not bringing a gun?"

"You gonna get naked in front of any strange men on the way home?"

"No."

"Then I don't need to shoot anybody, do I?"

•

Pipi's black Packard was in the driveway. I parked behind it and followed Brigid in. I waited in the marble-floored foyer and watched Brigid's hips as she moved up the large spiral staircase. Figured I was about to meet old Pipi, the fuckin' wife-beater himself. I hate men that hit women. Hate 'em.

Just as I peeked in at the Audubon prints on the walls of the study, Brigid screamed upstairs. I took the stairs three at a time and followed the screams up to a large bedroom with giant flamingo lamps, blond furniture and a huge round bed with the body of a man on it. The man's head lay in a pool of blood. Brigid had her back pressed up against a large chifforobe in the right corner of the room, next to the drapes. She covered her face with her hands and screamed again.

The man lay on his side. I leaned over to look at his face. I recognized Pipi de Loup from the society page, even with the unmistakable dull look of death on his waxen face and his eyes blackened from the concussion of the bullet. The back of his head was a mass of dyed black hair and brain tissue. Brigid turned around and started crying.

I looked at the mirror above the long dresser, looked into my own eyes and felt my stomach bottom out. I saw the word 'sap' written across my face.

I moved over and grabbed Brigid's hand and led her out of the bedroom and down the stairs and out to my car. I opened the passenger door and told her to sit. Then I went next door and called the police.

Brigid was still crying when I got back to the DeSoto. I leaned against the rear fender and waited. Two patrolmen arrived first. I knew neither. I pointed at the house. The taller went in, the other took out his note book and asked my name.

A half hour and fifty questions later, Lieutenant Frenchy Capdeville pulled his black prowl car behind my car. He stepped out and shook his head at me, took off his brown suit coat and tossed it back in the prowl car.

Short and wiry, with curly black hair and a pencil-thin moustache, Capdeville looked like Zorro – with a flat Cajun nose. He waltzed past me and stood next to the open door of my car and looked at Brigid's crossed legs. He pulled the ever-present cigarette from his mouth, flicked ashes on the driveway and told me, "You stay put."

He reached his hand in and asked Brigid to step into the house with him. He left a rookie patrolman with an Irish name to guard me while other detectives arrived, one with a camera case. I looked up at the magnolia tree and tried counting the white blossoms, but lost count after twenty. At least the big tree, along with the two even larger oaks, kept the sun off me as I waited. I looked around at the neighbors who came out periodically to sneak a peek at the side show.

A detective arrived and waved at me on the way in. He was in my class at the academy. He was the only white boy I ever knew named Spade.

Willie Spade came out of the house an hour later and offered me a cigarette.

"I don't smoke."

"I forgot." He shrugged and lit up with his Zippo. About an inch smaller than me with short carrot-red hair and too many freckles to count, Spade had deep-set brown eyes.

"I need to search your car. OK?"

He meant do I have your consent. I told him sure, go ahead, but didn't expect him to pat me down first. No offense he said. No problem I said.

While he was digging in my back seat he said we needed to go to the office for my statement.

"I'd like to drive," I said. "I'd rather not leave my car here."

Spade turned and wiped sweat from his brow. "You can drive us both."

•

"No," I said. "I didn't touch a fuckin' thing in the house. She opened the door and I didn't touch the railing on the way up the stairs. The only thing I touched was her arm, when I dragged her out."

Spade narrowed his deep-set eyes. "You touched more of her than her arm."

I nodded and leaned back in the hardwood folding chair in the small interview room. I looked out the lone window at the old wooden buildings across South White Street from the Detective Bureau Office on the second floor of the concrete Criminal Courts Building at Tulane and Broad. A gray pigeon landed on the window ledge and blinked at me.

"We found the murder weapon on the floor next to the bed."

"Yeah?"

"A Colt .38. The misses says it's Pipi's gun. He kept it in the night stand next to the bed. The drawer was open."

"I didn't notice." I picked up the cup of coffee on the small table and took a sip. Cold.

"The doors and windows were all locked," Spade said, watching me carefully for a reaction.

"What time did the doctor say he died?"

"Between two and four a.m. Give or take an hour."

I nodded.

Spade leaned back in his chair and put his arms behind his head and I saw perspiration marks on his yellow shirt. His brown tie was loosened.

"So you're her alibi and she's yours," he said.

I nodded again and felt that hollow kick in my stomach.

There was a knock on the door and a hand reached in and waved Spade out. A couple minutes later Spade returned with a fresh cup of java, along with my wing-tips. He dropped my shoes on the floor and put the coffee in front of me. He pulled my keys out and put them on the table before sitting himself.

"Find anything?" I said as I leaned down and pulled my shoes on.

"Nope." Spade didn't sound disappointed. He sounded a little relieved. He put his elbows up on the table and told me how they knew the killer came in the kitchen door. It rained last night. The killer came in through the back with muddy shoes, wiped them on the kitchen mat and still tracked mud all the way up to the bedroom, then tracked mud right back out.

"That's why we had to search your pad and office," he explained the obvious. They had to check out all my shoes, and everything else in my fuckin' life.

"Let himself in with a key?" I asked when I sat up.

"Or." Spade shrugged. "The door was unlocked and the killer flipped the latch on his way out, locking it. We have some prints, but smudges mostly."

I nodded.

Spade let out a tired sigh and said, "You know the score. Whoever finds the body is automatically the first suspect."

"Until you prove they didn't do it. I know."

I didn't say – especially when it's the wife and the man who's fuckin' the wife.

"I'll be right back," Spade said and left me with my fresh coffee and my view of South White Street.

A while later, just as I was thinking how an interview room would be better for the police without a window, the door opened and Frenchy Capdeville walked in with Spade. Capdeville took the chair. Spade leaned against the wall.

Capdeville smiled at me and asked if I knew anything about the pictures they found in Mr. de Loup's darkroom. I told them everything. Fuck, they knew it anyway.

I ended with a question. "Did your men sniff my sheets?"

Capdeville smiled again. "Who found the photographer?"

I waited.

"You come up with a nigger photographer for her, or did she?"

"She told me Pipi found him."

Capdeville blew smoke in my face and gave me a speech, the usual one. I could leave for now, but they weren't finished with me yet. They'd be back with more questions, he said, flicking ashes on the dirty floor. He made a point to tell me they weren't finished with Mrs. de Loup by a long shot. Her lawyer was on his way and they expected an extended interview.

"One more thing," Capdeville said, looking me in the eyes. "You have any idea who did it?"

"Nope," I lied, looking back at him with no expression in my eyes.

They let me go.

•

I drove around until dark, checking to see if I was followed so many times, I got a neck ache. I meandered through the narrow streets of the Quarter, through the twisting streets of the Faubourg Marigny and over to Treme where I parked the DeSoto on Dumaine Street.

I jumped a fence and moved through back yards, leaping two more fences to come up on Joe Cairo's studio from the rear. As I moved up the back stairs, I thought how much this reminded me of a bad detective movie. Easy to figure and hard to forget.

I knocked on the back door. A yellow light came on and Joe's face appeared behind the glass top of the wooden door. His jaw dropped. It actually dropped.

"Come on, open up," I told him. "You don't have much time."

He opened the door and gave me a real innocent look, and I knew for sure he did it. I breezed past him, telling him to lock the door. I followed the lights to a back room bed with a suitcase and camera case on it.

"Going somewhere?" I sat in the only chair in the room, a worn green sofa.

Joe stood in the doorway. He looked around the room but not at me.

I put my hands behind my head and watched him carefully as I said, "She's gonna roll over on you."

Joe looked around the room again, his fingers twitching.

"If I figured it out, you know Homicide will. They're a lot better at this."

Joe started bouncing on his toes, his hands at his sides.

"They found the pictures. She'll bat those big blue eyes at them, roll a tear down those pretty cheeks and tell them, 'Look at the evil things my husband made me do... with a nigger'."

Joe stopped bouncing and glared at me.

"Don't be a sap," I told him. "She'll tie you up in a neat package. Cops like neat packages, cases tied up in a bow. Get out now. Leave. Go to California or Mexico. Just leave, or you'll be in the electric chair before you know it."

Joe leaned his left shoulder against the door frame. "There's nothing for her to tell."

"OK." I stood up. "Wait here. They'll be here soon." I looked at the half-packed suitcase and said, "Don't tell me you thought she was gonna run off with you."

Joe puffed out his cheeks.

"Look around. Look how you live. You saw how she lived." I stepped up to his face. "She used you, just like she used me."

Joe squinted at me. "What you mean, she used you?"

"She came over last night."

Joe shook his head. "She went to her mama's."

"Come on, wise up. She fucked us both. Only you're gonna take the hot squat."

Joe balled his hands into fists.

I looked him hard in the eyes. "What's the matter with you? You killed a fuckin' white man. You're history."

He blinked.

"Forget her, man."

I could see the wheels turning behind his eyes. He opened his mouth, shut it, then said, "He beat his wife."

"I know." That was the thing that tipped the scales, that brought me to Treme, instead of just going home. I hate wife beaters. I lowered my voice. "You killed a white man. You're in a world of shit, man."

"How... how did you... know?"

How? It was a gut feeling. It was the way Brigid looked at him, the way he looked back. It was that look of intimacy. Joe was the obvious killer, so obvious it was obscene.

"It had to be you," I told him, "because it wasn't me."

Joe blinked and I could see his eyes were wet.

"You willing to turn her in? You willing to tell the cops she was in on it?"

He looked at me and shook his head. "I'd never do that."

"Then you better beat feet. Go to California. Change your name. But get out now."

Joe looked hesitatingly at his suitcase.

"Forget her," I said forcefully.

"Forget her?"

"Like a bad dream."

I stepped past him. I knew if I was caught here, I'd be in a world of shit too.

Joe grabbed my arm, but let go as soon as I turned. He looked down at my feet said, "Why you helpin' me?"

"Because I'm more like you than I'm like them."

I'm not sure it registered, not completely.

"You're not getting rid of me to keep her for yourself," he said in a voice that told me he didn't believe that.

"She's done with both of us, man."

I went out the way I came, my heart pounding in my chest as I jumped the fences. I slipped behind the wheel of the DeSoto and looked around before starting it. I took the long way home.

•

It's night again. The French doors of my balcony are open, but there is no breeze. I'm on my fourth Scotch, or is it my fifth? I'm waiting for Capdeville and Spade. They'll be here soon, asking about Joe Cairo, wondering where the fuck he went.

I'll tell them I drove around and went to Cairo's on a hunch. Figuring someone must have seen a white man jumping fences, I'll tell them I tried to sneak up on Cairo, but he was gone.

They'll do a lot of yelling, a lot of guessing, but won't be able to pin anything on me. After all, I didn't do it. I was too busy fucking the wife at the time of the murder. I close my eyes for a moment and the Scotch has me thinking that maybe, just maybe she'll come. But I know better.

Rising from the sofa, I take my drink into the bedroom and look at the messed-up bed.

God, she was so fuckin' beautiful it hurt.

I sit on the edge of my bed. It still smells like sex. I'm sure, if I look hard, I'll find some of her pubic hair scattered in the sheets. That's all I have left – the debris of sex, the memories, and the fuckin' heartache.

END of EROTOPHOBIA

Erotophobia is for debb

Friscoville

I had my feet up on my beat-up mahogany desk, the small revolving desk fan flapping the front page of the morning paper as I read about how public enemy No. 1, Lou Jacoby himself, eluded an FBI dragnet on Bourbon Street last night.

I laughed just as the smoked-glass door of my office opened and a little girl walked in. She wore a blue, flowered cotton dress with white socks and black patent-leather shoes, the strap of a small black patent-leather purse draped over left shoulder. She batted her wide brown eyes at me and said, "Are you the detective?"

"Yeah," I said, pulling my feet off the desk.

She closed the door and walked up to the front of my desk and stuck her hand out for me to shake. I reached over and shook it.

"I'm Vivian Hartley."

"Lucien Caye." I let go of her hand and sat back down.

"Do you find missing people?" She looked about seven or eight. Her light brown hair was cut in a page boy.

"Sometimes."

Her lower lip quivered and she looked away. "I want you to find Amy."

She opened the purse and pulled out a picture and passed it to me.

It was a cat.

A tear rolled down her round cheek and fell on the collar of her dress.

I put the picture down and nodded to one of the chairs in front of my desk. She moved over and sat, carefully crossing her legs like a little lady.

"Amy's a calico. Two years old. She's been missing for two days and I can't find her anywhere." She had a deep voice, the kind that would drive me crazy if she was about fifteen years older.

"I prayed to St. Anthony all last night, but I still can't find her." She pronounced Anthony the old New Orleans way, "Ant–nee."

The old Catholic school rhyme echoed in my memory –

> *St. Anthony. St. Anthony.*
> *Please come around.*
> *Something I've lost.*
> *Cannot be found.*

The patron saint of lost things, St. Anthony's reputation was over-rated. I didn't tell her that.

"How old are you?"

"Eight and a half exactly. I was born New Year's Day, 1940. This is July first, so I'm exactly eight and a half." She punctuated it with a nod of her head.

I looked through the venetian blinds out at Cabrini Playground across the street and said, "Where do you live?"

"Almost next door." She pointed up Barracks Street.

"Your mother know you're here?"

"Heavens no."

It was at that moment I knew I was hooked. The way she said, "Heavens no" floored me. I pulled a note pad out of my desk and starting writing notes – Amy. Calico. Two years old. Missing since Tuesday.

"Um," she said, "how much do you charge? I have seventy-six cents. Is that enough?"

•

The French Quarter smells old, even with a breeze filtering in from the river on a bright spring morning. It's one of the things I like best about living and working here – the familiar musty smell of old buildings.

Stepping out of my office with Miss Vivian Hartley into the bright sunlight, I slipped on my sunglasses and took in a deep breath of musty air. Across the street the breeze rustled the branches of the oaks and the thick leaves of the magnolia trees.

I took the little miss home, up to her wooden shotgun double with its three small front steps at 925 Barracks Street. I hoped to meet Vivian's mother, figuring if the kid's that pretty, the original should be quite a looker. Vivian went in through the wooden louvered door. I waited, running my hands through my dark wavy hair.

Vivian came back and said, "She's not here. She went to the grocery."

I told her I was going to canvass now.

"You'll keep me posted, won't you?" She sure had a way with words, for an eight year old.

I told her of course, loosened by tan tie, which matched my pleated tan suit pants and tan-and-white wing-tips, and walked up to Burgundy Street to begin my canvass. I worked my way back down Barracks, knocking on every door. Nobody had seen Amy. At least someone was home at each house, except the other half of the double where Vivian lived.

I stopped when I reached the bookstore at the corner of Barracks and Dauphine. In the same two-story building as my office, the dusty bookstore was run by a lanky ex-fireman named John who hadn't seen Amy either. I leaned against one of the black wrought iron posts that supported the lacework balcony running along the second floor and wrapped around the corner of our brick building. Some of the masonry that covered the brick had worn away. I liked that. My office was at 909 Barracks. I lived upstairs in Apartment 2B.

I went back to Vivian's and knocked on her door. She answered and asked, "Have you found anything yet?"

"No." I pointed to the other side of the double. "Who lives next door?"

"They moved." She let out a long sigh.

"When?"

"Day before yesterday."

I pulled out my note pad. "What's their name?"

I wrote the names Frank and Nettie Gumm on my pad, winked at Vivian and walked back down to my office.

Settling in my desk chair, I picked up the phone and called a buddy at the light company. Marty and I were the police once, before he found better-paying work, before I went civilian. I asked for another favor.

"I'm looking for a Frank Gumm. Just moved out of 927 Barracks. Can you call me back?"

Marty said sure. I leaned my face in front of the desk fan, but it did little good. Three minutes later Marty called back. Frank Gumm switched his electricity from 927 Barracks to an address in St. Bernard Parish, on Friscoville Avenue. I reminded Marty I owed him another one and hung up.

Well, it was cooler outside and I hadn't been in the parish for a while, so I grabbed my hat and suit coat off the rack and walked back out into the sunlight.

My Bulova showed eleven a.m. exactly. I figured I'd go down to the parish, check out the Gumms and catch a bite at Gina's Diner across from the Chalmette Battlefield. Gina's had some good looking waitresses, a little on the hairy side. I like that in a woman.

I walked around the corner to my DeSoto and climbed in. It was a pre-war model, a light gray 1940 two-door coach with the most comfortable seats and a cool ceramic steering wheel. I rolled the front windows down to let in the river breeze, smelled the familiar musty old-building smell again and started the engine.

I took Barracks up to Rampart and hung a right over to St. Claude Avenue and followed the avenue through Bywater. Near St. Roch Avenue, I passed a streetcar rattling down the neutral ground along the center of St. Claude. A good looking blonde leaned out a streetcar window and winked at me and blew me a kiss. I smiled back and realized she looked familiar. I think I pinched her once for shoplifting on Canal Street.

Friscoville Avenue was only a little ways out of the city, running from St. Claude down to the river, where illegal gambling houses were still open for business, on the sly, except everybody knew. I hooked a right on the small, two-lane avenue and slowed immediately, trying to catch an address. I couldn't see an address on the first few houses, typical wooden singles half hidden behind trees, so I pulled over to the right and dug out the note I'd written with Gumm's new address.

The air was sweet with the humid smell of greenery. The avenue was tree-lined with oaks and magnolias and pecan trees all the way down to the levee. I spotted a pasture on the left with a black-and-white cow. Some of the houses had white picket fences in front. The two-story ones had wrought iron fences and front galleries with gingerbread overhang and front porch swings.

I couldn't read my own handwriting. When Marty called back, I jotted it down too quickly. Gumm lived either at 542 or 342 Friscoville. I ran into 542 first, along the uptown side of the street. A shotgun single in dire need of paint, it was recessed a little off the avenue behind a large magnolia whose dead leaves covered the front yard.

I avoided the hole in the front porch and knocked on the screen door. The bottom half of the screen was ripped and dangled. I heard someone move around and knocked again, louder.

"Yeah," a voice called out.

"Are you Frank Gumm?"

"No, who the hell are you?" The voice was rough and sounded like a Yankee.

"The name's Caye. Did you just move in here?"

The front door opened and a man looked at me through the screen door. In a soiled white undershirt and blue pants, his angry face was half-hidden in darkness. He gave me the once over and said, "You got the wrong house, stupid." Then he slammed the door.

On my way back to the DeSoto, I realized his face was familiar too. Unshaven and half-hidden, he still looked familiar. That's the problem being an ex-cop. I keep seeing faces from mug shots all the time, like the babe on the streetcar.

The single story bungalow with the cement steps and wide front porch at 342 Friscoville looked more promising. I rang the doorbell and shaded my eyes with my left hand to peek in through the screen door. A woman stepped into the living room, straightening her pink shirtwaist dress. I like to watch women do that.

She touched the sides of her shoulder-length brown hair, worn in a swirl, and smiled when she saw me.

"Are you Nettie Gumm?"

"Why, yes." She had green eyes and a nice figure.

I pulled a business card out of my wallet and pressed it against the screen and introduced myself. A little boy with crew-cut hair moved up behind her. He looked to be about Vivian's age. He wore a red striped shirt and jeans.

As Mrs. Gumm looked at my card, I pulled out the picture of Amy and pressed it against the screen and she said, "That looks like Amy."

The boy started crying. Nettie went down on her knees and asked him what was wrong. It took a minute to get the story out. Her son, Frank Jr., had told her the Hartleys gave Amy to him.

When Mrs. Gumm stood back up, her lips were shaking. I told her if she'd just give me the cat, then everything would be all right.

"Go get her," she told Frank, Jr. who hustled back through the front room.

Mrs. Gumm wrung her hands and said, "Does this mean my son will have a record now, officer?"

"I'm not the police. I'm a private-eye."

Frank arrived carrying Amy. Mrs. Gumm took the cat from her son, unlatched the screen door and shoved Amy at me. She re-latched the door quickly and wouldn't look at me. Frank Jr. wasn't crying anymore. He was sticking his tongue out at me.

•

Juggling Amy, I rang the Hartley's doorbell a half hour later. Vivian opened the door and leaped at me, grabbing at Amy. The cat jumped to her, digging claws in my arms in the process.

"Oh, my. Oh, my. Oh, my." Vivian was ecstatic. She hugged the cat and bounced in place, her face beaming.

"Is your mother home, yet?"

"No. Oh, thank you. Thank you. Thank you!"

I reached over and tousled her hair and winked at her and left. I love leaving females smiling and bouncing on their feet.

I climbed in the DeSoto and drove straight back to Friscoville, parking just up from the wooden shotgun in dire need of paint. I eased my snub-nosed Smith and Wesson .38 out of the glove box and kept it hidden behind my right leg as I walked around the magnolia and up to the porch. I knocked hard on the door.

The same voice said, "Yeah, who is it?"

"Are you sure you're not Frank Gumm?"

"What?" The door opened and that familiar face leered at me through the screen. "You nuts or something?"

"Come on," I said with a smile. "You gotta be Frank Gumm."

I watched his eyes move as he looked around me, checking to see if I was alone.

"Your face has a gummness about it, so you gotta be Frank Gumm." I said matter-of-factly.

He pressed his face against the screen and growled, "Get lost, stupid."

"You have a Gumm face." I made a sound like Goofy, the Disney character. Then I stuck my tongue at him.

He unlatched the screen door quickly and shoved it open. I took a hesitant step back as he came out, his fists clenched. His momentum took him right to me; and I shoved the snub-nosed barrel under his chin.

He stopped. I grabbed his undershirt with my left hand and twisted hard and told him to put his hands in his pockets. I pushed the barrel against the soft flesh under his chin, for emphasis. He obeyed, a hard glint in his dark eyes.

I cocked the hammer. "This has a hair-trigger." I gave him a cold smile.

He blinked his eyes and beads of sweat rolled down his right temple.

"Now," I said, "you got a phone?"

He said, "Uh, huh," but it didn't sound like that with the .38 pressed hard under his chin. I guided him, on his tip-toes, back into the house all the way to the black phone resting on an end table next to a tan sofa.

"Move and I'll blow your head off." I let go of the undershirt, picked up the receiver and dialed the operator.

"We need the sheriff's office at 542 Friscoville. It's an emergency." I hung up.

Lou Jacoby swallowed, his Adam's apple bouncing as he glared at me. I tapped the barrel against his chin and said, "Don't move. Scumbag."

•

I had my feet back up on my beat-up mahogany desk, the small revolving desk fan flapping the front page of the morning paper as I read about how public enemy No. 1, Lou Jacoby himself, was captured by a private-eye on a missing cat case. At least they spelled my name right and had my address correct.

I laughed and folded the paper and put my hands behind my head and dreamed about all the big money cases that were going to roll in now.

The smoked-glass door of my office opened. A woman stood in the doorway, her left hand on her hip, her piercing blue eyes staring at me. I pulled my feet off the desk.

She closed the door and walked straight to the desk, her eyes still staring at me. She wore a tight blue skirt with a pale blue silk blouse and black open-toe high heels. Her blonde hair was shoulder length and parted down the side of her face, like Veronica Lake.

She raised her large, black purse from under her left arm, opened it and pulled the front page of today's paper out and showed it to me.

"Lucien Caye," I said. "At your service."

The pearls around her creamy neck looked real; so did the diamond rings on each ring finger. The rest of her didn't look bad either. She let out a sigh – I love it when women do that before they talk – and said, "So you're the cat detective."

"Huh?"

Then she pulled a black kitten from her purse and said, "I just *have* to find her mother!"

END of FRISCOVILLE

Friscoville is for Dana

Lair of the Red Witch

It's always a good day when the client shows up.

On this bright, New Orleans autumn morning, my newest client opens the smoky-glass door of my office, peeks in and says, "Are you Mr. Caye?"

"Come in." I stand and wave her forward. Leaning my hands on my desk, I watch Mrs. Truly Fortenberry cautiously step in. A big woman, Truly has mousy brown hair worn under one of those turban hats, the kind Ann Sheridan made popular during the war. She wears a full brown skirt with a matching vest over a white blouse.

A typical-looking, 1948 housewife, Truly glances around my office, at my well-used sofa, at the hardwood floor in need of waxing, at the high ceiling with its water marks. She looks at the row of windows facing Barracks Street. With the Venetian blinds open, the oaks and magnolias of Cabrini Playground give this section of the lower French Quarter a country-feel in the middle of town.

Truly clears her throat, takes another step in and says, "I took the liberty of bringing a friend." Turning, she waves at the shadow I see through the smoky-glass.

"Uh," Truly says, stepping aside, "This is Diane Redfearn. My friend and neighbor." As the second woman steps in, Truly adds, "She wants to hire you too."

This one has my attention immediately. Diane Redfearn moves around Truly, stops and bats a pair of large brown eyes at me. Her blonde hair up in a bun, she wears a powder blue suit dress with sloping shoulders and a curving waistline. I had ogled a model in that same outfit, a upcoming '49 fashion. It was a D. H. Holmes ad in yesterday afternoon's *Item*. I like ogling fashion models. So sue me.

Diane, a long, cool blonde, makes the model in the paper look like a chubby, over-fed boy. She follows Truly across my wide office to the matching wing chairs in front of my desk (I bought the chairs at a furniture auction on Magazine Street.). Diane slinks into the chair on the left and crosses her legs.

Truly sits in the other chair, filling the seat with her broad hips. I sit in my high-back captain's chair.

"Any problem finding the place?" I ask as I notice the bevy of diamonds, two rubies and an emerald dotting their fingers.

"Oh no. Your directions were perfect." Truly blinks her deep set eyes at me and leans forward. "I told Diane how nice you were on the phone, Mr. Caye. And since she's in a similar position, I convinced her to come along."

Diane's keeps staring at me. Happens a lot with clients. Some expect a smooth Sam Spade some expect a debonair Nick Charles, some expect me to starting cleaning a .45 while spouting harsh language ala Mike Hammer.

"Lucien," I tell them. "My first name's Lucien."

"Oh," Truly leans back and digs something out of her oversized purse. She places a five-by-seven inch photo on my desk. "This is my husband."

I have to stand to reach the picture.

Diane opens her purse and pulls out a photo and leans forward, uncrossing her legs. Her breasts push nicely against the front of her dress. I smile and take the picture. She leans back and re-crosses her legs. I catch a whiff of expensive perfume. Nice. Very nice.

Sitting back, I look at Truly's picture first. It's a studio shot with Truly standing next to a mohair chair where a man sits. His hands in his lap and his legs crossed, the man has a Boston Blackie pencil-thin moustache and a goofy look on his wide face. His dark hair lies thick and curly on an oversized head.

We had a guy like that in our outfit back in Italy. Head too big for his helmet, so he never wore it. Never got hurt either.

Just a big jolly fella, he even came to see me in the hospital after that damn German sniper winged me back in '44. Monte Cassino. But that's another story.

Diane Redfearn's husband is another sort completely. He's alone in his photo, posing as he looks to his right, a cigarette in his raised right hand. He looks like Ronald Coleman, without the moustache, a distinguished looking gentleman wearing a cravat and what has to be a silk shirt. I hate cravats.

I put the photos down and pick up my fountain pen, holding my hand over my note pad. "So, what can I do for you ladies?"

Truly clears her throat and says, "Our husbands have left us. Mine two weeks ago. Diane's last week."

God, I hate domestic cases. But with the state of my bank account, I can't afford to be choosy. Truly looks at me as if I'm suppose to say something. Diane's brown eyes remind me of a sad puppy dog.

"So, Mrs. Redfearn. What can you tell me about your husband, besides he's blind?"

The women look at one another momentarily before Diane tells me her husband isn't blind.

Lord help me.

Truly clears her throat again and says, "They left us after visiting the red witch."

It's my turn to clear my throat.

"The red what?"

"The red witch." Truly points to my windows. "You can see her place from here. She's your neighbor."

I look out the windows for a moment before reaching over to turn on the small, black revolving fan that sits on the corner of my desk. The air feels good on my freshly shaved face.

"Um," I say as intelligently as I can.

They both speak.

"She always wears red," Truly says.

"She's not really a witch," Diane says.

Truly turns to her friend. "We don't know that. She calls herself a witch."

They both look at me and Truly says, "We want to hire you to... "

"Investigate this woman." Diane completes the sentence and brushes a loose strand of hair away from her eyes. She blows at it when it falls back, her lips purse in a nice red kiss. I try not to stare, but she's hard to look away from. Thin and buxomly and married... my kinda woman.

"We tried talking to the police," Truly says. "My uncle knows someone downtown."

I nod as I pull my gaze from Diane's lips.

"They sent someone to talk to the red witch's neighbors," Truly adds.

"But no one seems to know much about her," Diane says.

"Except cats and dogs have disappeared."

"Cats and dogs?" I put my pen down.

Both women nod. The strand of hair falls across Diane's eyes again. If I could only reach it. I pick up my pen and ask, "When do your husbands visit her?"

"Oh," Truly bounces in her seat. "They don't anymore. My husband's in Cleveland."

I look at Diane who tells me her husband is in Mexico.

"They moved out *after* visiting the red witch," Diane explains.

"We want you to find out what she told them," Truly says.

Diane looks down at her lap. "We want to know what happened... "

"When they visited this... sorceress."

I stand and move to the windows and open one. A nice breeze floats in, bringing the scent of freshly cut grass. I spot a city worker pushes a mower across Cabrini Playground. Shirtless, his brown skin shimmers with sweat under the bright sun.

"Where does she live?"

Truly clamors over and points up Barracks Street across the corner of the playground to a row of buildings on the lake side of Burgundy Street. Her elbow brushing mine, her perfume isn't the scent I'd caught earlier.

"See that second cottage from the end? The one painted yellow?"

I nod.

"That's the place. Her cauldron."

Cauldron? Isn't that some sort of kettle? I don't ask. I turn around and Diane is standing. Truly notices and hurries back to pick up her purse. I move back to my desk.

"There's nothing more we can add," Truly says as she pulls a white envelope out of her purse and hands it to me. "If you need more money, just let me know." I place the envelope on the desk and shake Truly's hand. It's sweaty. Diane's hand quivers when we touch and she smiles softly before pulling it back.

She brushes the loose strand of hair from her eyes again. "You'll let us know as soon as you can?"

"Absolutely." I reach for my pen and paper. "I have your number Mrs. Fortenberry, but... "

"Both numbers are in the envelope," Truly says as both women move quickly to the door and leave without looking back. The door closes and I stretch and yawn, then pick up the envelope. Inside, an ivory-colored sheet of paper is wrapped around a C-note. Ben Franklin never looked as good. On the paper are their names, and phone numbers: Fortenberry *CHestnut-0719;* Redfearn *CHestnut-0729.* Cozy.

The electric wall clock reads ten-fifteen. The red witch should be up, even on a Saturday. I reach into my desk drawer and pull out my snub-nosed .38 Smith & Wesson, slipping it into its tan leather holster on my right hip. I pick up Fortenberry and Redfearn's pictures, my pen and pad and tuck them into my tan suit coat, which I don on my way out. I wait for my eyes to adjust to t he sunlight. I don't wear hats. They mess up my hair.

The warm autumn breeze feels almost cool, flowing through my damp hair. It's wavy brown and in dire need of a haircut. I'm thirty, six feet tall and have standard-issue Mediterranean brown eyes. I'm half-French and half-Spanish – old blood, pre-American occupation blood. No aristocracy, however. Both sides of my family have been laborers forever, even after emigrating to Louisiana long before Washington and Jefferson started their little revolution.

Moving under the shade of the balcony, I stop next to one of the black, wrought iron railing that supports the second story balcony running the length of the building – I rent the apartment above my office – and check my pre-war 1940 DeSoto parked against the curb. A trail of cat prints dot the hood, reminding me the car needs a good washing. Gray, the DeSoto provides good cover on surveillances and hides most of the dirt, until a cat strolls across it.

I cross Barracks Street and walk next to the low brick wall, with its own black wrought iron railing, that surrounds the playground. The lower French Quarter has certainly seen better days, before everyone around here started speaking harsh Yankee English. Abutting the sidewalk, the houses across the street are connected by party walls. Masonry plastered over brick and cypress, and painted in muted pastels, the buildings look tired and time-worn.

At the corner I look at the row of Creole cottages lining Burgundy Street. The second one, painted yellow, is a typical one-story brick cottage with a roofed dormer. The address 1233, in bright crimson is prominent on the left cypress post that supports the gingerbread overhang above the small front gallery.

I take the three bricks steps up to the small gallery and spot another sign, this one hand painted in black letters next to a scarlet door. "Sorceress Eros" the sign reads. Love Sorceress.

"Yeah." I chuckle as I ring the doorbell. "Right."

I ring it a second time and the door opens.

She puts a hand up on the door frame and says, "Yes?" Her light green eyes stare at me so directly, it's almost startling. Women don't usually stare like that, unless they're a different sort. And she's clearly not.

In her early twenties, she has a perfectly symmetrical face with a small, pointed chin and cupie-doll lips also painted a deep red. Her straight hair is long and dark brown, parted in the center. She's a looker, all right, even if she wasn't wearing a tight, blood red dress and matching heels.

"Yes?" She repeats as I look back up at her big eyes.

I realize I have no game plan, so I opt for the direct approach. I pull a card from my pocket and hand it to her. As she looks at it, I tell her I'm a neighbor, pointing over my shoulder toward Barracks Street. She takes a step back and, still looking at the card, asks me in and closes the door.

The front room is dark and stuffy with the strong scents of incense and scented candles – vanilla, cinnamon, lilac maybe. A line of candles sits atop a chest of drawers to my right, two more are on the coffee table. Incense smolders in an urn on an end table next to the maroon sofa, reminding me of high mass. I cough.

"Oh," she says, "it's cooler in back." She leads me through the front room, down a narrow hall, past two bedrooms on the right, to a brightly lit kitchen. The rear door opens to a small patio filled with banana trees. She moves to a window and flips on a window fan, then pulls the chain on the ceiling fan above the small, aqua Formica table. She slips my card in a breast pocket and asks if I'd like some coffee.

"Sure." I watch her nice, round hips move away. She's about five-three and slim, but not skinny. Shapely slim. My kinda woman.

She turns to the stove and lights a burner beneath a white porcelain coffee pot. Turning back, she smiles, moves up and says, "Give me your coat. You look hot."

I pull off my jacket and she takes it and drapes it over the back of a chair next to the table. She points to another chair and says, "Sit down, Mr. Caye."

She sits across from me. The fan-driven breeze feels good, especially on the perspiration collecting around my temples. Her creamy, white skin looks paler in the bright light. She's very pretty. I notice she isn't sweating at all.

"So," she says, "What can I do for you?" Her gaze is penetrating, almost invasive.

"I never noticed your sign before. You're new to the neighborhood, aren't you?"

She nods. "Moved in last month."

I loosen my navy blue tie and unbutton the top button of my white shirt. Then I smile and ask, "What does a sorceress do, these days?"

"Help people."

"So a love sorceress must help people with love problems?"

"Sometimes." She stands and moves to a cabinet next to the sink, where she digs out two cups and saucers. "Cream or sugar?"

"Black."

She fills our cups, puts them on the table and sits again.

I wait. It's an old police trick. People will automatically restart a conversation if you just wait.

"You have a love problem?" Her right eyebrow rises.

I look into those light eyes, which seems suddenly different. She looks at me in an innocent, child-like way, the kind of look you'd see on a grade-school girl. The atmosphere seems intoxicating again, thick, even with the air blowing over me. Slowly, almost imperceptibly, her head nods. She takes a sip of coffee and says, "You're here about someone else's problem. Why don't you just come out and ask?"

I take a sip of the strong coffee and chicory.

"Two actually." I put the cup down. "Fortenberry and Redfearn. Sounds a little like a British law firm."

"Actually Mr. Fortenberry is an architect and Mr. Redfearn, an industrial engineer. But I can tell you little else about them."

"Why not?"

"It's confidential."

I grin. "As I recall, the law recognizes doctor-patient, priest-penitent, lawyer-client confidentialities. I don't remember anything about sorceress-confessor?"

She takes another sip of coffee.

"How long were you a police officer?" She smiles again.

She's bright. I like that.

"Seven years." I want to ask her how old she is, but down south we just don't do that. She can't be much over twenty. So I ask, "How long have you been a sorceress?"

"Professionally? Two years."

I take another sip. "You from around here?"

"Born and raised. Went to Sacred Heart. Where'd you go to school?"

I should have known. When someone doesn't have a recognizable accent, they're usually from where you're from.

"Holy Cross," I tell her. Like dogs, we've just sniffed each other. Sacred Heart – she's an uptowner – upper class. Holy Cross – I'm a from the lower part of town – working class.

She pulls her hair away from her face with both hands. I like watching women do that.

"So how did you become a sorceress? They teach it at Sacred Heart?"

She laughs lightly, then her face turns serious. She looks at the window fan and says, "I was born a sorceress." She turns to me with ovaled eyes. "I have a gift, Mr. Caye. I can sense feelings in people."

And it occurs to me – I don't know her name, but I don't ask. I wait for her to continue her train of thought. She doesn't disappoint me.

"I can sense things about people. Sometimes before they do."

She finishes her coffee and asks if I'd like another cup. I shake my head and finish mine.

"We're not talking about witchcraft here, are we?"

"Hardly." She unbuttons the top button of her dress, reaches in an pulls out a gold chain and crucifix. "I'm still a practicing Catholic."

"Then you don't sacrifice cats and dogs." I watch her face carefully and the surprise there turns into a wide smile.

"No. I love animals."

"Then you don't know why so many cats and dogs are missing in the neighborhood?"

She picks up our cups and saucers and moves to the sink. She wipes her hands on a red checkered dishcloth. Turning, she rests one hand along the kitchen counter and lifts her hair off her nape with her other hand to let the fan cool her neck. Her eyes stare at me. I almost smile, because she's waiting now – for me to restart the conversation.

"So what do you do, exactly?"

"People come to me with problems." Her voice is deeper. "Sometimes, I'm able to help them."

"So you have the power to make people happy?"

"Sometimes I can point them in the right direction. It's up to them."

I wait a second before saying, "Mrs. Fortenberry and Mrs. Redfearn think you seduced their husbands. Caused them to leave their wives." Her eyes still look innocent as she shakes her head. She lets her hair fall. The doorbell rings.

"Sounds like my eleven o'clock appointment is early."

She starts for the door and I scoop up my coat and follow her back through the house, back into the insufferable front room. When she turns back to me and looks up with those soft eyes, I apologize.

"I put you on the spot and you didn't throw me out. Thanks."

She turns to open the door and I have another question.

"What's your name?"

"Maggie. Maggie LeRoux."

Nice French name.

She opens the door to a young man with wavy brown hair and glasses. He wears a tweed suit and looks soft, almost effeminate as he stands there awkwardly.

"Come in, Thomas," Maggie says with a warm smile.

Thomas extends a hand for me to shake and says, "And you are?"

I tell him my name as we shake hands. His hand is clammy and limp. I resist wiping my hand on my pants after he pulls his hand away.

"And what do you do?" Thomas asks, his eyes suddenly intense.

"Detective."

"Oh, my." He smiles and there's something familiar about his face. "I'm a playwright." He turns to Maggie and says he's ready. She ushers him in.

I step out, toss my coat over my shoulder and walk away. I don't go home. I turn right and walk up Burgundy, past more Creole cottages and multi-story townhouses, passing beneath more lacework balconies. An early lunch at the Napoleon House sounds like a good idea to me.

•

Starting my canvass at the corner of Governor Nicholls and Burgundy, I find no one in the first few houses who know anything of the woman in yellow house down the block.

Four doors from Maggie's cottage, the door stands open on another cottage, this one painted pale blue. I knock on the screen door and a woman's voice answers, "Hello?"

I knock again.

A slim woman with her hair in a bun steps into the front room. She wears a casual off-white dress and has a mop in her hand.

"I'm not buying anything today," she tells me.

"I'm not selling anything."

She huffs and leans on the mop handle. "Then what do you want?"

"I'm a detective. I'd like to ask you a couple questions."

She moves forward and I see she's not a bad looking woman at all. No make-up on her face and a little perspired from housework, she's not bad at all.

"It's not about that woman again, is it?"

I turn toward Maggie's house and smile slightly. "Woman?"

"The red witch."

"Actually, it is."

"Well, come on in."

We talk in her living room. Me on a green easy chair. She on the matching sofa. The room smells of old cigarette smoke. The ashtray on the end table next to me has a gray line of ashes still in it. Her name is Agnes English and no, her husband hasn't left her. He's at work at Hibernia Bank. No, she's never even seen Maggie, but her cat's been missing for two weeks.

"A yellow tabby. Maybe you've seen her. Name is Judy and she's such a love."

"Just disappeared?"

Agnes nods and tears well in her eyes.

A half hour later, I'm knocking on another screen door, this one on the house next to Maggie's. Another woman with a mop moves into the front room, squints at me and asks what I want.

As soon as I tell her I'm a detective, she shushes me and moves quickly to the screen door.

"Keep your voice down," she says as he unlatches the door and lets me in.

In a light-weight sky blue blouse and white short shorts, she's a sight with her long strawberry-blonde hair pinned with two barrettes. She leads me through the front room, which smells faintly of pine oil, back to a bright kitchen. I can make out her visible panty line along her ass as she moves in front of me. I like that in a woman.

"Coffee, officer," she asks. Her eyes are the same color as her blouse.

"Sure."

I watch her bend over for the grounds and flutter back to he sink to fill the percolator.

"I'm Lola Kinks." She plugs in the percolator. She's suddenly self conscious, standing with the strong sunlight behind her and the way I'm leering at the front of her shorts and the dark patch between her legs. She moves to the small wooden table, sits and crosses her legs. I sit across from her as the blush slowly fades from her pretty face. As soon as Lola tells me she's a widow, something inside stirs, something down south. I readjust myself as I sit.

When she mentions Okinawa, the stirring fades.

"My husband was killed in the last day of battle. Sniper."

She's a war widow. Dammit. I hate moving in on war widows. Like most surviving veterans, I feel a little guilty that I lived. It just seems slimy to ease in on a war widow, even three years after Hiroshima.

As the coffee perks, Lola tells me how she'd married her high school sweetheart, spent a whirlwind honeymoon in Mexico, then sent him off to the Pacific. He fought at Eniwetok and Saipan before Okinawa.

Damn, he'd seen some of the heaviest action.

When the coffee's ready, she fixes us some and I try not to leer at her, although I do steal another peek at her ass as she's pouring cream in her cup.

"Didn't mean to get off the subject," she says as we start in on our coffee. "I guess you're here about the red witch again, aren't you?"

"Why do you call her that?"

"Ever see her? She's spooky and with that sorceress sign. Who knows what she's up to next door."

I take out my note book. "Ever see anything unusual?"

"All the time."

Lola tells me about moaning and wild laughter, about boogie-woogie music, about strange smells, about hearing incantations and voices whispering harshly late at night.

"Smells?"

"Not cooking smells. But like in church. Incense and other strange odors." She goes on but tells me nothing new. I remind myself how good detective work is done in details, not broad strokes. But these details are redundant. I close my note book and thank the widow Kinks. As she leads me out I ask if she's heard of any missing animals.

"My dog ran away the same week the witch moved in. Dug a hole under the fence and I haven't seen him since."

A black lab, he answers to the name "Nigger."

Jesus, lady –

She shakes my hand and gives my hand a gentle squeeze. And there's something there, for a moment, in those sky blue eyes. But she blinks and looks away and it's gone.

"She's a flirt, you know."

"Really?" I act surprised.

"She flirts with my fiancé."

Fiancé? Did she say fiancé?

"In the backyard last Saturday. I saw her smiling at him and her in a silk robe with God knows what underneath."

A war widow with a fiancé. If there's one thing a man like me knows, a woman with a fiancé is as approachable as a nun. Women with fiancés are newly in love. Bored housewives are more my style. It takes a few more minutes, but I manage to escape from the widow Kinks' house and those pretty blue eyes.

•

The electric clock on my bedroom wall shows it's almost midnight.

I sit in my easy chair, just inside my balcony's French doors as a light rain wets the Quarter. A cool breeze floats in through the partially opened doors. With the porch light on outside Maggie's, I can see the red door clearly. I raise my glass of my Johnnie Walker Red and compliment whoever laid out Cabrini Playground. The trees are interspersed perfectly to give me a clear view of Maggie's. A dull light flickers in her front room. Candles probably, but I haven't seen the red witch since I got back – unless I close my eyes.

Maybe it's the smoky scotch or maybe she put a spell on me, but when I close my eyes, I see those hips moving lithely, like a cat, beneath that tight dress. I see those ovaled, green eyes staring back at me. The cupie-doll lips, pursed as they come in close for a kiss, touch my lips and...

I down the scotch and yawn.

Tomorrow, I tell myself. I think it's time I become a client of the red witch. What have I got to lose?

That night I dream, but not about Maggie's lips. I'm back in Italy, crouched on a dusty hill, a German machine gun strafing around me. The rat-tat-tat of the automatic rifle burps and the ground shakes and I stand up. No. *Yes.* I stand up, take careful aim at the German helmet behind the machine gun and squeeze the trigger of my M-1.

A stream of banana pudding gushes from my rifle and I know if I can cover the bastard with enough banana pudding, he'll drown. Only I run out of banana pudding. So I race down to the

Italian fruit peddler at the bottom of the hill and ask him to hurry with the bananas. I point up the hill and tell him the Germans are dug in and need to be drowned. He shakes his head and tells me not to worry. He points overhead at a formation of heavy bombers.

We move to the side of the hill and watch the bombers destroy the Sixth Century Benedictine Monastery atop Monte Cassino. Germans were using the monastery to spot for their field artillery. The bombers reduce the ancient citadel to rubble, which only provides better cover for the crack troops of the First Panzer Division who'll kept us at bay for weeks.

I try to explain to the fruit peddler that the Germans up our small hill have machine guns and we need banana pudding right away. He calls me *pazzo Americano* – crazy American. I run off in search of another fruit peddler.

Only, when I turn around I'm back at Anzio beach where hellfire rains down on us from long range German artillery. You know, the guns of Krupp. A dogface next to me in the foxhole turns and shouts, "Pray! Pray to God for help!"

I start praying and he grabs my arm.

"But tell him not to send Jesus. This is no place for kids!"

A shell blows up next to us and I wake up.

Rain slams against the balcony doors. I roll over and try to force myself to dream of the cupie-doll lips. Thankfully, I don't dream at all.

•

Maggie answers the door wearing a flowered sarong skirt and a red blouse with black piping. She's barefoot, a coffee cup in her hand. I raise the brown bag in my hand. She smiles and her lips are candy-apple red this morning.

"Beignets," I tell her. "From Morning Call."

She leads me back through the house, through the smoldering incense and candles to the kitchen where both fans are already blowing. As she pours me a cup, I pile the half dozen beignets on a saucer and place them in the center of the Formica table.

In a short sleeved white shirt and dungarees, I'm casual today. I even wear tennis shoes. She sits across from me, picks up a beignet and takes a dainty bite of the French pastry – powdered sugar sprinkled on square donuts without holes. I pick up a beignet and tell her, "I came as a customer today."

She smiles. "I figured that would be your next move."

"I have problems," I tell her. Only I can't help the wicked grin from crossing my lips.

"I know," she says seriously.

A half hour and two cups of coffee later, I'm in the living room, reclined on the maroon sofa with candles burning around me and incense smoking up the place. Maggie moves next to me and rubs a potion on my forehead and the back of my hands. It's cool and smells like over-ripe bananas.

She moves to the chest-of-drawers and lights two large green candles, then comes back and sits on the coffee table, crossing her legs, closing the sarong that gave me a quick look at her pale thighs.

"Close your eyes," she says softly.

I go along. The air becomes stuffier and I smell something else. The green candles. Musty, they smell like mud. No, they smell like an old shoe left out in the rain.

"Tell me your most pressing problem." Her voice sounds distant, but I open my eye and she hasn't moved.

"I dream about the war a lot." My eyelids close by themselves. I try to force them open, but they're too heavy. I drift and hear her breathing close to me now. Her breath brushes my cheek.

"That isn't your problem," she says and I feel her rub lotion on my forehead again. She takes my hands in hers and rubs my knuckles. It takes a moment for me to realize she's humming softly. A sweet tune, her voice is soothing. And I drift again, further and further. I'm carried on her voice and feel as if I'm floating.

"So," she says when I open my eyes. "Feel better?"

I sit up and stretch. I feel much better, rested, as if I've slept for hours. I look at my watch and it's been less than an hour. Sitting up, I realized I've a raging hard-on. Glad my pants are baggy. She stands and moves to the green candles and blows them out.

"Come back to the kitchen," she says. I follow the easy movement of her hips beneath the sarong to the well-lit kitchen where she pours us each a fresh cup of java.

As I take a sip, she says, "Your dreaming about the war is your way of working it out. You're dreams will become less violent. They have already, over the last year, haven't they?"

The rich coffee and chicory warms me. I'm cold and can't understand why.

"The war isn't your problem."

"What is?" I ask, half jokingly.

"Sex."

The big eyes look innocently at me.

Sex, huh? I gotta admit, she knows how to keep it interesting.

"You want sex."

"What, now?" I laugh.

"Always." She's serious.

I take another sip and lean back in the chair.

"What red blooded American boy doesn't want sex all the time? I'm an ex-cop, and ex-GI. I'm French and Spanish. I've got hormones coming out of my ears."

She shakes her head, pulls her hair back with one hand as she takes a drink of coffee. She puts the cup down and I smell her perfume for the first time. Less sweet than Diane Redfearn's scent, it's nice and subtle.

"I've never met a man with as powerful a sex drive as you." She says it so seriously, I can't laugh, although I want to.

"You want sex now with me and you want sex with your clients." She props her elbows up on the table. "You want sex with just about every woman you see. The attractive ones, anyway."

"What's abnormal about that?"

"Your sex drive is super potent. Insatiable. You want mind-numbing sex." She says it matter-of-factly as if she just told me I wanted to be a fireman when I grow up.

I laugh aloud. And I wonder were she's going with this. She's right about one thing. I've love to screw her – right now. On the kitchen table. Jesus! Maybe I am insatiable. I shake the thought away.

"Your sex drive is quite similar to a male cat's."

She catches me with my cup to my lips. I cough and spill coffee on the table. She reaches back, pulls a towel off the counter and tosses it to me. I shake my head as I wipe up the spill.

Me – a tom cat?

"That's right," I tell her. "You're good with animals too. You tell this stuff to the tom cats in the neighborhood?"

She takes a drink of coffee.

"What'd you do, liberate all the cats and dogs in the neighborhood?" I say, facetiously as I raise my cup again.

"I freed them. I felt their desires, the inner dreams and set them free. They ran away. Just like your clients' husbands." She gives me that big-eyed, innocent look again.

I put the cup down. "Wait." I raise an index finger. "Let me get this straight. Fortenberry and Redfearn went through what I just went through and you told them their secret desires and they left their wives?"

She nods and finishes her coffee.

"It took several sessions," she says as she stands and puts her cup in the sink.

"What did you tell them? What are they looking for? Other women?"

She puts her hands on the table and leans toward me. "That's confidential."

The doorbell rings.

"I have an appointment. Thanks for the beignets." She shakes her head. "And the interesting walk through your psyche."

I'm dismissed, I guess. She leaves and I follow her down the hall. She turns into a bedroom. I stop outside just as she comes out brushing her long hair.

"How much do I owe you?"

"Five dollars."

I pull a fin out and follow her into the front room. She moves to the door and lets in a middle-aged woman in a cardigan suit. No I don't want to immediately fuck her new client! Although, I must admit, the woman has a nice, shy smile and her full lips look –

•

A picture of Thomas the playwright in the afternoon's *Item* catches my attention as I wait in my office for my clients. No wonder his face is familiar. He's Tennessee Williams, author of "A Streetcar Names Desire," the play that's got Broadway sizzling. Seems he just won the Pulitzer Prize. Maggie's got some clientele.

My office door opens and Truly Fortenberry leads the way in. In another full dress, green this time, she wears a floppy hat with a pink carnation. Diane Redfearn, wears a slim-fitting, yellow dress. Her hair in a bun, she wears no hat. They sit in the same chairs, Diane crossing her long legs.

Freshly shaved, I have on my best blue suit, a starched white shirt and powder blue tie. Women have told me blue goes well with my dark complexion. With the windows open and the ceiling fans on high, the room feels almost cool.

"I'm not sure what to make of this," I start. "So I'll just tell you straight. The red witch is more like a hypnotist. She claims to be able to discover people's inner desires and frees them."

"Frees them?" Truly leans forward.

"She claims that's why all the cats and dogs have left the neighborhood. She freed them."

Truly bats her confused eyes at me. Diane looks down at the purse in her lap.

"I don't think she had sex with your husbands."

Truly looks even more confused. Diane lets out a long sigh.

"Mrs. Redfearn, what did your husband tell you when he left?"

She looks up and shakes her head.

"Did he tell you he was going to sail around the world or something like that?"

She shakes her head again and looks at the windows. Her chest rises as she takes in a deep breath. "He said he was going to Mexico to find a lost city and that he wants a divorce."

I turn to Truly who clears her throat and digs a handkerchief from her purse.

"Mine told me he was tired of living with me, tired of being married and wants to live in Cleveland." Her eyes glisten and she has that look on her face. I've seen it before, the look of desertion, the look of betrayal, the look of an abandoned lover. It's not a pretty sight, especially on Truly Fortenberry's puffy face.

"Why?" she moans. "Why would he leave me for – Cleveland?"

Diane stands and wraps an arm around her friend.

I wait as Truly cries. What the hell can I tell her? Who, in his right mind, would leave New Orleans for Cleveland? Even if the Indians lead the American League at the moment. The obvious answer was whoever was married to Truly. I don't say that, but I can't help thinking it. And I wonder if she thinks it too. It's an unwritten law of nature. Unattractive people know they're unattractive.

God, I feel terrible. Really. I know I'm superficial when it comes to women, but I wish there was something I could do for Truly Fortenberry. But I'm no wizard. And I'm sure, if she visited the red witch, Maggie would discover Truly's inner desire was to be married to Mr. Fortenberry.

I look out the window as a mockingbird lands on the wrought iron part of the playground fence across the street. Immediately it goes through its long litany of calls – bouncing, ruffling its gray and white feathers. A male probably, advertising its voice to passing females.

Finally, Truly stops crying and fixes her face. She stands and thanks me. I tell them I'll try to find out more about the red witch, if I can. Diane says it won't be necessary as I shake her soft hand. For a moment there's some eye contact between us, but I can't read it. They leave me with a good whiff of Diane's strong perfume. As I said – nice. Very nice.

•

The rain started an hour ago; and as I sit in the easy chair behind my closed balcony doors, windblown rain washes across the balcony in waves. It's so dark outside, it looks as if the rain has put out the yellow electric streetlights.

The bathroom light is still on behind me, so I know the electricity hasn't gone out. Leaning back in the chair with my tie loosened and an untouched glass of scotch in my left hand, I watch the rain. The nearly full bottle of Johnnie Walker Red lies next to my foot in case I need a quick refill.

The persistent drum of the shower has me drowsy. Leaning back, I close my eyes and envision the cupie-doll lips in candy apple red, pursed in a sweet kiss. I see those hips moving away from me, lithely, in a smooth feline movement. I see her legs crossed in the sarong. I watch her uncross them slowly. The sarong falls open and the front of her sheer white panties come into view. I see the dark mat of her pubic hair through the panties.

I hear her humming again, her voice echoing in my mind. The tune fades, then rises again. I try to open my eyes, but my eyelids are so heavy, I can only crack them. I try harder. Then I feel her fingers on my chin. Softly, she traces her fingertips down my throat, then back up to my chin.

I'm on her sofa and strain to open my eyes. I think I see her face above me but it fades and her fingers leave my throat. The humming is to my right, hovering above me. Turning my head I try to look, but everything's hazy. I feel myself fall into a deep well. It's so hot I can barely breathe. I have to open my eyes. Concentrating, focusing all my strength, I pull myself back.

The humming returns, still above me and to my right. I force my eye-lids to open but no matter how hard I try, I only manage to crack them. The darkness fades slowly and I see her, swaying next to me, her hands clasped behind her head. Her eyes are still closed. Her hands move down the back of her neck and around to her throat. And slowly she unbuttons her blouse, pulls it out of the top of her sarong and drops it on the coffee table behind her.

She reaches back and unfastens her white brassiere and I strain to focus my eyes on her round breasts. Her pink nipples are pointed as she continues swaying. She reaches to the knot on the side of her sarong. She drops the sarong atop her blouse and bra.

I crane my neck more to the right. Her white panties are sheer enough to reveal her dark triangle of pubic hair. She turns her back to me, her hips still moving slowly to her humming. She pulls off her panties, her nice round ass not three feet from my face.

She turns back and continues her rhythmic gyrations. I stare at this naked vision, my gaze roaming from her pubic hair up to her breasts up to her lovely face. She leans forward, her breasts falling toward me. Moving from side to side, she rocks her breasts above me like a pendulum. I want to touch them but my hands won't move.

Her eyes open now, she pulls back and steps closer to the sofa. Still swaying, she presses her bush forward and her silky pubic hair brushes the side of my face, back and forth, back and forth, ever so lightly.

She takes a step back and goes down on her knees. Her face moves forward and her lips touch my cheek. It takes a few moments to realize she's kissing me. Her lips move to mine. Her kiss is so soft I can barely feel it. But she presses harder and I try to kiss her back, but my lips won't respond. Her tongue slips into my mouth and she kisses me deeply.

Pulling back, she stands and I feel my hand rising. She's lifting it. She rubs my open palm along the side of her leg, then around to her ass. I feel her crack but can't get my hand to squeeze in response.

Maggie moves my hand around to her bush. She opens her feet and slips my hand between her legs. She rubs my fingers along her inner thighs, then turns my hand palm up. My fingers press against her pussy and she moves her hips back and forth on my hand. My middle finger slips into the folds of her pussy, into the hot wetness.

The humming is replaced by heavy breathing. Holding my arm with her left hand, maneuvering my hand with her right, she fucks herself with my finger. My thumb massages her clit as my middle finger works inside. Am I moving my fingers or is she?

Maggie gasps. Her gyrations increase, the weight of her body pressing harder against my hand. Waves of pleasure cross her face. She throws her head back and cries out and I feel her climax on my hand in deep spasms. Gasping, Maggie collapses next to me. I see her reach up and close my eyelids. She speaks in a distant voice.

She tells me I will remember nothing. And I fall into that well again. There's something else, something suddenly cool on my hand, the hand that fucked Maggie. It's a face rag. She's wiping my hand before she wakes me. My eyes snap open as a rush of wind and rain rattles the French doors.

Jesus – What a dream.

Wait. It'd didn't feel like a dream. It felt more like a memory. In that hour I was on Maggie's sofa, is this what happened? Did that little woman take advantage of me? Use me? I reach down to straighten my swollen dick. Leaning forward, I look at the darkness of Cabrini Playground. She's so close I can almost feel her.

Maybe, when the rain lets up, I'll creep over, like an alley cat. Maybe, just maybe, she wants me to slink over to her. Telling me all that about my sex drive. Maybe that's what she wants. At thirty, I should know women by now; but the older I get the less I seem to know.

My doorbell rings and I almost kick over the scotch bottle. I swallow my drink in one gulp. It burns my throat and warms my belly. I put the empty glass on the coffee table on my way through the living room. The doorbell rings again as I step out the door to the landing. I look down the stairs and see a shadow outside the building's pebbled-glass front door, which is locked at night.

As I descend the stairs the shadow moves slightly; and I see it's a woman. I hurry to pull open the door. It takes me a second to recognize her with her long hair dripping wet around her pretty face. Her hair looks darker wet.

Diane Redfearn pulls her hair back with both hands, steps into the doorway and cranes her neck to the side. Her lips pursed, she leans toward mine and we kiss. Softly, she presses her rain-washed lips against mine. Her lips part and her tongue probes for mine.

We French kiss in the doorway, my arms pulling her close, her drenched coat soaking me. The heat of our kiss and the cool water against my skin is electrifying. I feel her arms around me. A rush of wind and rain blows over us and Diane pulls her mouth away, takes my hand and leads me up the stairs and into the open door of my apartment.

"I'd noticed," she says softly, "your name next to apartment number 2B on the ringer outside the first time we came. I almost rang it, but Truly said your office was downstairs." I close the door and she turns and pulls off her dark blue coat, dropping it next to the sofa.

She wears the same yellow dress. It clings to her damp body. She reaches back and unbuttons it, pulling it off her shoulders. Her lacy white bra is sheer revealing nice, round nipples. I pull off my tie and unbutton my shirt.

Her velvet brown eyes watch my eyes carefully as she steps out of her dress and drops her half-slip.

My shirt tossed aside, I drop my pants and step forward as she starts to unfasten her stockings.

"Let me," I say as I go down on my knees in front of her. I unhook her right stocking from her garter belt and work the stocking down her long, cool leg. Tracing my fingers up her left leg, I unhook the second stocking, my fingers following it down her leg. She drops her bra on my head.

My face is inches from the front of her panties. I reach up and unfasten her garter belt, dropping it next to the stockings. My fingers rise along the back of her legs, across her ass to the top of her panties. I pull them down slowly, my gaze never leaving her crotch. Her mat of dark blonde pubic hair is damp. I lean forward and kiss it. She gasps as she reaches down and pulls me up by the ears. Her bra falls off my head.

It's her turn now. She goes to her knees and runs her fingernails along the back of my legs. She pulls my shorts off and kisses the tip of my swollen dick. She kisses her way down my dick to my balls and kisses her way back up.

Her tongue flicks the tip of my dick, which throbs in response. Her mouth opens and slides over my dick. She sucks for a second and then works her head up and down, her tongue rubbing my dick. I pull her up, shove my tongue into her mouth and feel the length of her hot body against mine. I scoop her up in my arms and carry her into the bedroom, without losing a stroke of our French kiss.

I lay her on the bed and stand over her. God, she's gorgeous naked. Unbefuckinlievable! Her breasts, even as she lies on her back, rise firm and full. Her round nipples are erect. She opens her legs and I climb atop this beautiful woman. I kiss my way down from her lips to her breasts, sucking each nipple, nibbling each before kissing my way to her flat stomach and down past her bush to her the soft, inner thighs.

She raises her knees, her legs wide and her gorgeous, pink pussy is open in front of my face. I kiss each side and kiss her soft, silky pubic hair. My tongue flicks across her clit. She lets out a little cry. I press my tongue against her clit and rub it up and down and up and down and up and down.

She grinds her hips against my tongue. I reach around her legs and grab her breasts. I knead them as I continue tonguing her clit. She moans and gasps and cries out. She shoves her hips against me and bounces and grinds and I keep on licking until, with a jolt, her hips lift from the bed and she comes in a deep climax, her thighs squeezing against my ears until they ache.

I keep licking. I lick as she gyrates, as her hips dig for the pleasure. I lick until her legs fall open and she pulls me up to her eager mouth. I feel her hand reach down to guide my dick into her wet pussy. It takes my thick dick a few seconds to work its way in. She gasps and puffs as she tries to catch her breath.

I moan as I start grinding my dick in her hot pussy. The muscles in her pussy pull in response. Jesus! And I fuck her in long, deep strokes, in and out and in and out, back and forth, riding her until I feel it coming. I stop. She pulls at me, works her pussy around my dick, but I hold still. When it subsides, I go back to the screwing. I keep this up for as long as I can, holding it back at the last moment, until I can hold it no more and I gush in her in long, deep spurts.

Rolling off, I scoop her in my arm and she kisses my face and snuggles against me. It take a while for my breathing to return to normal. Pressed against me, she raises a hand and gently rubs my belly. Her fingers eventually work their way to my pubic hair.

"You sure your husband isn't blind?"

Smiling now, she tickles my dick with her fingernails.

"Then he's just stupid, right?"

She strokes my dick. I'm not ready, but my dick, which has a mind of its own, gets hard between her fingers. She climbs on me, straddles me and rubs her pussy against my dick.

I reach up and grab her breasts, squeeze them and crane my neck up to suck each nipple, to nibble each, as she rubs her pussy up and down the length of my hardening dick. She reaches down and guides the tip of my dick into her and rides me like I'm a fuckin' horse.

"Come on," she gasps. "Fuck me. *Fuck* me! *Fuck me*!

I want to tell her that's what the fuck I'm doing, but why spoil the mood? Instead I watch this gorgeous blonde bounce on my dick. The second time always take longer and I savor the good fuck. She comes again, bucking against me, just before I come. Her pretty face reaches for the pleasure. Man, there's nothing to compare to this – fucking a beautiful woman and seeing all the pleasure I'm giving her.

Diane rolls off me and lies panting on her back. I get up immediately and crack open the French doors, using the bottle of scotch to keep it from opening too far. The rush of cool air is invigorating. I climb back into bed and lie on my belly next to Diane.

Her eyes closed, she breaths softly and I begin to drift. Later, she rolls over and wakes me. I go to the bathroom and on my way back, I fetch my glass from the living room. I refill the glass, reposition the scotch bottle against the French doors. The rain has stopped.

The lair of the red witch is completely dark and looks ghostly, its yellow paint pale beneath the amber streetlights. Sipping the scotch, I stare at the house for a while, then turn to watch Diane sleep. On her back, her legs open, she's a vision in the soft light.

Finishing my drink I go back out into the living to make sure my front door's locked. When I turn around, Diane's in the bedroom doorway, her hands high on the door frame as if she's blocking me from going back in the bedroom with a naked body from a school boy's wet dream. With her arms raised, her full breasts look even fuller.

My dick stirs.

She smiles wickedly and moves to me. I meet her half-way and she pushes me back on the sofa.

"No, sit up," she tells me as she kneels in front of me. She opens my knees and kisses her way up to my semi-hard dick. She licks it, kisses it, brushes it with her teeth, sucks it. Her head rising and falling, she sucks until I'm nice and stiff.

Standing, she climbs on me, her hands on my shoulders, those luscious breasts in my face. Her pussy rubs against my dick and Diane slowly positions herself until she impales herself on my dick. She sinks on me and I feel those pussy muscles grab my dick.

She starts a slow, grinding fuck. I cradle her ass in my hands. My mouth move again from nipple to nipple, sucking each as this woman fucks me, rides me, bucks me. It is so delicious, so hot and wet and I finally come after such a long time, I feel I'm about to pass out.

By the time we get to fifths, I'm shooting blanks, but it's just as good.

•

Frying eggs and bacon the next morning, I make sure the bacon doesn't splatter. I'm still naked. My sofa is dotted with wet spots and my bed's a wreck and Diane is long gone. She didn't even leave a note, the hussy. My kinda woman.

I pour myself a thick cup of coffee and chicory and take a deep sip. Hot and strong – I need it. I'm wasted. I feel like I've been on Anzio beach for a week, until I move and my balls remind me of all the pleasure and I smile.

An hour later, after a shave and a long shower, I walk out of my building into the bright sunshine. I pull on a pair of aviator's sunglasses and yawn. The warm air smells musty as it always does in the old quarter after a long rain. The ancient mortar and bricks and cypress absorb the rain and seems to remain perpetually damp.

I wear a blue shirt today and dress gray pants with my new black Florsheims. No hat, of course. Moving up Barracks I cross over to the playground side and make my way up to Burgundy to the red door of Maggie, the Love Sorceress.

To my surprise, it's open. I knock and peek in. The sofa's missing and a chest-of-drawers and an end table are against the far side of the room. No lit candles, the room is bright with the curtains open.

"Good," Maggie calls out from a back room. "You made good time."

She steps into the front room, blinks at me and giggles. "I thought you were the movers." In a pink tee shirt and red shorts, her hair in a pony tail, she looks like a high schooler – a damn good looking high schooler. The cupie-doll lips are a deep scarlet today.

I hold up the palms of my hands and ask what's going on.

"I never stay more than a month or two in one place." She folds her arms across her chest and looks around me, not at me.

"What?"

"I'm moving to Mid-City. I'll send you the address, although you don't need me anymore. Even when you get horny again." She says it matter-of-factly, without feeling, as if I'm not there. She taps her fingers on her arms.

"I don't understand."

"I like moving to new places," she says quickly, takes in a deep breath, then stops tapping her fingers. She looks right at me and says, "Diane Redfearn came to you last night, didn't she?"

My mouth opens, but I say nothing.

"I thought she might."

And it comes to me. "She came to see you."

Maggie nods.

"You sent her to me?"

"She sent herself."

"Her deepest desire?"

She looks down and shrugs.

"Wait. You mean to tell me she came to me for 'mind-numbing sex' at your suggestion?"

Maggie takes in a deep breath looks up, focusing those large green eyes at me.

"You have a right to know, I suppose."

"Yeah."

"She didn't go to you for 'mind-numbing sex'."

"Then what for?"

She gives me a long stare and says, "A child."

And I can hear my heart beating as I stand in the doorway. It sounds like thunder.

END of LAIR OF THE RED WITCH

The Heart Has Reasons

For two days she came and sat under the WPA shelter in Cabrini Playground with her baby, sometimes rocking the infant, sometimes walking between the oaks and magnolias, back and forth. Sometimes she would sing. She came around nine a.m. and around lunchtime she'd reach into the paper bag she'd brought and nibble on a sandwich. After, she would cover her shoulder with a small pink blanket and nurse her baby beneath the blanket. Around five p.m., she would walk away, up Dauphine Street.

On the third morning the rain swept in, one of those all-day New Orleans rainstorms that started suddenly then built into monsoon proportions. The newspaper said to expect showers brought in by an atypical autumn cool front from Canada, which would finally break the heat wave that has lingered through the sizzling summer of 1948. I grabbed two umbrellas and found her huddled under the shelter.

"Come on," I told her, "come get out of the rain." I held out an umbrella. When she didn't take it immediately, I stood it against the wall and stepped away to give her some room. She looked younger up close, nineteen, maybe eighteen and stood about five-two, a thin girl with short, dark brown hair and darker brown eyes, all saucered-wide and blinking at me with genuine fear.

I took another step away from her, not wanting to tower over her with my six foot frame, and smiled as warmly as I could. "Please. Come take your baby out of the rain." I opened the second umbrella and handed it to her.

Slowly, a shaky white hand extended for the umbrella, those big eyes still staring at me. I took a step toward the edge of the shelter. A loud thunderclap caused us both to jump and the baby started crying.

I led the way back across the small playground, the umbrellas pretty useless in the deluge, and hurried through the brick and wrought iron fence to narrow Barracks Street, having to pause a moment to let a yellow cab pass. She moved carefully behind me and I held the door to my building open for her. I closed the umbrellas and started up the stairs for my apartment. "I'll bring towels down," I called back to her, then took the stairs two at a time.

Moving quickly, I grabbed two large towels from my bathroom, lighting the gas heater while I was in there and pulled the big terry-cloth robe I never wore from the closet, draping it over the bathroom door before leaving my apartment door open on the way out. She stood next to the smoky glass door of my office, rocking her baby, who had stopped crying. She still gave me that frightened look when I came down and extended the towels to her.

"Top of the stairs, take a left. My apartment door's open." I reached into my suit coat pocket and pulled out a business card. "That's my office behind you. The number's on the card. Go upstairs. The heaters on in the bathroom and take your time. Lock yourself in. Call me if you need anything."

I shoved the towels at her and she took them with her free hand. I pressed the business card between her fingers as she moved away from my office door. She took a hesitant step for the stairs, stopped and watched me with hooded eyes now.

Stepping to my office door, I told her, "I'm Lucien Caye," and nodded at my name stenciled on the smoky glass door. "I'm a detective."

Her lower lip quivered, so I tried my warmest smile again. "Go on upstairs. You'll be safe up there. Lock yourself in."

The baby began to whine. She took in a deep breath and backed toward the bottom step. Glancing up the stairs, she said, "First door on the left?"

"It's open," I said as stepped into my office. "I'll start up some eggs and bacon. I have a stove in here." I left the door open and returned to the row of windows along Barracks Street where I'd been watching her. A louder thunder clap shook the old building before two flashes of lightning danced over the rooftops of the French Quarter. The street was a mini-canal already, the storm washing the dust from old my gray, pre-war 1940 DeSoto coach parked against the curb.

"Bacon and eggs," I said aloud and turned back to the small kitchen area at the rear of my office. I had six eggs left in the small refrigerator, a half-slab of bacon and milk for the coffee. I sniffed the milk and it smelled OK.

I called my apartment before going up. She answered after the sixth ring with a hesitant, "Yes?"

"It's Lucien. Downstairs. I'm bringing up some bacon, eggs and coffee, OK?"

I heard her breathing.

"I'm the guy who got you outta the rain. Remember? Dark hair. Six feet tall. I brought an umbrella."

"The door's not locked," she said.

"OK. I'll be right up." When she didn't hang up immediately, I told her, "You can hang up now."

"All right." She did and I brought a heaping plate of breakfast and a mug of café-au-lait. I'd left my coat downstairs, along with my .38 revolver. Didn't want to spook her anymore than she was already spooked.

She was sitting on the sofa, her baby sleeping next to her. In the terry-cloth robe, a towel wrapped around her wet hair like a swami, she looked like a kid, not a mother. The baby lay on its belly, wrapped in a towel. I went to my Formica kitchen table and put the food down, flipping on the light and telling her I'd be downstairs if she needed anything else.

"Is that a holster?" she asked, staring at my right hip.

"I told you I'm a detective." I kept moving toward the door, giving her a wide berth, hoping the fear in her eyes would subside.

"Thank you," she said, standing up, arms folded across her chest now.

I pointed down the hall beyond my bathroom. "There's a washer back there for your clothes and a clothesline out back, if it ever stops raining."

She nodded and said, "I'm Kaye Bishop." She looked down at her baby. "This is Donna."

I stopped just inside the door. "Nice to meet you Kaye. If you need to call anyone, you know where the phone is."

I hesitated in case she wanted to keep talking and she surprised me with, "You're not how I would picture a detective."

"How's that?"

Her eyes, like chocolate agates, stared back at me. "You seem polite. Maybe too polite."

"You've been out there for three days. You all right?"

"We'll be fine when Charley comes for us."

"Charley?"

"Charley Rudabaugh. Donna's father. We're not married, yet. That's why I'm staying with the Ursulines."

Nuns. The Ursuline convent on Chartres Street. Oldest building in the Quarter. Only building which didn't burn in the two fires that engulfed the city in the Eighteenth Century, or so the story goes. For an instant I saw Kaye Bishop in a colonial costume, as a casket girl, labeled because they'd arrived in New Orleans with all their belongings in a single case that looked like a casket. Imported wives from France, daughters of impoverished families sent to the new world to marry the French settlers. The Ursulines took them under wing to make sure they were properly married before taken off by the early, rough settlers. Looks like they're still taking care of young girls.

"The church took us in." Her eyes were wet now. "We're waiting until Charley can get us a place."

Donna let out a little cry and Kaye scooped up her baby and moved to my mother's old rocking chair next to the French doors that opened to the wrought iron balcony wrapping around my building, along the second floor. As she rocked her baby, she reached up and unwrapped the towel on her head, shook out her hair and rubbed the towel through her hair.

The baby giggled and she giggled back. "You like that?" She shook her hair out again and the baby laughed. Turning to me, she said, "Can you get my purse? It's in the bathroom."

I brought it to her and she took out a brush and brushed out her short brown hair. Donna peeked up and me, hands swing in small circles, legs kicking.

"She's a beautiful baby," I said backing away, not wanting to crowd them.

Kaye smiled at her daughter as she brushed her hair, the rocker moving now. I was about to ask if the eggs and bacon were OK when she started humming, then singing in a low voice, a song in French, a song that sat me down on my sofa.

My mother sang that song to me. I recognized the refrain… "*le coeur a ses raisons que la raison ne connait point*." Still don't know what it means. I wanted to ask Kaye but didn't want to interrupt her as she hummed part of the song and sang part.

I closed my eyes and listened. It was hard because I could hear my heart beating in my ears. When the singing stopped and I opened my eyes, Kaye was staring at me and I could see she wasn't afraid of me anymore.

•

Two hours later, I was about to call upstairs to suggest I go over and pick up Charley, bring him here when she called and said, "Could you get a message to Charley for me?"

"Sure."

"He's working at the Gulf station, Canal and Claiborne. He's a mechanic," she said with pride.

Slipping my blue suit coat back on, I looked out at the rain still falling on my DeSoto. It wasn't coming down as hard now but I took the umbrella anyway after I went back and slid my .38 back into its holster. I started to grab my tan fedora but left it on the coat rack. Hats just mess up my hair.

It took a good half hour to reach the station on a drive that normally took fifteen minutes. Every car in front of me drove so slowly, it was as if these people had never seen rain before in one of the wettest city in the country. I resisted leaning on my horn for an old man wearing a hat two sizes too large for his pin head, wondering why he couldn't get his Cadillac out of first gear.

Forked lightning danced in the sky, right over the tan bricks of Charity Hospital towering a few blocks behind the Gulf station as I pulled in. The station stood out bright-white in the rain, illuminated by its lights normally on only at night. I parked outside the middle bay with the word "tires" above the doorway. The other bays, marked "lubrication" and "batteries" were filled with jacked-up vehicles.

Leaving the umbrella in my DeSoto, I jogged into the open bay and came face up with a hulking man holding a tire iron.

"Hi, I'm looking for Charley Rudabaugh."

He lifted the tire iron and took a menacing step toward me. I stumbled back, turning to my right as I reached under my coat for my revolver.

"Sam!" a voice boomed behind the man and he stopped but kept leering at me with angry eyes.

I kept the .38 against my leg as I took another step back to the edge of the open bay doors so he'd have to take two steps to get to me. I'd have to run or shoot him. Neither choice was a good one. A second hulking man, even bigger, came around the man with the tire iron. Both wore dark green coveralls with the orange Gulf Oil logos over their hearts.

The bigger man growled, "Who the hell are you?"

"Kaye Bishop sent me with a message for Charley."

"Kaye? Where is she?" He took a step toward me and I showed him my Smith and Wesson, but didn't point it at him.

"I'm a private detective. You wanna tell me what's goin' on?"

"You got an ID?"

Don't remember ever seeing Bogart, as Sam Spade or Philip Marlowe, showing his ID to anyone, but I had to do it – a lot. I reached into my coat pocket with my left hand and opened my credentials pouch for him and asked, "Where's Charley?"

The bigger man looked hard at my ID. "I'm Malone," he said. "Charley works for me. Where's Kaye?"

"At my office." I slipped my creds back into my coat pocket.

Malone turned his face to the side and spoke to his buddy with the tire iron. "He's too skinny to work for Joe. And his nose ain't been broke. Yet."

The man with the tire iron backed away, leaning against the fender of a Ford with its rear jacked up.

"I told you where Kaye is. Where's Charley?" I re-holstered my revolver but kept my distance.

"Don't trust the bastard," said the man with the tire iron.

I could see, in both sets of eyes, there was no way they were telling me anything. Maybe they'd tell Kaye. I suggested we get her on the phone. I stayed in the garage as Malone called my apartment from the office area. When he signaled for me to come in and get the phone, the first hulk finally put the tire iron down.

"Kaye?"

"Charley's in the hospital," she said excitedly. "Can you bring me to him?"

"I'll be right there." I hung up and looked at Malone. "You wanna tell me what happened now?"

Charley Rudabaugh was a good kid, a hard worker, but he borrowed money from the wrong man. Malone learned that tidbit that very morning when a goon came by with a sawed-off baseball bat and broke Charley's right arm.

"I was under a Buick and couldn't get out before the goon got away."

"The 'Joe' you thought I was working for?"

"No. A goon works for Joe Grosetto."

Malone explained Grosetto was a local loan shark. I asked where I could locate this shark but neither knew for sure. Charley would.

•

Kaye and Donna were waiting for me in the foyer of my building. I brought them out to the DeSoto under the umbrella and drove straight to Charity Hospital, parking at an empty meter outside the emergency room.

Charley Rudabaugh was about five-ten, thin build with curly light brown hair and green eyes. He smiled at Kaye and kissed Donna and finally noticed me standing behind them. His right arm in a fresh cast, Charley blinked and said, "Who are you?"

I let Kaye explain as she held his left hand, bouncing a gurgling Donna cradled in her free arm. He looked at me suspiciously, sizing me up, giving me that look a male gives another when he just showed up with his woman. When Kaye finished, more nervous now, she asked Charley what happened to him.

He turned to her and his eyes softened. He took in a deep breath and said, "Haney." She became pale and I pulled a chair over for her to sit, then went back to the doorway.

"He didn't ask where I was?" asked Kaye.

Charley shook his head. "He just wanted the money."

Kaye's eyes teared up and she pressed her face against his left arm and cried. Charley's eyes filled too and he closed them but the tears leaked out, down his lean face. Donna's arms swung around in circles as she lay cradled and I waited until one of the adults looked at me.

It was Charley and I asked, "How much money are we talking about?"

"This doesn't concern you."

Kaye stopped crying now and wiped her face on the sheet before sitting up.

I tried a different tack. "What school didya' go to?" The old New Orleans handshake. This was no public school kid. He told me he went to Jesuit. I told him I went to Holy Cross. Two Catholic school boys who'd gone to rival schools.

"Your parents can't help?" Jesuit was expensive.

"They don't live here anymore. And don't even ask about Kaye's parents. This is our problem."

"Everyone needs help, sometimes."

"That's what you do? Some kinda guardian angel?"

I shook my head, thought about it a second and said, "Actually, it's what I do most of the time. Help people figure things out."

"We can't afford a private-eye."

I tried still another tack. "How do I find this Grosetto? This Haney?"

Charley shook his head. Kaye wouldn't meet my eyes so I left them alone, went out in to the waiting area. Ten minutes later a blond-headed doctor went in, then a nurse. I caught the doctor on the way out. It was a simple fracture of both bones, the radius and ulna between wrist and elbow.

"It was a blunt instrument, officer," the doctor said. "Says he fell but something struck that arm."

I thanked the doc without correcting him that I wasn't a cop. The nurse was obviously finishing up, telling them how Charley had to move on soon as the cast was hard. Kaye turned her red eyes to me and I took in a deep breath. "I'll take you to the Ursulines, OK?"

Her shoulders sank. I turned to Charley. "So where have you been staying?"

"He's been sleeping at the Gulf station," Kaye said.

He shot her a worried look.

"They don't know," Kaye added. "He stays late to lock up and sleeps inside, opens in the morning."

I put my proposition to them to use my apartment and stepped out for them to discuss it, gave them another ten minutes before walking back in. Kaye shot me a nervous smile, holding Donna up now, the baby smiling too as her mother jiggled her.

I looked at Charley who asked, "I just wanna know why you're doing this."

"How old are you, Charley?"

"Twenty. And Kaye's eighteen. We're both adults now."

I nodded slowly and said, "I watched a young mother and her baby spend three days in that playground, avoiding the kids when they came, keeping to themselves until the rain blew in. I've got two apartments, one converted into an office downstairs with a sofa bed, kitchen and bath. I've slept down there before. You got a better offer?"

•

Charley and Kaye wouldn't volunteer any information about Grosetto and Haney and there was no way Malone and his tire-iron friend were going to be much help. But I knew who would. He was in too, sitting behind his worn government-issue gray metal desk, in a government-issue gray desk chair in an small office with gray walls lined with mug shots, wanted posters and an electric clock that surprisingly had the correct time.

Detective Eddie Sullivan had lost more of his red hair, making up for it with an old-fashioned handle-bar moustache. Grinning at me as I stepped up to his desk, he said, "I was about to get a bite."

"Me too."

So I bought him lunch around the corner from the First Precinct house on South Saratoga Street at Jilly's Grill. Hamburgers, French fries, coffee and a wedge of apple pie for my large friend. Sullivan was my height exactly but out-weighed me by a hundred pounds, mostly flab.

Eddie Sullivan was the Bunco Squad for the First Precinct, since his partner retired, without a replacement in sight. He handled con artists, forgers, loan sharks and the pawn shop detail, checking lists of pawned items against the master list of stolen articles reported to police. I waited until he'd wolfed down his burger and fries and was starting in on his slab of pie before bringing up Grosetto and Haney. He nodded and told me he knew both.

"Grosetto's a typical Guinea, short, olive-skinned, pencil thin moustache, weighs about a hundred pounds soaking wet. Haney is black Irish, big, goofy-looking. Typical bully." He stuffed another chunk of pie into his mouth.

"Grosetto? He mobbed up?"

Sullivan shook his head. "He wishes but he ain't Sicilian. I think he's Napolitano or just some ordinary Wop. You got someone willin' to file charges against these bums?"

"Maybe. I need to know where they hang out."

"Easy. Rooms above the Blue Gym. Canal and Galvez."

I knew the place and hurried to finish my meal as Sullivan ordered a second wedge of pie. He managed to say, between mouthfuls, "I'd go with you but I gotta be in court a one o'clock. Drop me by the court house?"

As he climbed out of my DeSoto in front of the hulking, gray Criminal Courts Building, Tulane and Broad Avenues, he thanked me for lunch, adding, "See if you can talk your friend into pressing charges. I could use a good collar."

"I'll try."

·

The Blue Gym was hard to miss, sitting on the downtown side of Canal and Galvez Streets. Painted bright blue, it stood three stories high, the bottom two stories an open gym with six boxing rings inside, smelling of sweat, blood and cigar smoke. I weaved my way through a haze of smoke to a back stairs and went up to a narrow hall that smelled like cooked fish. A thin man in boxing shorts came rushing out of a door and almost bumped into me.

"Oh, 'scuse me," he said.

"I'm looking for Grosetto."

He pointed to the door he'd just exited and rushed off. I reached back and unsnapped the trigger guard on the holster of my Smith and Wesson before stepping through the open door to spot a smallish man behind a beat-up wooden desk. The man glared at me with hard brown eyes, trying to look tough, hard to do when he stood up and topped off at maybe five-three and skinny as a stick-man. He wore a shark-skin lime green suit.

"Who the hell are you?" he snarled from the right side of his tiny mouth.

I stepped up, keeping an eye on his hands in case he tried something stupid and said, "How much does Charley Rudabaugh owe you?"

"Huh?"

"How much?" I kept my voice even, without a hint of emotion.

The beady eyes examined me, up and down, then he sat and said, "You ain't Italian. What are you? Some kinda Mexican?"

I wasn't about to tell this jerk I'm half French, half Spanish, so I told him, "I'm the man with the money. You want your money, tell me how much Charley owes you."

"Three hundred and fifty. Tomorrow it's gonna be four hundred."

"I'll be right back." And I didn't look back as strolled out, making it to the nearest branch of the Whitney Bank before it closed. My bank accounts, I have a saving account now, were both in good shape after the Duponceau Case. As I stood in the teller line, I remembered the salient facts that brought such money into my possession –

It was a probate matter. When it got slow, I'd go over to civil court, pick up an inheritance case. This one was a search for any descendants of a recently deceased uptown matron. Flat fee for my work. If I found someone, they got the inheritance, if not, the state got it. I'd worked a dozen before and never found anyone until I found Peter Duponceau, a fellow WWII vet, in a VA Hospital in Providence, Rhode Island.

Not long after I caught a bullet from a Nazi sniper at Monte Cassino, he collected a chest full of shrapnel from a Japanese bombardment on a small island called Saipan. Peter was the grandson of the recently deceased uptown matron. His mother was also deceased. When I met him to confirm his inheritance, he was back in the hospital for yet another operation. At least the last months of his life were lived in luxury in an mansion overlooking Audubon Park. He left most of his estate to several local VFW chapters and ten percent to Lucien Caye, Esquire. When the certified check arrived, I contemplated getting an armored car to drive me to the bank. I couldn't make that much money in five years, unless I robbed a bank or two.

•

Grosetto was back behind his desk but there was an addition to the room, a hulking man standing six-four, outweighing me by a good hundred pounds of what looked like grizzle, with a thick mane of unruly black hair and a ruddy complexion. He wore a rumpled brown suit as he stared at me with dull, brown eyes, Mississippi River water brown. My Irish friend Sullivan described Haney as black Irish, probably descended from the Spanish of the Great Armada, the ones who weren't drowned by the English. The ones who took the prevailing winds, beaching their ships along the Irish coast to be taken in by fellow Catholics to later breed with the locals. I would have given Haney only a cursory look, except I didn't expect he'd be so young, early twenties maybe.

Stepping up to the desk, I dropped the bank envelope in front of Grosetto. "Rudabaugh sign anything? Promissory note? IOU?" I knew better but asked anyway.

Grosetto picked up the envelope and counted the money, nodding when he was finished. I turned to Haney. "You still have that baseball bat?"

He looked at Grosetto for an answer and then looked back and I could see he wasn't all there.

"Try that stunt again and I'll put two in your head. And I'll get away with it."

"Alls I want is the girl," Haney said.

"What?"

He looked down at his feet, all shy-like and said, "I seen her," looking up now with those dull eyes, "*Real* pretty." He followed with a childlike chuckle.

I turned back to Grosetto, "Better let him in on the real world."

Grosetto was smiling now, or trying to with that crooked mouth. "He usually gets what he wants."

"Not this time," I said.

No use arguing with idiots. When I got back to my office, I located my black jack, a chunk of lead attached to a thick spring, covered with black leather, brand named the Bighorn because it allegedly could cold-cock a charging bighorn ram. I only used it twice back when I was a patrolman and it worked well enough to incapacitate bigger, combative men. Then I put away my .38 and brought my army issue Colt .45 caliber automatic and loaded it, switching holsters now. I needed something with stopping power.

I called upstairs and Kaye answered, telling me the baby and Charley were asleep.

"I need to get a couple things, OK?"

She let me in and I quickly packed a suitcase with essentials, grabbed a couple suits and fresh shirts. Before stepping out, I waved her over and we whispered in the hall. I told her they owed Grosetto nothing. How? I told her someone had given me a lot of money and now I was giving them some.

"Charley won't stand for it. We'll pay you back."

I shrugged, then watched her eyes as I told her I'd met Haney. She blanched, so I followed it with, "Back at Charity, why did you ask Charley if Haney asked where you were?"

She took a step back, crossed her arms and said, "Haney's my half-brother."

•

Sitting at my desk in my dark office, I watched the rain finally taper off.

"What about your parents?" I'd asked Kaye up in the hall. She told me her father was dead and her mother had abandoned her when she was five and wouldn't say anything else about the matter, not even who'd raised her.

I was thinking – at least they were safe for now – just as I spotted Haney standing next to the playground fence across the street. Didn't take him long to find us. He stood there for a good ten minutes before coming across the street. I expected the baseball bat, not the revolver stuck in the waistband of his suit pants as he stepped in the foyer of my building. I'd moved into the shadows next to the stairs, black jack in my left hand. Slowly, I eased my right hand back to my .45 as he saw me and said softly, "Where is she?"

The sound of squealing tires behind him made him look over his shoulder. When he looked back I had my .45 pointed at his face and said, "That'll be the cavalry."

Two uniforms alighted from the black prowl car and came into the building with their guns out. It was Williams and

Jeanfreau, both rookies when I was at the Third Precinct. I lowered my weapon. "He's got a gun in his waistband."

Williams snatched Haney's revolver and Jeanfreau cuffed him and dragged him out.

"Aggravated Assault, right?" Williams checked with me for the charge.

"Yeah. Hopefully he's a convicted felon." A felon with a firearm would hold Haney for quite a while.

"Thanks," I called out to my old compadres. Williams called back, "Your call broke up the sergeant's poker game. But only for a while."

•

Charley sat shirtless at my kitchen table holding Donna with his good arm, Kaye in my terry cloth robe again, getting us coffee, them looking like a family now and I had to tell them about Haney. Kaye blanched at the news; Charley just nodded while Donna gurgled.

"How close are you?" I asked.

"I'm not even sure he's my half-brother," Kaye answered. "He claims to be. Claims my dad was his father. I never met him until he showed up at the hospital when Donna was born." She didn't volunteer any more and I didn't want to cross-examine her, sitting at my table, all three adults sipping coffee which wasn't bad and I'm picky about my coffee.

I turned to Charley and said, "We need to press charges against Grosetto. I'll back you and we'll put the slime-ball away. My buddy Detective Sullivan is chomping at the bit to nail him."

Charley shook his head and told me, in careful, low tones how he wanted Grosetto and Haney and all of it behind him, how he was going to pay me back whatever it cost me. I tried for the next half hour, but there was no changing his mind. He said he didn't want to be looking over his shoulder for the rest of his life. God, he was so young.

The coffee kept me up a little while, but the rain came back that night, slapping against my office windows as I lay on my sofa-bed. Why was I lying there? Why wasn't I out on the town, dancing with a long tall blonde in a slinky dress? Maybe bringing her here or going to her place and helping her slip into something more comfortable, like my arms.

I knew the answer. It was upstairs with those kids, so I lay waiting for trouble to return, knowing it would.

•

Arriving at the Criminal Courts Building early, I searched the docket for Haney's name, wanting to get a word in with the judge before his arraignment. When I couldn't find his name, the acid in my stomach churned. I snatched up a pay phone in the lobby and called parish prison, speaking to the shift lieutenant who took his time, but looked up the name for me.

"Haney. Yeah. Bonded out four-thirty a.m."

I asked more questions and got the obvious answers, a friendly judge and an friendlier bail bondsman had Haney out before sunrise. The only surprise was that Haney had only two previous arrests, both misdemeanors, no convictions.

I should have gotten a speeding ticket on the way home, but no one was paying attention. Catching my breath when I reached the top of the stairs, I tapped lightly on the door. Even a bachelor knows better than to ring a doorbell with a baby inside. Kaye answered and I let out a relieved sigh, which disappeared immediately when she told me Charley wasn't there.

"Where'd he go?"

"To work. Malone picked him up." Her eyebrows furrowed when she saw the worried look in my eyes. I pointed to the phone and she opened the door wider, telling me, "Malone said a one-armed Charley was better than any of his other mechanics."

She knew the number by heart and I dialed. Malone answered after the fifth ring and I warned him about Haney being out of jail.

"Didn't know he was in jail."

"Well, he had a gun last night, so be on the lookout."

Then I called Sullivan to make sure the patrol boys did a drive-by at the Gulf Station before I went to see Grosetto.

•

He was behind the desk wearing the same lime green suit, sporting that same crooked slimy grin when I walked in on him, the place reeking of fish again.

"Where's Haney?"

Grosetto tried growling, which only made him look like a randy terrier, instead of a gangster. His hands dropped below the desk top and I turned my left shoulder to him, pulling out my .45, letting him get a look at it.

"Put your hands back on your desk and they better be empty."

"Who da' heller you comin' in here, tellin' me what to do?"

"Where's Haney?"

He tried smiling but it looked more like a grimace. "I'm glad you come by. You needa tell Charley he owes another fifty. I, how you put it, miscalculated the amount." This time it was a smile, sickly, showing off yellowed-teeth.

I shot his telephone, watched it bounce high, slam against the back wall, the loud report of my .45 echoing in my ears. Pointing it at his face now, I said. "Put your hands back on your desk."

He did, his eyes bulging now. I backed up and locked the door behind me and came back to the desk as I holstered my weapon, slammed both hands against the desk, shoving it across the linoleum floor with him and his chair behind, pinning him against the wall.

"Tell Haney I'm looking for him."

Three boxers and two trainers were in the narrow hall. I opened my coat and showed them the .45 and they backed away cautiously, none of them saying anything until I started through the gym. A couple brave ones cursed me behind my back, but kept their distance.

•

I figured Haney was loony enough to come by but it was Grosetto, just before midnight. He wore a gray dress shirt and black pants, hands high as he stepped into my building's foyer. I was sitting in darkness, half-way up the stairs, sitting in my shirt and pants with my .45 in my right hand.

"That you?" he called out when I told him to freeze. I'd unscrewed the hall light.

"What do you want?"

"I come to tell you somethin'."

I went and patted him down, closed and locked the building door then shoved him into my office, leaving the door open. He smelled like cigarette smoke and stale beer. I made him stand still as I moved to my desk and leaned against it.

"All right, what is it?"

"I made a mistake. Charley don't owe me nothin'."

"Good."

He tried smiling again, but it still didn't work. "I checked on you. You got some rep. You know. War hero. Ex-cop. Bad when you gotta be bad." He looked around my office for a second. "You check up on me?"

"In the dictionary. Under scum bag."

"You funny. You owe me a phone, you know."

Maybe it was the twitch in his eye or the way he sucked in a breath when I heard it, a thump upstairs. Grosetto should never play poker. It was in his eyes and I was on him in three long strides, slamming the .45 against his pointed head, tumbling him out of my way.

I took the stairs three at a time, reaching the top of the stairs as a gunshot rang out. My apartment door was open and a woman's screaming voice echoed as I ran in, scene registering as I swung my .45 toward the figure standing with a gun in hand.

The gun turned toward me and I fired twice, Haney bouncing on his toes as the rounds punched his chest. The gun dropped and he fell straight back, head ricocheting off an end table.

Kaye, with Donna in her arms, moved for Charley as he lay on the kitchen floor, a circle of bright red blood under him. Holstering my weapon, I leaped toward them as Kaye cradled his head in her arms. He was conscious, a neat hole in his lower abdomen, blood oozing through his white undershirt. I jumped back to the phone and called for an ambulance. When I turned back, Charley was trying to sit up.

"Don't!" I jumped into the kitchen, snatched an ice tray from the freezer, broke up the ice, wrapped it in a dishcloth and got Kaye out of the way with Donna screeching now. I pressed the ice against the wound and told Charley to keep calm, the ambulance would be right there. Then I remembered I'd locked the foyer door and had to go down for it.

Charley was still conscious when they rolled him out with Kaye and Donna in tow. Williams and Jeanfreau had accompanied the ambulance and used my phone to call the detectives.

"What'd you shoot him with?" Williams asked, pointing to the two large holes around Haney's heart. I pointed to my .45 which I'd put on the kitchen counter before they came in.

It was then I remembered Grosetto and brought Williams down to my office. The little greaseball was just coming around and Williams slapped his cuffs on him and brought him up to have a look at Haney. The dead man looked younger in death in a yellow shirt and dungarees, his eyes even duller now, his face flaccid. To me he looked like an eighth grader trying to pass himself off at a high school. His shoes were tied in double knots as if his mom had made sure they wouldn't come undone.

It took the detectives forty minutes to get there. I made coffee for all and was on my second cup when Lt. Frenchy Capdeville strolled in, trailing cigarette smoke, a rookie dick at his heels. Frenchy needed a haircut badly, his black hair in loose curls over the collar of his brown suit.

His rookie partner had tried a pencil-thin moustache, like Frenchy's but his was lopsided. "Joe Sparks," Frenchy introduced him to me. Sparks, also in a brown suit, was sharp enough to keep quiet and let Frenchy run the show, which he did, quickly and efficiently.

After the coroner's men took Haney away, they took me and Grosetto to the Detective Bureau, Frenchy calling in Eddie Sullivan. While they booked Grosetto, I gave a formal statement about the first man I'd shot since the war. Self-defense, defined in Louisiana's Napoleonic Code Law was – justifiable homicide.

•

It didn't take a detective to discover how Haney had come in the back way, through the broken fence of the building next door, across the back courtyard and up the rear fire escape to break the hallway window.

"How'd he get in the apartment?" I asked Kaye as we sat in the hall at Charity Hospital the following morning, while Charley slept in the recovery ward. Dark circles around her eyes, she looked pale as she rocked Donna slowly. Thankfully the baby was asleep.

"I heard scratching against the door and thought it was the cat, the black one that's always around."

"Did he say anything?"

"No. He just shoved past me and shot Charley. Then he stood there looking at me."

A nurse came out of Charley's room and said, "He's awake now."

I didn't go in. I went back home to look up my landlord.

•

Charley Rudabaugh spent six days in the hospital. When I brought him home and walked him past my apartment door to the rear apartment, he balked until Kaye opened the door and smiled at him.

"What's going on?"

Kaye pulled him in and I stood in the doorway, amazed at what she'd done with the place in a few days. It came furnished but she'd brightened it up, replaced the dark curtains with yellow ones, the place looking spotless. Donna, lying on her back in a playpen in the center of the living room was trying to play with a rubber duck, slapping at it and gurgling.

It took Charley a good minute to take in the scene as Kaye eased up and hugged him.

"Here's the deal," I told them over coffee at their kitchen table. "The landlord gave us a break on the place. I'm fronting y'all the money. You don't have to pay me back, but if you insist, you can, but get on your feet first." I'd just put any money they gave me in a bank account for Donna's education.

Then I explained about how it really wasn't my money. It had been a gift and I was sharing it. "Everyone needs help sometimes. And you two have had a bad time recently."

I could see Charley was still confused, but not Kaye, beaming at him, paying little if any attention to me. I thanked her for the coffee and stood up to leave. Charley's eyes narrowed as he asked, "I understand what you say, but it's just hard to figure you ain't got some kinda motive. Everybody does."

I started for the door, turned and said, "Sometimes things are exactly as they appear to be."

Kaye moved to her daughter and began humming that same song, repeating the line in French again, "*le coeur a…*"

"What is that?" I had to ask.

"It's the reason you're doing all this." She smiled at me, looking like a school kid in her white shirt and jeans. "An old French saying that goes, 'The heart has reasons of which reason knows nothing'." She smiled down at her baby.

It wasn't until later, as I sat in my mother's rocker looking out the open French doors of my apartment, out at the dark roofs of the Quarter with the moon beaming overhead, that I heard my mother's voice back when she was young, a voice I haven't heard for so long, as she sang, "*le coeur a…* "

Then it hit me.

The heart has reasons of which reason knows nothing. Kaye hadn't mean just me. It cut both ways. She'd also meant Haney and I felt the hair on the back of my neck standing up.

END of THE HEART HAS REASONS

Kissable Cleavage

As I enter Etienne's Ladies Shoe Store, shortly before noon of another steamy New Orleans day during the sizzling summer of 1948, a tall brunette in a low-cut, red dress steps up to me and says, "What to you think of these?"

My gaze lowers to her plunging neckline and she laughs.

"No, silly. The shoes."

I look down and see she's wearing black, patent-leather high heels. She turns and walks away to give me a better look. I checked out her sleek legs and nice round hips and wipe my sweaty brow with the back of my hand.

As she approaches my old war buddy, Freddie, sitting on one of those stools, the woman turns back to me and says, "Well, Mr. Caye. Do you like them?"

She *knows* me?

Freddie rolls his eyes as the woman sits in the chair in front of his stool.

"Y'all know each other?" Freddie asks.

I step up to them as the woman pulls her tight dress up past to her knees and raises her left knee to put her foot up on the stool. When she leans back, I can see the front of her sheer, white panties.

Freddie's already staring between her legs as he slips off the black high heel.

"I'm sorry," I say as I look up at the woman's blue eyes. "Do I know you?"

"We met last week." She smiles as Freddie slips a red high heel on her left foot. Dropping her left leg, she raises her right knee, exposing even more of her panties as her dress rises.

I look at her face again and it hits me. She's the woman who just moved into my apartment building. She has a husband, little guy, looks like a jockey.

She must see the recognition in my eyes and extends her right hand and says, "Evelyn Bates."

"Lucien Caye." I shake her soft hand and she holds mine for an extra second before letting go. I wonder if she knows I'm already sporting a helluva hard-on.

She stands and walks back to the front of the store in the red heels, her hips moving nice and languidly. Returning, she's shaking her head. She moves around Freddie and I have to step back out of the way. I catch a whiff of perfume.

She sits with her hands on her knees, which are pressed together, nice and proper now. Leaning forward, she reaches down for the shoes and the top of her plunging neckline falls open to give us a nice long look at her round breasts inside her lacy, low-cut bra.

She says she can't decide. Freddie tells her he doesn't get off until five. Evelyn says she might come back. He helps her out of the red high heels and into her own heels. Rising, she extends her hand to me and we shake again.

"See 'ya around, Sport." With that, she pivots in her toes and walks away.

As she reaches the door, a burly man in a rumpled brown suit enters and glares at her on his way in. Freddie introduces the man as his boss.

"Come on," Freddie says. "Let's get a bite." He grabs his hat on our way out.

"No extended lunch break," his boss calls out as we reach the door.

Stepping out on narrow Royal Street, I look up and down but don't spot Evelyn.

"She'll be back around five," Freddie tells me as he leads the way down Royal toward Canal Street. He puts on his hat. The bright sun is hot on my head, but I never wear hats. Don't like to mess up my hair.

Freddie is exactly my age and height. Thirty. Six feet. Only he's balding already and soft, with a little pot belly. He's grown a moustache since we got out of the army. I'm clean-shaven, as always. My half-Spanish, half-Mediterranean French complexion is a couple shades darker than freckle-faced Freddie with his Irish red hair.

"Who was that? Etienne?" I ask.

"His name's Ernie Zumiga. He figured *Etienne* sounds like a shop you'd find in the French Quarter."

As we approach Iberville Street, I feel a slight breeze from the river and smell crawfish boiling. One of the little restaurants along here has its crawfish boiler directly beneath its exhaust fan. My stomach grumbles.

"Zumiga doesn't like women."

"You mean he's... "

"Naw. He's no fruit. Just doesn't like waiting on women, who can be picky as hell with shoes." Freddie chuckles. "In the wrong business. Now that *last* woman. She'll come back around five. Probably without panties."

We turn on Iberville and make for the rear entrance of D. H. Holmes Department Store.

"No panties?" I ask as we cross the street in front of a yellow cab who punches his horn because we made him take his lazy foot off the accelerator.

"No panties," Freddie repeats. "Happens all the time."

We enter the store and head for the Holmes Café. It's much cooler inside. Typically, Freddie doesn't bother lowering his voice as he explains how he's got it down to an art, looking up skirts. Even the longer skirts. The women don't think he can see, so they throw their legs all over the place and his face is right there at knee level.

"If you noticed, I push my stool up close so they have to lift their knees extra high."

We sit at a table next to the windows and I can't help wonder why I'm having lunch with this lunatic. OK, so he saved my life. That was four years ago, May '44, on that dusty hill outside Monte Cassino. Freddie kept me from bleeding to death after a goddamn Nazi with a Mauser slammed a round into my left arm, knocking me on my ass.

I order a chicken salad sandwich and coffee. So does Freddie. He doesn't have to tell me how good the chicken salad with the poppy seed dressing is here, but he does anyway.

"The Babe died today," I tell Freddie when he finally pauses to catch his breath.

"Babe Ruth?"

As if there's another fuckin' Babe.

"Heard it on the radio."

Our waiter drops off our iced teas.

"Man-o-man. The Sultan of Swat." Freddie shakes his head. "Seven hundred, fourteen home runs. Nobody'll ever break that record."

I don't remind him records are made to be broken. I just look at his comical face and smile. Son-of-a-bitch saved my ass with bullets ricocheting around us, when no one else, including the medics, would come forward to help me. Buying an occasional lunch for this man, who decided New Orleans was warmer than his home town of Moose River, Maine, is the least I could do.

"What's so funny?" Freddie asks.

"You."

"What? Lookin' up skirts. You didn't look at Evelyn's lily-white panties?" You didn't see her pubic hair right through the fabric?"

Thankfully our waiter arrives with our sandwiches.

Freddie takes a quick bite and talks with his mouth full. "Maybe I'll get lucky. Screw her in the back room."

The chicken salad is nice and cool, the poppy seed dressing sweet and tangy.

"I screwed a woman in the back room last week. We got a couch back there."

"Did Porky watch?"

"Naw. Zumiga leaves at four. On the dot."

I wait until I finish what's in my mouth before telling Freddie, in a low voice, "Evelyn's got a husband."

"Good. I don't wanna marry her." Freddie's voice echoes. "Just screw her."

A blue-haired woman with a black hat that looks like a tarantula, gives us a haughty look as she throws down her money and leaves the table next to us.

"Freddie," I say as I pick up my sandwich.

"Yeah?" He wipes his mouth with his shirt sleeve.

"Glad you asked me to lunch." I grin at him. "I can always use a laugh."

"Well," Freddie says. "You wanna come by the store 'round five to see what happens?"

I shake my head. Hell, my hard-on is just going away now.

•

Sitting in my high-back chair, behind the beat-up mahogany desk I bought at a used furniture store on Magazine Street (it would be an *antique* if I'd bought it in the Quarter), I look through the open Venetian blinds of my office windows at the commotion going on outside.

Two mockingbirds are dive-bombing a hapless alley cat across the street in Cabrini Playground. The cat races to this side of the street to hide under my pre-war, gray DeSoto, parked against the curb. A mockingbird lands on my car's roof and squawks so loud I hear it through the windows.

I flip the switch to "high" on the small, black revolving fan, perched on the edge of my desk and turn back to my typewriter to continue pecking out my report on the Choppel Case. The sooner it's done, the sooner I get paid. My old Corona is one of those big models and works well, except the "e" gets stuck once in a while.

Living in the low-rent, lower end of the French Quarter has its advantages, besides being in the center of town. Clients can easily find Barracks Street and the parking's no problem. So what if most of the buildings are decaying.

I hear footsteps in the hall outside my smoky-glass door. My electric clock reads four-thirty. Is it a panty-less Evelyn on her way back to Etienne's? The outer door of my building opens and I see the old Englishman who lives across the hall from my upstairs apartment. He walks leisurely up the sidewalk next to my windows. Turning my way, he waves.

It's hard to concentrate on typing my report while I'm thinking of Evelyn Bates and her round, kissable cleavage. I adjust my dick and continue typing. No, I'm not going to knock on Evelyn's door, casual-like. Just passing, I could say and wondering how your breasts are hanging, if they need adjusting or re-alignment. I used to be a bra fitter, I'd tell her. She'd invite me in, of course and I'd slip my arm around her waist, pull her close and start nibbling her neck...

Damn – Now I'm getting another hard-on.

I'll never get this fuckin' report done –

•

As I'm shaving the next morning, my phone rings. It's Freddie.

"Can you meet me for a cup 'a Joe?" he asks.

"What's up?"

"I'll tell you over coffee." There's a catch in his voice.

"She came back?"

"You want details, meet me at Morning Call. Half hour."

I climb into my light blue seersucker suit and new brown-and-white Florsheims, matching brown belt of course. Stepping into the bright, morning, I'm taken aback. Something's wrong. The humidity is gone. It isn't cool, but the insufferable combination of heat and steamy air is gone. Guess some sort of autumn front has breezed through the city.

I walk down to Decatur Street, past Creole brick cottages with their upstairs dormers and pastel colored houses with louvered shutters covering their windows and doorways. I turn right on Decatur before reaching the French Market where I smell the fresh fruit and vegetables – bell peppers, garlic, onions, apples and oranges.

Freddie is unshaven, in a wrinkled white shirt and equally wrinkled black pants. Seated at the long, marble counter of the coffee stand, he's looking at his reflection in the mirror that runs the length of the counter. There's a bruise on his jaw and his left eye is swollen and will be a regular black eye by this afternoon.

A waiter, clad in all white, including a ridiculous white, paper hat similar to the cunt caps we wore in the army, asks my pleasure before I sit.

"Two coffees."

"Beignets?"

I tap Freddie on the shoulder. "You want beignets?"

Freddie shakes his head so we pass on the French pastries – donuts actually with no holes, generously sprinkled with powdered sugar. The place reeks of sugar as several customers pound on tin shakers, inundating their beignets with even more sugar. As I sit on the stool next to Freddie, our waiter returns with our coffees in thick, off-white cups and matching saucers. I pour a teaspoon of sugar into the strong café-au-lait mixture and take a sip.

"So, what's up?" I ask.

Freddie starts laughing and can't stop. Pointing at himself in the mirror, he laughs so hard he almost falls off his stool. I drink most of my coffee before he recovers and tells me, between chuckles how Evelyn Bates came back, but still had on her panties. It didn't take Freddie long to get her out of them and into the back room where they went at it, "like rabbits."

An elderly couple at the closest table are listening, the man grinning, the woman's eyes glaring at Freddie as if he just pinched her ass. Taking my friend's shoulder I tell him to lower his voice.

He leans close and says, "Just before I get a nut, her goddamn husband comes in." Freddie rolls his eyes. "He musta been following her."

Freddie notices his coffee, dumps two spoons of sugar in it and takes a hit. I finished mine and wave to the waiter for another.

"Short bastard's like a bantam rooster," Freddie goes on. "He tore into me with those little, pointy fists and there we are, shoe boxes falling all over the fuckin' place, me with my pants around my ankles. I finally shoved him into the store room to get away. Only I ran into my damn boss, who was supposed be gone, and he fired me on the spot."

The old couple gets up and the woman pulls her husband out the door.

Freddie rubs his jaw and speculates that Mr. Bates might have been a boxer once.

"So what are *you* doing today?" Freddie asks as picks up his cup.

"Have to see a lawyer. Get paid for a case."

The waiter brings my second cup.

"He didn't hit Evelyn, did he?"

"Nope. Just me."

I wonder if she's all right.

"Well, I'll let you know when I get another job." Freddie finishes his coffee and reaches into his pocket. I tell him it's on me. He thanks me and says he's on his way to pick up his last check from good ole generous Ernie Zumiga.

"Before you go looking for another job," I tell him. "Take a shower and change."

He laughs and walks out, rubbing his jaw.

•

Back on Barracks Street, I spot Evelyn and her husband standing in Cabrini Playground. She's in a white dress, one of those loose-fitting cotton dresses New Orleans women wear to fend off the heat. Her husband, in a black tee-shirt and black pants, is a head shorter. His black hair is slicked back and he has a two day growth of beard on his face. He's got his hands in his pockets as he digs the toe of his shoe into the grass. They're talking.

They don't notice me as I pass next to the brick and wrought iron fence alongside the playground. I cross the street to our building, glancing over my shoulder to see they're still talking.

I go over my report one last time, proofreading my typing. It's only nine a.m., so I have plenty time before my one o'clock appointment with the attorney who hired me.

A good twenty minutes later a movement outside catches my eye. Evelyn and her husband come out of the playground and cross the street. With the sun behind her, I can see the outline of her body, the curves and the dark spot between her legs. When they reach my side of the street, I can almost see her nipples through the dress. Evelyn looks in and waves at me.

I wave back, hesitantly.

The outer door opens and I see their shadows through my smoky-glass door. The husband continues toward the stairs. Evelyn taps on my door and opens it, leaning in to smile at me.

"Are you busy?"

"Nope." I stand.

"I'll only be a second," she says as she steps in. She's unbuttoned the top two buttons of her dress. Her cleavage, like a deep, inviting chasm seems to dare me to stare, to leer, to want to kiss –

I look up at Evelyn's face. At least she isn't beat up.

"How's your friend?" she asks.

"He'll live."

She sighs and asks me to tell Freddie she's sorry. Those penetrating, blue eyes stare at me for a long moment before she turns and leaves.

Three minutes later, I see her husband out on the sidewalk. A tool box in hand, he raises the hood of their black, '47 Buick sedan, which is parked behind my DeSoto. Although only a two-door, the Buick's much bigger and swankier with its wide, chrome grill. He starts working under the hood.

I finish my proofreading, deciding I need to re-type only three pages.

Putting a pot of coffee on the small stove in the tiny kitchen at the rear of my office, I go to work. It takes me nearly an hour and three cups of coffee before the report's acceptable to me. I carefully file away the carbon copy and slip the original into a manila folder. Rechecking the invoice, I have to smile. Haven't made this kind of money in a long time.

Finally, I get to sit back with the morning paper to check what's new with the world. Today the big news is Truman calling the House Un-American Activities Committee more Un-American than anyone they've investigating. Man's got a point. I turn to the sport section to read about the Babe. At eleven-thirty, I put away the paper, wash up and head out for lunch.

Just as I step out of my building, a black prowl car pulls up, along with a black and white marked police car, both stopping in the middle of Barracks Street. A squat man with stubby arms and a regretfully familiar face, jumps out of the passenger side of the prowl car and heads for Mr. Bates.

Flashing his silver star-and-crescent NOPD badge, Detective Jimmy Hays snarls, "You Billy Bates?"

"Yeah." Billy pulls his head from under the hood.

Hays grabs Billy's right arm as two uniformed officers I don't know chip in to cuff my startled neighbor. Hays shoves Billy toward the prowl car. I hear someone behind me and Evelyn steps out.

"What's happening?"

Hays notices me for the first time and freezes. I lift my left hand and wave slowly, my face remaining expressionless.

"You Mrs. Bates?" Hays snaps.

Evelyn rushes forward, "What are you doing with my husband?"

The two uniforms move around Evelyn and take her by the elbows. She stiffens and asks again what's going on.

"We'll tell you at the precinct," Hays says. Taking two steps toward me, he points a finger at my face and growls, "What the fuck are *you* doing here?"

I stick my tongue out at him. His partner, still sitting in the prowl car, starts laughing. He's an old timer named Frank Lemon. Hays takes another menacing step toward me, narrowing his dull gray eyes, as if that'll scare me. "What were you just doing with the man's wife?"

"Fuck you!"

Hays doesn't take the bait. I'm braced and ready to drop him, as I did before when we were both in uniform, rookies right out of the academy, back before the war. He shot a dog that had knocked over the garbage can outside the Third Precinct Station. I decked him with one punch. Glass jaw.

A jack-o-lantern smile comes to the face as Hays says, "Your pal Freddie O'Hara should be over at the coroner's office 'bout now."

I feel a hollowness deep in my belly.

"And *I'm* the one who caught his killer." Hays pulls on the lapels of his ill-fitting brown suit, backs into the prowl car and continues eye-fucking me as the cars pull away.

•

I drop off the Choppel report with my client's secretary on my way to the morgue. Parking on South White Street, next to the gray, cement Criminal Courts Building, I walk up the steps of the building's side entrance to the Coroner's Office.

Immediately, I smell the putrid scents from the morgue downstairs – formaldehyde, ammonia, human waste. A large black man behind the counter looks up as I ask if any of the coroner's investigators are in. He waves me to my right and I go down the hall to a narrow office with ancient wooden desks and wall-to-wall filing cabinets. Behind one of the desks sits Sean Harrigan, a burly man pushing sixty with a receding hairline and droopy brown eyes. He recognizes me and waves me in. I ask about Freddie.

"We won't post him until morning," Sean tells me on our way down the narrow stairs to the morgue.

Freddie is in the first cooler. Eyes half open in that dull look of death, my friend still wears the same wrinkled white shirt and pants. I take a long look at him, reach over and touch his hand, already cold now and stiff.

I have a flashback of that dusty hilltop and Freddie's grinning face as he drags me away from the line of fire. Guess I always suspected Freddie wasn't long for this world. My throat tightens and my heart stammers as I pat Freddie's hand and back away from the drawer.

"Cause of death?" I ask Sean in a voice I have trouble controlling.

"Blow to the back of the head. Blunt object."

"When was he brought in?"

Sean closes the drawer, shoving Freddie back into the cooler.

"Eleven o'clock. Cops found him around ten this morning." Sean wipes his hand on his black pants as he leads me away. "He was lying in Exchange Alley between Bienville and Conti."

Jesus.

"Did he have a check on him?"

"Personal effects are upstairs."

There's no check, just a wallet, keys, Sin-Sin breath mints, a pack of Lucky Strikes, Zippo lighter and seven dollars and fifty-three cents.

I pick up the phone and dial the operator who puts me through to the operator in Bangor, Maine. Three minutes later I hear the scratchy voice of Freddie's uncle with the unforgettable name Harry O'Hara of Moose River, Maine. He gotta be pushing eighty, a veteran of the first World War, he was middle-aged back then. It takes a minute for my message to sink in.

"Freddie's folks have passed away," Uncle Harry tells me. I tell him I know and ask about Freddie's sister who lives in one of the Dakotas.

"Yes. Priscilla. I'll have to look up her number."

Uncle Harry thanks me for calling and tells me he'll contact Priscilla himself. "Aren't you the friend in New Orleans Freddie talks about?"

"Yes I am."

"Good that you're there for him."

Yeah. Fat lot of good.

I pass the phone to Sean Harrigan who wants to get mailing information for Freddie's personal effects.

When I leave ten minutes later, I stop at the bottom of the steps. Taking in deep breaths of fresh air, my face lifted to the sun, my eyes closed, I fight it as best I can. My heart aches and my stomach feels like marbles are rolling around inside. But I can't let it get to me. Not now.

I've got a killer to catch.

Billy Bates didn't kill Freddie.

Fuckin' Hays arrested the wrong man.

•

I park on Conti Street, within view of the Third Precinct Building on Chartres Street, where they're holding Billy and Evelyn, I walk into Exchange Alley. The uneven bricks cause my ankles to turn as I move through the alley that's as wide as our narrow French Quarter Streets, which were built for horse and buggies.

Ancient wrought iron light posts dot the center of the alley, which services the rear of the small shops and eateries of Royal and Chartres Streets. Long ago, young blades practiced here. The small buildings of Exchange Alley once housed the finer fencing schools, where Creole Frenchmen and Spaniards learned the art of dueling.

There's a man emptying garbage into a large bin. He saw nothing this morning. Neither did any of the other people I speak with as I move up and down the alley. A nervous antique shop owner admits she saw police in the alley, but nothing else.

Since the alley's only two blocks from Etienne's Ladies Shoe Store, I pay Ernie Zumiga a visit. He's finishing a sale. A silver-haired woman with an umbrella figure, an opened umbrella, snorts as she counts her change and leaves. Zumiga doesn't seem to recognize me, so I play it like this –

"I have some follow-up questions about Freddie O'Hara."

His dull brown eyes reveal nothing. He wipes sweat from his brown with the sleeve of the same rumpled brown suit coat he wore yesterday.

"I thought y'all already arrested that Bates lunatic." Zumiga moves through the store, repacking several pairs of shoes the umbrella woman must have gone through before making her big decision.

"We have information that Freddie O'Hara was heading here to collect his last check around the time he was killed."

Zumiga turns and glares at me.

"I gave him his check." The brown eyes widen as he says, "Hey, ain't you Freddie's pal?" He takes a menacing step toward me, a vicious-looking pair of brown mules dangling from his fingers. I stand my ground and tell him the check wasn't on Freddie.

"Where's your checkbook?" I ask casually. "We'll need the check number so whoever took it, doesn't cash it."

Zumiga steps right up to me, fists balled up against his hips, mules dangling from his hands.

"Let me see ya' badge."

I look at his eyes and tell him I turned mine in.

"Then get the fuck outta here!" He makes the mistake of moving forward but quickly sees I'm not moving backward so he does a little dance before falling back a step.

"I'll call the real cops," he says on the way around the counter.

"Good," I tell him as I step up to the counter. "Then we can all check out your checkbook."

The door opens and three women breeze in, middle-aged ladies in nice outfits. Wives out shopping. One smiles shyly at me as I step out of their way. Zumiga grabs a black checkbook from next to the cash register. He opens it on the counter for me, then steps around to help the women. He tells me to knock myself out.

It's right there, two checks back. In the name of Freddie O'Hara for forty-two dollars and seventeen cents. Zumiga has his back to me and doesn't turn around as I close the checkbook and leave it there on my way out.

•

It's four o'clock by the time I step back into my building. There's a note taped to my office door. It's from Evelyn, asking me to come see her, if I can. She doesn't answer her doorbell until the third ring. Breathless, she leans out and says, "Oh, Mr. Caye. Thanks for coming." She opens the door wider and I step in.

Evelyn is in a shortie, blue silk robe with lots of bare legs showing. She also wears blue pumps as she stands there, staring at me, hands behind her back. Her face is made-up as if she's going out tonight, her hair freshly washed and curled, hanging to her shoulders. Only thing that's out of place is her eyes. Red-rimmed and ovaled, she bats them at me, so innocently.

"Where's Billy?" I ask as I force myself to look away from those legs. Her apartment has the same layout as mine, only everything's on the opposite side. We have the same light green curtains, but her sofa's dark green and there's a matching loveseat and a desk and bar with plenty of liquor stacked atop. The place smells faintly of pine oil.

"They're still holding him," she answers.

"They won't for long."

She tilts her head to the side, the way a puppy does when you make a funny noise. Her brow furrows in confusion. So I tell her I'm Billy's alibi. No way he could have killed anyone.

"I had coffee with Freddie this morning until eight forty-five. Came back and y'all were out in the park. We both how know Billy came right down to work on his car and he was there until the cops came."

Her eyes become wet as she tells me she told that to the police, but they didn't believe her.

"They'll have to believe me," I say. "I'm good on the witness stand."

She wipes a tear from her left eye as I tell her that I used to be the police and used to testifying in court. They won't shake me. Billy has a good alibi because Freddie was my friend and I know Billy didn't do it.

"You have a lawyer?" I ask.

She shakes her head.

"I know a couple." I point to the door behind her. "Down in my office. I have their numbers and can make a call for you."

"Let me slip into something," she says as she moves past me quickly toward the master bedroom. She doesn't close the door, but I don't peek. I call out, reminding her we need to call right away. Lawyers are nine to fivers.

She hurries out carrying a pair of brown high heels, a tan blouse and brown skirt draped across her arm. She drops them on the sofa next to me and pulls off her robe and I can't help staring at her lacy, white bra and semi-sheer white panties.

"You've seen my panties before," she says in a husky voice. "When you looked up my skirt at Etienne's."

I watch her pull on her blouse and oouch into the tight skirt. She puts a hand on my shoulder as she pulls on each shoe. I catch a whiff of Chanel as she finishes, looks up and pulls her hair away from her face, which is only inches from mine.

She smiles and thanks me, then leans up and brushes her lips across mine. I have trouble rushing downstairs with the lumber between my legs. We have to catch the lawyer who hired me for the Choppel Case before he leaves for the day. He agrees to see us and I can pick up my check at the same time.

"He might be a little expensive," I warn Evelyn on our way back out of my office. "But he's very good."

"That's what we need."

She takes my hand and squeezes it and doesn't let go until she climbs into my car.

•

Unlocking her door just before seven that night, Evelyn looks back at me and says, "Don't be silly. The least I can do is fix you supper."

She moves to her small kitchen and puts a pot of water on the stove. Reaching into her refrigerator, she pulls out left-over spaghetti and meat balls. As she warms them, she offers me a drink.

"Beer will be fine."

She passes me a Schlitz on her way to the sofa where she kicks off her shoes and climbs out of her clothes and puts on the robe. Only she doesn't bother tying it shut. I'm about to get lucky, I guess. If she isn't a little fuckist, I'm a goddamn bomber pilot, instead of an ex-infantryman.

We have dinner at her small Formica table, her robe open the entire time. I watch her breasts rise and fall, rise and fall as she breathes, as she talks to me about how she and Billy met. They met cute, him helping her fix a flat along Gentilly Boulevard.

"But he's tiny," she says, finishing off her spaghetti.

I know where she's going with this.

"Everything's tiny." She stands and drops her robe on her chair, picks up her plate and goes back into the kitchen, bending over to scrape off her plate in the trash can, pointing that round ass at me.

She comes back and pulls her bra straps off her shoulders. She reaches around and starts to unfasten it, but hesitates, waiting for something from me. In the long seconds that follows, I know its time to decide. Get out now or listen to the beat of the hard-on throbbing between my legs.

"Let me help you with that," I say as I stand, readjusting my dick.

She smiles seductively, opening her arms.

I step over and reach behind her to unsnap her bra in one smooth movement. It falls to the floor and I stare at her full breasts, at her pink aureoles and small, pointed nipples.

My hands move to her hips as I lean down and kiss each nipple softly, then run my teeth over them. She gasps and pulls my mouth up to hers. We French kiss, our tongues rolling, our arms wrapping around each other tightly. The kiss continues as my hands slip down to her ass. I squeeze and she tightens her arms around me. I kiss my way down her throat back to her breasts, cupping them in my hands, kneading them as I suck each nipple. I continue massaging her breasts as I kiss my way down to her panties.

I lick the front of her silky panties, momentarily sucking at her crotch. Her breath comes fast and she moans and spreads her feet apart. I yank her panties down and bury my face in her bush, my tongue working its way inside her. She's already nice and wet.

She cries out and rolls her hips to my tonguing. I continue and she grinds her hips against my tongue. She tugs at my hair, but I won't stop. Moaning louder, she grabs my ears. I keep licking. She pulls harder until my ears hurt. I flick my tongue against her clit. She yanks on my ears, pulling me up to her mouth.

We barely make it to the sofa, her tugging at my pants, me trying not to fall. She lays back on her sofa, legs spread and guides my dick into her. As I slide in, she cries out and freezes, then starts gyrating and we fuck there on her sofa.

It's frenzied. It's hot. It's a ball slamming fuck. Trying to hold back isn't an option and she lets out a high-pitched cry as I come in her in long spurts. We catch our breath and kiss softly before I climb off.

Evelyn takes my hand and leads me into her bedroom, to her brass bed for a long, smooth, deep penetrating second fuck. And as I'm on top of her, looking down at her lovely face in the dim light, seeing those bright blue eyes looking up at me, eyes filled with passion, I think of Freddie, lying in the morgue.

I don't lose my stroke. I keep grinding her, and think of Freddie and her husband, illegally in jail, and here I am nailing this gorgeous woman. I know – a hard-on has no conscience.

For a moment I almost waiver, but only for a moment. I catch my stride again and continue fucking her in long, deep strokes. I do it because we both want it. I do it because she's beautiful. I do it because Freddie didn't get a nut and I'm about to get my second one in her.

I'm finishing what my friend only got to start.

If there's one thing I know about Freddie – he'd want me to.

•

Something wakes me and it takes a few seconds for me to realize I'm in Evelyn's bed, alone. The curtain from the French doors of her bedroom swirl in on the night's breeze and I see her standing beneath a dim yellow light out on the rear balcony of her bedroom.

I get up and slip out on the balcony behind her, my hand caressing her naked ass for a moment. She turns and kisses me.

"That feels so nice," she whispers in my ear. "Don't be obvious," she continues whispering. "See the window across the courtyard, on the first floor?"

I nod.

"There's an old man sitting inside watching me."

She turns her naked body toward the old man, raises her arms and stretches. Her breasts rise as she arches her back.

Craning her neck back to me, she whispers how the old man is there every night, watching her. She comes out naked like this every night for him.

"He probably hasn't seen anything like this in a long time," she says.

"Maybe never."

"That's sad."

Evelyn reaches back for my dick, which is already semi-hard. She hardens it, leans her ass against me and bends over, spreading her legs. She guides the tip of my dick to her pussy lips and we fuck on the balcony, Evelyn holding on to the railing, those luscious breast bouncing back and forth as I screw her while the old man watches.

•

It takes less than a day to solve my friend's murder.

A visit to the coroner's office confirms Freddie died of a skull fracture. One blow to the back of the head.

At nine-thirty, I'm in Exchange Alley looking for people who were there the same time yesterday. Several kids are tossing pennies against a warehouse wall. I pick out the boy who appears to be the leader and talk to him man-to-man. He's about ten, tall and skinny with cocoa skin and black hair. Of the seven kids there, three are white. The leader tells me he's Michael. I lose a few pennies to them, then pull out some bills to loosen their tongues. It still takes a good half hour.

Eddie, the smallest in the crowd, a boy with skin so dark it has a blue hue, saw it. He saw Freddie bopping into the alley, saw the fat man come in behind him, saw Freddie turn. They argued. Over money. Freddie cursed the fat man and turned to walk away. The fat man pulled a pipe from his coat pocket and hit Freddie across the back of the head.

"Got a good look at the fat man?"

Eddie nods and points across the alley to a restaurant worker cleaning stainless steel trays. "He saw too."

I walk over to the young man. He's reluctant to talk at first. He gives in after I point to the Holy Cross ring on his finger. We went to the same high school, although he's a lot younger. His name is Charlie Parker and works part-time at the restaurant, before his afternoon classes at Loyola.

We get permission from his boss to take a walk. I ask the kids to come along.

"I'll give each of you another buck to take a walk with me."

They make me pay first and we all go around to Royal Street to Etienne's Ladies Shoe Store where Ernie Zumiga is just opening up.

Eddie points through the front window at Zumiga and says, "That's him!"

Charlie confirms it and follows me in. Zumiga stops straightening stools and stands there with a queer look on his face as I go around the counter, pick up his phone and call the Third Precinct. As I hang up, I spot a metal pipe under the counter. I think I see a strand of red hair clinging to the end of the pipe.

We wait. Zumiga sees Charlie and sits heavily in one of his chairs and closes his eyes. He shakes his head and says, "They arrested *Bates*!"

When Jimmy Hays rushes in, snarling, "What the fuck is this?" I ignore him. I turn to his partner and lay it out methodically to Frank Lemon.

"But what happened to the check?" Hays growls.

"Probably in the trash can." I point to one under the cash register.

When Frank Lemon pulls out the crumpled check, Zumiga starts shaking. his lower lip quivering, liquid pooling around his shoes.

I can't help thinking of the old police cliché – *thank God criminals are stupid.*

•

The day after the newspaper runs the story of Ernie Zumiga's arrest by two of New Orleans' finest, I'm sitting in my high-back chair, my brown and white Florsheims propped up on the corner of my desk.

The heat and humidity have returned with a withering vengeance so I'm dressed casually today in a tan and white shirt and brown pants as I read the sport section of the morning paper. There's a tribute to the Babe. I didn't know he broke into the major with Baltimore in 1914, didn't know he tossed a record twenty-nine consecutive scoreless innings in a World Series. How he was sold to the Yankees by Boston, I knew. How Boston's never won much since, even with Ted Williams...

Someone taps at my office door and I can see, through the smoky glass who it is before the door opens. Evelyn slinks in. She's in navy blue today, another low cut dress that's too tight around the hips. She stops in front of my desk and folds her arms beneath those luscious breasts.

"I just came from that lawyer's office." The little fuckist licks her crimson lips. "Now I'm here to pay you."

"For what? I solved my friend's murder."

"My husband was released this morning." Evelyn reaches back and starts unzipping her dress. I shake my head and smile, pull my feet down as she works the top of her dress down to her waist, then starts working it the rest of the way down.

Evelyn unsnaps her bra and drops it on my desk. I realize the blinds are open and move over to shut them. When I turn back, Evelyn's naked. She does a slow pirouette for me. I move back behind my desk and readjust my dick as I sit. Evelyn comes around and reaches for my belt.

"Look, um... " is the only intelligent thing I can think of, taking in a deep breath as Evelyn runs her fingers across my erection. I reach for those breasts hovering in front of me, softly squeezing them, pinching her nipples.

Evelyn unbuckles my belt and pants and unzips me. She pulls out my dick and squeezes it. She sinks her mouth on mine and we French kiss as she climbs on me. I instinctively grab her ass. Rising, she guides my dick to her pussy and sinks on it.

We fuck right there on my chair, Evelyn riding my dick, bouncing and groaning.

"Fuck me!" She moans. "Yes. Oh. Oh. *Oh*!"

She's hotter than ever and wetter than ever and I pounding her when I think I hear my door open. I shove my face around and Billy's there, wearing all black, glaring at us like a bull terrier.

I lift Evelyn and she wails passionately. I put her ass up on my desk as Billy comes forward, fast, fists rising, face contorted in anger.

"Wait!" I gasp.

"No!" Evelyn cries back. "Fuck me, you big bastard!"

I try to pull away, but she's got her arms around my neck like a vice.

Billy runs around the desk and tries to punch my face, but I duck forward and his fist bounces off the back of my neck.

Evelyn sees him and cries out.

Billy punches me again, on the side of the head as I disentangle myself from his panting wife who's up on my desk now, legs spread.

Billy howls and lunges at me with both fists and I block his blows as I fall back. I shove the high-back chair at him and hobble around my desk, trying to kick my pants off.

He comes at me, face red with rage. Screaming, he rushes right into the left jab I throw at him in self-defense. It slams against his nose and he screams. He bounces back and runs his left hand under his nostrils, then looks at it for blood.

"Hey," I call out. "This is enough."

There's no blood and Billy leaps at me again. I block his punches with both arms.

"Stop!" I shout. "Quit hitting me!"

Billy tries a roundhouse right, but I back away. Stumbling, he tries to come back with a left, but I catch him with my own left hook, right on the temple and he tumbles against the bookcase.

"Let's stop," I try but Billy keeps coming, swinging wildly.

I slam another left to the side of his head and the little man goes down.

"Don't get up!" I back away but Billy jumps up again and I block his shots with my left. Damn little fists hurt like hell.

He pivots to his left and runs smack into the right cross I throw. It lifts him off his feet momentarily. His knees buckle and he goes straight down.

Evelyn hovers over him, rolling him on his back.

He seems to be breathing OK.

I pull up my boxers and pants and fasten them quickly.

Satisfied her husband's not hurt badly, Evelyn gets up and moves back to me with that hungry look in those blue eyes.

She tries to put her arms around my neck, but I grab her wrists.

"What the fuck?"

She smiles and leans forward to peck my lips.

"Watching me get fucked gets Billy juiced."

I let go of her wrists and she kisses me, tonguing me as she grabs my stiff dick again. I try. I really try to resist, but I'm only human. Evelyn yanks down my pants and drawers and we do it on my desk, right on top of the Sports Section, her unconscious husband on the floor.

Our mouths fish each other, tongues rolling together. I come up for air, not missing a stroke and ask, "Why did he hit me?"

She gasps and says I'm pretty naive for a detective.

"Watching me like this gets Billy hot and his blood boils, so he wants to hit you. Then he'll screw the hell out of me later." She grunts with my grinding. "Actually, he'll try. Get his little dick wet. But I get my pussy reamed by you, big boy. Come on!"

She closes her eyes and bounces under me, nearly lifting me.

"What... are... you... com... plaining... about?" Her voice is husky with passion. "You get to do this with me!"

Jesus. These are my neighbors.

I feel myself close to coming and try to hold back. Evelyn wants no part of that and bucks me wildly.

"We're... going... to have... lots... of fun... this summer!" Her eyes are closed and this gorgeous woman is flushed with passion. I come in her, jamming my dick in her, making her cry out in pleasure.

Just as we finish, I see her husband stirring.

Here come the little fists again.

This is what I get for thinking with the wrong head.

Again.

END of KISSABLE CLEAVAGE

Hard Rain

Through my office windows I see heavy, gray rain clouds move over Barracks Street and darken the blue morning sky of the lower French Quarter. I watch the first fat raindrops plop on the hood of my gray, pre-war DeSoto parked against the curb. The rain bounces high off the hood and dances in the street. The boys playing baseball across the street in Cabrini Playground scramble for cover. The rain comes down quickly in sheets, sweeping over the dark roofs of the Creole cottages and the Spanish townhouses, washing the black wrought-iron lace balconies, drenching the tall oaks and wide magnolias along the edge of the playground.

I prop my feet up on my old mahogany desk and watch the rain, thinking how the spring of '49 is the wettest and coolest spring since the war. The morning paper predicted the high would be in the low sixties. That's almost as rare in New Orleans as snowfall. The paper also predicted scattered thunderstorms, which are as common here as red beans and rice.

I close my eyes. The small black revolving fan atop my desk blows air across me in waves as the rain storms outside. My mind drifts to a vision of a sultry brunette with a wicked smile and cobalt-blue eyes. She wears a tight black skirt and a white blouse sheer enough that I can see the outline of her lacy bra.

A loud crack of thunder brings me back from the edge of sleep. I see the rain has transformed Barracks Street into a mini-canal. And just as suddenly as it arrived, the rain goes away, as if God turned off a spigot.

I close my eyes again to the sultry brunette, only I wind up thinking about my bank account. I've been living off the money I'd made on the Choppel Case for a while now, with only a handful of paying cases since. Good thing I set up my one-man detective agency on low-rent Barracks Street. It doesn't attract many high-rolling clients, but the rent is easy to make. Living upstairs helps.

I feel drowsy again. And just as I drift away with the brunette hanging on my arm, I hear the building's outside door open. I hear footsteps, followed by the sound of my office's smoky-glass door opening. I pull my feet off my desk as a blonde steps in.

"Is this the detective office?" she asks in an uptown, sing-song voice.

"Yes." I stand and brush down my tie with my left hand.

She moves across the room to the desk.

I button the top button of my white, dress shirt and tighten my tie. I record her vitals before she reaches my desk – late-thirties, about 5'6", slim build (nice round hips), blonde hair worn up in a bun, make-up as professional as a model's. Her tan suit is the latest fashion, a short jacket over a high-collared white blouse and a snug skirt. Her high heels are the same shade of brown as the purse dangling from her left arm.

She stops in front of my desk and gives me the kind of look a woman gives when you don't open the door for her. I point to one of the cushioned chairs in front my desk and she sits, placing her purse in her lap and crosses a leg.

I check out her hardware – a pearl necklace and three rings, one with a ruby the size of a silver dime, one with an emerald the size of a nickel and a wedding ring set with a diamond as big as the Ritz (Okay, I stole that line from F. Scott Fitzgerald, so sue me.). Up close now, she has the confident look of the well-fed, well-manicured, well-comforted uptown wife.

"I'm Lucien Caye," I say as I sit. "What can I do for you?" I would have said ma'am, only a man of thirty-one doesn't call a woman pushing forty 'ma'am', at least not down south, we don't.

She looks at the windows and swallows hard and the confident look on her face fades a little. I wait.

"Um," she says, "I uh..." She turns her money-green eyes to me and lets it out. "I need something done. Confidentially."

I nod slowly. The fan's picked up her perfume. Chanel. Sure is a popular scent.

She lets out a sigh. "My maid is missing."

"Go on."

"A week ago today, Monday, she said she wasn't feeling well. I paid her for the entire day and she left. And she hasn't come back."

I look at the calendar on my desk. Last Monday was May 30th. I remember the kids outside whooping it up. It was the last day of school. I pull a notepad from my side desk drawer, along with a pen.

"You don't know how to get in touch with her?" Sometimes you have to ask the obvious to keep the conversation moving.

"I don't know anything about her." Her face reddens slightly. She opens her purse and pulls out a pack of Chesterfields, taps out a cigarette, and raises it for me to light.

I shake my head. "I don't smoke."

She nods curtly and drops the pack and the loose cigarette into her purse.

I pick up my pen and ask her name.

She lets out another sigh. "Mrs. Julia Eindhoven."

While writing it down I ask her how she got her maid in the first place.

"Oh. Sadie knocked on my door eight years ago. Just before the war. And asked me about work." Her sing-song uptown accent is in full swing. "She does the laundry and cleans up, sweeps and mops, every Monday, Wednesday and Friday. I'm worried about her."

"You said Sadie. What's her last name?"

Mrs. Eindhoven shakes her head.

"What does she look like?"

"Well, she's attractive. Colored. Good shape for her age. I think she's about fifty. It's hard to tell with coloreds."

I write – Sadie. Negro Female. About fifty.

"She lives downtown. At least she told me that once, I think. She always catches the streetcar."

I look up at her again and her face looks pained.

"She's such a good worker. I don't know what I'm going to do without her." She uncrosses her legs then re-crosses them. "I'm worried."

"How tall is she?"

"I guess five-three. Maybe a hundred and twenty pounds."

"Hair color?"

"Black."

"Any gray?"

"No." She pats her hair with her left hand.

"You said she cleans up. Do you have any other servants? A cook?"

"I do my own cooking."

I watch her carefully as I ask, "Would your husband know anything else about her?"

She blinks and sits up straighter. "He barely knows her first name." Her eyes widen slightly as she adds, "Why did you ask that?"

"Did he ever drive her home? Maybe when it was raining or something?"

"She carries an umbrella."

Mrs. Eindhoven opens her purse again, pulls out a small wad of bills and places them on my desk. Then she pulls out a piece of paper and shoves the paper and bills toward me.

"My address and phone number are there. You can call me at home during the day. I don't want my husband finding out I hired you." Her round jaw seems to tighten. "He wouldn't understand me spending money to find a – Sadie."

Mrs. Eindhoven stands. I stand, brushing down my tie again. She points to the money. "I think that should cover it." I see a fifty on top and nod. She turns, takes a step then turns back. "You have connections, I presume?"

"Sure."

She puts her left hand on her hip. I love it when women do that.

"I mean – in the colored sections."

"No problem, Mrs. Eindhoven. I was a cop for six years."

"Good. I'll rely on your discretion." She turns again and I watch her hips move out of my office.

I breathe in deeply and smell her Chanel again. I open the piece of paper she left next to the money and she's written, "7020 St. Charles Avenue. Walnut-1115."

Eindhoven – has to be Eindhoven Jewelers. I've seen her husband's face on the society page. Alfred or Albert. Big money. Big in the Lutheran Church. Big deal. I pick up the money and count six fifties. Nice. Very nice.

The sun peeks through the trees across the street and falls across my office windows. I sit and loosen my tie. I can't call my power company contact, not with only a first name. Can't use the phone book.

Don't laugh. I clipped a lawyer last month for a cool fifty using the phone book. He couldn't find a witness the day before trial. The witness had moved since the lawyer spoke with him. I found the witness in the book, waited a half day, then told the lawyer.

I look at my watch. It's pushing ten o'clock now. I stand and stretch and feel a twinge just below my left elbow where that damn German sniper got me outside Monte Cassino. I rub it and figure it's just the rain. I straighten my tie in the mirror by the door. Tan seems to be the color of the day. My tan tie is only a shade darker than my suit. I pull on my suit coat and scoop up my brown fedora, which matches my brown and white wing-tipped shoes. I hesitate, then put the fedora back on my coat rack. I'm tired of wearing hats. They mess up my hair.

The kids are back in the playground. Throwing a football now, it's more fun on wet grass. The air smells of wet leaves. I climb into my two-door, light gray, 1940 DeSoto Coach and crank up the engine. It purrs nicely as I slip it into gear and ease my way up Barracks Street to Rampart. Waiting at the stop sign, I roll down the windows before hanging a left to meander through town.

The porcelain steering wheel feels cool, as does the breeze through the open windows. I turn on the radio and catch a news report on the fifth anniversary of D-Day. "Everyone remembers where they were when they heard the news," the reporter says.

Hell, I was convalescing in a hospital outside Monte Cassino, flirting with a blonde nurse who wound up marrying the New Yorker in the cot next to me. I switch the station until I find a nice blues number. I take Canal Street down to St. Charles Avenue, through the concrete central business district, and then through the Garden District. I look around at the stately mansions, Neo-Classical, Greek Revival, Southern Gothics, at elegant gardens and finely-trimmed lawns of China grass.

I pass Loyola University's red brick buildings on the right, Audubon Park's towering oak with their Spanish moss beards on the left, then Tulane University's gray stone buildings again on the right before I reach the 7000 block of St. Charles.

The Eindhoven mansion is on my left and is surrounded by oleander bushes. In full-bloom now, the bushes cradle the three-story white Greek Revival like a pink scarf. The manicured front yard is dotted with white camellia bushes behind a black wrought-iron fence.

I pull over to the right, park and cross over to the median we call a neutral ground, where I wait for a streetcar to rattle past. A little boy waves at me form the car while a bigger boy leans out the open window and sticks his tongue out at me.

Two fat raindrops plop on my shoulder from the canopy of oak branches that nearly cover the neutral ground. Looking again at the Eindhoven mansion, I see two cars parked in its long driveway, a blue '49 Chrysler and a red, two-door '49 Del Mar convertible. I jot the license numbers in my notebook.

I walk over to the house on the uptown side of the Eindhoven's and ring the doorbell. Also three story, this Victorian has a cut-glass front door that is answered by a short maid in a standard-issue white maid's dress. Her salt-and-pepper hair is close-cropped. Her brown face smiles at me as she asks my business. I pull out a business card and hand it to her.

"I'm looking for Sadie." I tilt my head toward the Eindhoven's. "She's missing."

The smile disappears. She looks over her shoulder and then back at me, nervously.

"What's your name?" I ask.

It's like pulling teeth, but I get her to tell me she's Prudence and doesn't know Sadie well. She tries to hand my card back to me and says, "You need to talk to Molly. Molly Jones."

I don't take the card.

She points toward the Eindhoven's. "Molly works in the blue house on the other side." She looks over her shoulder again.

"I gotta go." She closes the door slowly, no longer looking at me. If this was an interrogation, I'd figure she was hiding something. I write the name 'Prudence' in my notes and put a little star next to it.

The blue house on the other side of the Eindhoven mansion is another Victorian. The doorbell is answered by a tall, light-complected Negro maid.

"Hi, are you Molly?"

She nods and looks around me to make sure I'm alone, I guess. I hand her a business card and introduce myself, then tell her I'm looking for Sadie.

"She's not next door?" Molly leans out and looks at the Eindhoven mansion.

"She's missing."

"What?" Her brown eyes widen. "You sure?"

I can't stop this one from talking, which is rather nice, actually. I jot the pertinent details in my notes. Molly says she'd started working at the blue house a year before Sadie started with the Eindhovens. She says Sadie Martin is a very quiet person and lives in a yellow shotgun house in Treme, the oldest Negro section of town. Molly explains, "It's at the corner of Dumaine and Villere. It's the only yellow house there."

As I start to leave, Molly adds, "Lord, I hope she's all right."

•

The yellow shotgun is actually one house from the corner of Dumaine and North Villere, sandwiched along a row of narrow, wooden, shotgun houses with no front yards. I park across Dumaine. The people sitting out on the front stoops watch me cross the street, including the kids playing in the street. I take the three steps up the front stoop of the yellow house, which is in dire need of painting, as are most houses in the area, and knock on the screen door.

A woman's voice calls out, "Yeah?"

"I'm looking for Sadie," I call back.

The house is too dark to see inside. I hear footsteps approach. I step down the stoop and pull out a business card. The woman fits Sadie's description, except her hair is white. She wears a blue cotton dress and is barefoot. She puts both hands to her throat and says, "Oh Lord. Have you found her?"

"No ma'am. I'm looking for her." I hold my card up.

A small hand reaches around the woman's leg and then a little face peeks out at me from behind her. A little boy, around four years old, blinks his brown eyes at me.

"You police?" the woman asks.

I tell her I'm a private detective. I don't think she knows the difference. The little boy pulls on her dress and she reaches down and scoops him up. Then she opens the screen door and invites me in. I follow her through a front room of old furniture – a faded blue sofa, mis-matched end tables and two green rockers. The place smells damp and mildewy. We pass through a master bedroom and then another bedroom where I see a picture of the little boy with a pretty woman wearing a crooked smile. I stop at the picture.

"Is this Sadie?"

The woman turns back and nods. "She my sister. I'm Loretta." She looks at the boy. "This is Joe-Joe. He's Sadie's."

The boy points a finger at me and smiles shyly. I smile back, then follow Loretta into the kitchen. She sits at an unpainted wooden table with Joe-Joe in her lap. He immediately picks up a spoon, dips it into a white bowl in front of him, and eats oatmeal.

I take out my notepad and learn that Sadie left for work before eight last Monday morning and never came back. Sadie Martin is thirty-nine. So much for Mrs. Eindhoven's description. Sadie's husband, Desmond, has been checking at Charity Hospital before he goes to work and after. Desmond's a garbage man.

"I ask all my neighbors," Loretta says, shaking her head, "but nobody seen Sadie.

She gets up and goes to the small refrigerator. There's only a few items inside. She returns with a quart of milk and pours some in the oatmeal for Joe-Joe, who dips his spoon back in and continues eating.

I wait until the boy finishes before asking for a picture of Sadie. Loretta leads me back through the house, stopping at a chest-of-drawers to pull out a smaller copy of the same picture of Sadie and Joe-Joe. The chest has no legs. It rests on old telephone books.

"I know somethin' done happened to Sadie." Loretta sounds as if she's resigned to inevitable pain.

I promise to return the picture. She nods and I let myself out, fanning my coat to capture some of the cool air outside. The sun comes out from behind a cloud again and shines brightly off the windows of my DeSoto. As I pull away, I see a host of people moving toward Sadie's house. They look hard at me as if I'd just delivered bad news.

After a quick burger at the Clover Grill, I go back to my office to make some calls. The kids are still playing football, even though the ground is dry by now. I call the Third Precinct Station and then the Seventh, but the French Quarter police and the Uptown police have nothing for me. I call Charity Hospital next and they've got nothing too. Then I call the coroner's office and an investigator tells me they got a body that fits Sadie's general description.

"When did she come in?" I ask, sitting up in my desk chair.

"Tuesday a.m."

"I'll be right over."

"I'm thrilled," the investigator sounds like he's fighting off a yawn.

Twenty minutes later, I park my car on Tulane Avenue, in front of the Criminal Courts Building. The big building's cement facade is streaked with water stains. I walk around to the South White Street side and up the side steps to the Coroner's Office.

Investigator Nathan Stack yawns as I step in. At six feet, he's exactly my height, although he's got twenty pounds on me at least, most in a little paunch of a stomach. He runs his hands through his flat top and says, "Come on."

We follow the acidic smell of formaldehyde downstairs to the morgue. Stack leads me to the refrigerator units next to the autopsy room and pulls out a bottom drawer labeled "Colored." When he pulls back the cover, Sadie Martin's lifeless face lies in front of me.

I show Stack the photo and he focuses his bored gray eyes on it and says, "At least we can unload her." He shoves the drawer shut. "We need the room."

And it strikes me immediately. "It's been a while. Why isn't she in the pauper's cemetery?"

Stack yawns again. "She's a homicide victim."

I taste the onions from my burger again and swallow it back down as we go upstairs to Stack's cluttered office. He sits behind a wooden desk that has a twenty degree list. I stand between the filing cabinets and pull out my notepad. He asks me the pertinent details – victim's name, age, address.

"They got a phone over there?"

I tell him I didn't see one.

Stack shakes his head. Now he has to go over to Treme, personally, to notify the next of kin. He fills out a form in a big hurry. I pump him and learn Sadie was found Tuesday morning around seven-thirty by two schoolboys cutting across Audubon Park.

"Goddamn people should have phones." Stack reaches over to a wood filing cabinet and opens a drawer marked 'Active'. He pulls out a brown paper bag with what I figure to be the victim's personal effects

"I guess these people don't read the papers either." He rises. "It's been in the papers."

"You eat lunch yet?" I ask as he steps around his desk.

"No!"

"Come on. I'll drive you over to Treme and then buy you lunch."

Stack pulls his gray suit coat on and says, "Why you so nice to me?"

"I want you to tell me about the homicide."

"Figures." Stack is so proud of himself for figuring, he grins at me as he leads the way out. "You ain't the police any more, you know," He says with an unfriendly wink.

On the way back to Treme, Stack shows off his cleverness. First, he tells me the body had been moved after the murder. "Lividity," he says. "Gravity don't change. Once that blood settles, it settles. She had lividity along her backside and was found lying face down."

"Where was she found, exactly?"

"In one of those gazebo things, one close to Magazine Street."

"How long had she been dead?"

He shrugs. "Twelve. Eighteen hours."

Then he tells me she probably scratched her assailant. He found skin and blood under the fingernails of her right hand.

"What was she wearing?" I ask.

"A white maid's dress." Stack grins again. "Her left stocking and left shoe were missing."

"Anything else?"

Stack reaches into the brown paper bag and thanks me for reminding him of something. He pulls out a button and holds it up.

"I have to pass this on to Homicide." He's grinning like the Cheshire cat now. "Found this in the cuff of her left sleeve."

The button is brass with the emblem of an eagle imprinted on it.

"What's the cause of death?" I ask.

"Strangulation."

People are still out on Dumaine Street when I park in the same place I'd parked earlier. They glare at me now as I lead Stack with his paper bag back to the yellow house. This time Loretta stands in the doorway.

"Ma'am," I say. "This is Investigator Stack from the Coroner's Office."

I can't reach her in time, not with the screen door in the way. She collapses like a Venetian blind.

Stack puts a hand on my shoulder and says, "Usually they wail and roll around the floor like a flounder."

I brush his hand away, open the door and help Loretta to her feet. Then I step out and flag some neighbors over to help. Later, when I hang around to make sure Loretta is all right before leaving, Stack isn't too thrilled.

I take him to Ruby's Grill back on Tulane and pay for his lunch. Then I get away as fast as I can, not wanting to spend another minute with the jerk. Instead, I go to see my buddy Frenchy Capdeville, lieutenant, Homicide Division. My luck, Frenchy's off so I get to see another jerk. Detective Jimmy Hays also has gray eyes, but even duller than Stack's. He's a muggle-head, as thick-headed as a brick. I have to tell him three times that the "Colored Case" he'd deep-sixed has a victim's name now and an address.

"So?"

"So, I guess you got to work, huh?" I should be more diplomatic. Waving his stubby little arms around, Hays says, "We worked it. We canvassed the hell out of the area!" Then he tells me to get the hell out.

So I leave, reminding myself to listen more and talk less.

By the time I park across St. Charles from the Eindhoven mansion again, a third car is in the driveway, another '49 Chrysler, this one black, parked behind the Del Mar. I add its license number to my notes as I cross to the mansion. The air smells of rain again. I open the iron gate and take the brick walkway to the front steps. Fifteen steps later I'm up on the wide front gallery. I ring the doorbell next to the cut-glass front door. I ring it a second time and see someone approach quickly. I step back as the door opens and a teen-aged boy looks out at me. He's got his mother's green eyes and round face.

"Hi," I say, "Mrs. Eindhoven, please."

He bounces on his feet and says, "She's busy in the kitchen. Can I be of assistance?" He wears jeans and a long-sleeved blue dress shirt and black tennis shoes. It's hard to tell his age, but he's about five-nine and thin, very thin.

"My name is Lucien Caye. Please tell your mother I'm here."

"You're not a salesman are you?" He's having fun now.

I shake my head.

"If you are, I'll sick my Dad on you. He's here, you know."

"Does he bite?"

The boy laughs. "Ha! That's a good one."

I smile, and stick my hand out for him to shake and ask his name.

"Albert Eindhoven the fourth," he says as he shakes my hand. "But everyone calls me Alb."

Still holding his hand, I lean close and say, conspiratorially, "I'm a private detective." I let go of his hand. "So, could you tell your mother I'm here?"

His eyes are round and his mouth forms a big 'O'. Then he says, "Let me see your Roscoe."

My luck – I have a movie nut here. I reach into my coat pocket, pull out a business card, and hand it to Alb.

He takes it, looks at it, and says, "Really, what kinda Roscoe do you carry? A Colt? Smith and Wesson?"

"Don't carry one."

He looks at my coat, looking for a bulge, obviously. My snub-nosed Smith & Wesson .38 is neatly tucked in its holster at the small of my back. No way he'll spot it. I smell cooking now, wafting from inside the house. I ask Alb again if he'll just go get his mother.

He folds his arms.

"How old are you?" I ask.

"Nineteen. What about you?"

"Thirty-one."

Just then, Mrs. Eindhoven shuffles into the foyer. She wears a white apron over a pink dress and pats her hair as she approaches. Her face is flushed as she slips past her son and tells him to go stir the gumbo. He steps back but doesn't leave. Her money-green eyes leer at me as she cocks her chin and says, "I asked you to call first."

"She's dead."

I watch her eyes go blank. Alb's eye-brows rise and his mouth becomes a slit. He folds his arms again. Mrs. Eindhoven places a hand on the door frame.

"What?" She blinks at me as if I'm in a fog.

"She's dead," I repeat.

Mrs. Eindhoven looks over her shoulder quickly and says, "I'll... uh... I'll have to call you in the morning." She starts to close the door, then stops as she sees something in the foyer.

I see a movement behind the boy and a man steps around him. Tall, about six-three, Albert Eindhoven, the third, turns a pair of cold-blue eyes toward me and says, "What's all this?"

"Something's happened to Sadie," Alb says. He's bouncing on the balls of his feet again.

Mrs. Eindhoven leans her back against the door frame and waves at me. I start to tell Mr. Eindhoven who I am but Mrs. Eindhoven interrupts, telling her husband she'd asked me to find Sadie. She's suddenly very nervous. She tells him my name and says, "You know, like Sam Spade and Philip Marlowe. You like those movies."

I watch the man's square jaw grind as he stares at me. He wears a short-sleeved, white dress shirt with his gray tie loosened and navy blue suit pants. I can't help noticing a cut on his neck, maybe from shaving, maybe not.

He raises a hand and Mrs. Eindhoven stops talking.

"So, I suppose we'll have to find a new maid," he tells me.

Alb leans in and says, "How'd she die?"

"Murdered. Monday night."

Eindhoven doesn't react. Mrs. Eindhoven takes a step back, places a hand over her mouth, then turns and hurries through the mansion. Alb puts his left hand on the open door and says, "Gee. Murdered!"

"It happens," Eindhoven says. He's still leering at me. "Remember three years ago when our gardener was shot outside that barroom? Happens all the time in the colored sections." Eindhoven reaches around his son and grabs the doorknob.

"She was murdered around the corner," I tell them. "In Audubon Park."

"Gee," Alb says.

Eindhoven gives me an annoyed look, then glances over my shoulder for a moment and says, "That's a shame."

I nod slowly. Eindhoven turns to his son and takes my business card from the boy's hand and examines it. Then he looks back and me and says, "Caye. What kind of name is that?"

I don't answer.

His left eye narrows as he says, "Are you, by any chance, Hebrew?"

Where did that come from? I'm French and Spanish and Catholic, first time anyone asked if I was Jewish. For a second I see the face of my buddy Brian Epstein who'd bought it on the beach at Anzio.

"Yes," I say. "I'm a Jew."

"Yes," he says. "I thought so." He looks closely at my face, examining it.

"And what are you," I ask, "German?"

He looks surprised. "No, why did you ask that?"

I look at his face as if I'm examining it as I say, "You look like a jackass, so I figure you're German."

Alb laughs immediately and covers his mouth with both hands. Eindhoven takes a menacing step forward and growls, "I'm Dutch!"

I don't retreat. But I also can't think of anything bad to say about the Dutch.

"You're not funny," Eindhoven says.

"Yeah?" I point to Alb. "He thinks I'm funny."

Alb laughs again and steps way as his father glares at him. Then Alb leaves. Eindhoven turns back to me. "You've taken my wife for enough money, Mr. Caye. So get lost."

He closes the door slowly, shooting me the meanest look a jeweler possesses. I yawn and step back. I see Alb peeking out a front window at me. I wave and he waves back and I remember how he said, "Something's happened to Sadie," right after I said, "She's dead."

How did he know I was talking about Sadie? Unless his mother told him. Or he's a good guesser. Or he knows something.

I make it back to my DeSoto just in time. The rain attacks with a vengeance, washing over my windshield in giant sweeps. I sit for a while, leaning back in the seat and closing my eyes. I see Sadie's face again, from the picture, and then from the morgue. Then I see Joe-Joe's face as he peeked out from behind his aunt at me. Then I see the empty refrigerator.

Cranking up the engine, I turn on the defroster to unfog the windows. I creep up St. Charles all the way to Carrollton. I hang a right and then a U-turn to park in front of the Camellia Grill. One of the waiters is outside, leaning against one of the white ante-bellum columns as he puffs a cigarette. I wave to him on the way in, grab a seat at the W-shaped counter and order a plate of red beans and rice, a breaded pork chop and iced tea. After all, it's Monday.

Rubbing my eyes, I think of my mother. Like most New Orleans mothers, she cooked red beans and rice every Monday, the traditional wash day after the weekend. While she washed the clothes, the beans would simmer all day until supper. The smell of cooking beans is as familiar as the scent of my mother's hair and the sting of my father unshaved face when he hugged me.

The waiter slides my plate of beans and rice in front of me, and I can't help wondering what Joe-Joe's eating tonight. Suddenly, my stomach feels sour.

•

The boys are playing baseball again in Cabrini Playground the next morning. Standing next to my desk, the phone receiver in my right hand, I watch them as I wait for Lieutenant Frenchy Capdeville to get on the line. A dark-haired boy slaps a liner over the first baseman's head. By the time the right fielder gets to the ball, the batter's rounding second. It's a stand-up triple. The batter claps as the pitcher throws his glove down.

I hear movement on the other end of the line and then Frenchy's familiar gruff acknowledgment, "Talk."

"Lou, it's Caye. How ya' been?"

"Cut the small talk and tell me what ya' want." He's in a foul mood.

"I'm calling about the Sadie Martin murder."

"Figured. Hold on." I hear mumbling. He's put his hand over the receiver. Then he says, "Hays just brought in the husband."

Damn.

"He got something on the husband?" I ask, not expecting a straight answer, just knowing Hays is gonna lean on the husband. Maybe hard.

"Looks like the husband has some explaining to do." Frenchy doesn't sound convinced.

"What?" I'm pushing it.

Frenchy clears his throat and says, "He told everyone he's been checking with the police, but he hasn't checked here."

It takes me a second, then I realize. "Maybe he's been checking with the man on the beat."

"Maybe."

"Well, I just called to tell you I'm going back uptown, in case you get a call about me."

Frenchy lets out a long breath, probably exhaling from his ever-present cigarette. "Just don't ruffle too many feathers." It's subtle, but the way he says it tells me he doesn't really mind me shaking up the rich, so long as it doesn't come down on him.

"I plan on talking to a couple maids," I tell him.

"Just tread carefully, buddy. See ya'." He hangs up.

I look out at the kids and the dark-haired boy is still at third. The pitcher throws a fastball and a red-headed boy swings and misses. I move over to the coat rack and pull on my navy blue suit coat. The pitcher winds up and my phone rings. The red-headed batter swings and sends a slow grounder to the third baseman, who charges the ball. The phone rings again. The runner on third races home. The catcher sets up, straddling home plate. I'm moving toward the phone now. It rings a third time. The throw beats the runner home, but he slides between the catcher's legs and is safe. An argument starts immediately. I answer the phone. It's Julia Eindhoven.

"Oh," she says, "I thought you weren't there."

"I'm here."

"Good. My husband is quite angry with me. And you."

I want to say – big deal, but I don't.

"I called... uh. I called to ask. Um. I know you're not an employment agency, but since you seem to do so well with the coloreds, I thought maybe you could find a relative of Sadie's who needs a good job."

The kids are still arguing. I close my eyes and try, real hard, not to tell her what I'm really thinking. I try counting to ten.

Her lilting voice cuts in as I reach five. "It was just a thought."

Then I realize something and say, "Let me get back to you, okay?"

"Okay. Just don't call after four and don't come here."

"Fine." I hang up before she can say anything else. Now I have an excuse to keep on the case. I'm still working for the lilting Mrs. E. On my way out to my DeSoto, I see the boys haven't settled it yet. So I call out, "He was safe!"

They all look at me. I point to my office windows and tell them I saw it and the dark-haired runner slid under the tag. He was safe. Half of the boys jump up in triumph. The pitcher throws his glove back on the ground and the catcher gives me the same look Eindhoven gave me the previous evening.

I drive up to Rampart and take the same route back uptown and park in the same spot across St. Charles from the Eindhoven mansion. I cross the neutral ground and then walk over to the Victorian on the uptown side of the Eindhovens and spot Prudence outside wiping off the white lawn furniture. I ask her to sit. She does, reluctantly. I tell her about Sadie and she sags.

I give her a couple seconds before I ask, "Was Sadie afraid of Mr. Eindhoven?"

"Yes." Then she tells me Eindhoven was just unfriendly. It's the son that gave Sadie the creeps.

"What do you mean by that?"

"He watches her. He watches me too." Then her eyes grow wide and she stands suddenly. I look over my shoulder and see Alb moving across his yard to the white picket fence between the properties. He waves. Prudence retreats toward the Victorian. I stand and wave back at Alb who hurries to the fence and rests his arms atop. He wears a yellow, long-sleeved dress shirt today with jeans.

"Hey," he says as I approach, "you got your Roscoe today?"

"Naw. This is a safe neighborhood, isn't it?"

"That's what the police said during the Leopold-Loeb case."

"What?" I get to the fence and lean my left hand on it. "Leopold and Loeb? Now that's a pair of names that don't come up in conversation often." Leopold and Loeb, thrill killers, killed a little boy just to see what it was like to murder someone. Chicago, I think.

"I just read all about them. Don't you read true crime magazines?"

I shake my head and wait for him to re-start the conversation.

"Know why they killed that little boy?" Alb's face beams.

I shake my head again.

"Because they could. Thought they were supermen, you know, like Nietzsche said. Super intelligent. You read any Nietzsche?"

"Not lately."

"He said the superman is not liable for anything he may do, except for the one thing that is impossible for him to do – to make a mistake."

I feel a chill along my back as I look at the plain, young face standing across the fence from me. "They got caught," I tell him.

"Yeah. They made a dumb mistake."

I nod and try not to be too obvious when I say, "I'll bet you're pretty smart, huh?"

"Top of my class. What about you? You a regular copper turned P.I., or were you too smart to stay a copper?"

"I'm pretty regular."

Alb taps his fingers atop the fence. They are long and thin and look delicate. "Naw," he says. "Private-eyes are smarter than regular detectives. Sherlock Holmes is smarter than those Scotland Yard clowns."

"That's fiction."

"Come on," he says, looking at my side now. "Let me see your gun. I know you're carrying one."

When he looks back at my eyes, I say, "How'd you know I was talking about Sadie when I told your mother, 'She's dead'?"

He blinks and says, "What?"

I lean closer. "When I told your mother, 'She's dead', you knew I meant Sadie. How?"

He shrugs and presses the heel of his hand against his left eye. "I guessed." He looks around and then looks back at me. "She *was* missing."

The back door of the Eindhoven mansion opens and Mrs. E. leans out. She spots us and takes a step out and calls to Alb to come in. Her hair is down and she wears a sleeveless, white cotton dress. She looks younger and very nice, especially with that deep red lipstick.

"Aw, Mom!" Alb backs away from the fence slowly. "We *just* started talking."

She gives me the same look the nuns used to give me back in grammar school when I did something to disappoint them, which was often. Alb waves at me and says, "See ya'."

"See ya'."

They go in so I walk over to the blue house on the other side of the Eindhovens and speak with Molly Jones. She's shook and has little to add, except that Sadie told her she didn't like Alb at all. "She said he's a smart-aleck."

The words 'smart-aleck' echo in my mind as I walk back to the DeSoto. I feel that chill again, thinking about Leopold and Loeb and a dead little boy, about self-appointed supermen with super intelligence.

I take off my coat, fold it and climb in the car. I look at the Eindhoven's Greek Revival mansion and try hard to remember what I can about Leopold and Loeb. They were sons of the very wealthy and were brilliant students, or something like that. They were caught because one of them lost a pair of glasses when they dumped the body; a pair of rare glasses, I think, glasses the police traced to them. Yeah, and that sharp lawyer Clarence Darrow got them off with a life sentence. Then I remember how one was murdered in jail before the war.

I also remember one of them pretended to help the police. Could Alb be that devious? Could he be arrogant enough to kill someone, then tell me about Leopold and Loeb? Could he be arrogant enough to think he can outwit me?   What the hell's going on?

Then I remember something Frenchy Capdeville told me at a murder scene.   Back when I was in uniform, I was nosing around one of his murder scenes, asking dumb questions and Frenchy told me how a good homicide detective gathers evidence until it leads him to a suspect.   A bad detective finds a suspect and gathers only the evidence that fits that suspect.   I guess that's what Hays is doing right now with Sadie's husband.

I start up the DeSoto and ease into traffic to hang a U-turn at Broadway and drive past the Eindhovens, in case anyone's watching.   I go down a ways, take another U-turn, and park a little ways down from where I've been parking, still across from the mansion, but not within easy view.   I turn off the engine, roll my windows down, and settle in.

I run it all through my mind – the frantic wife, the missing maid, the discovery of the body in Audubon Park early Tuesday morning, the missing stocking and shoe, the fingernail scrapings, the brass button with the eagle, the fact the body had been moved, the cut on Mr. E's neck.   And what about Alb?   Does he know something?

An hour creeps by until Eindhoven comes out, climbs into the black Chrysler, backs out and head downtown on St. Charles. I start up my engine and spot Alb hurrying out of the house and looking down the street after the Chrysler.   He opens the trunk of the Del Mar and tosses a brown paper bag into the trunk, inside and climbs into the convertible, all in a big hurry.   He backs out of the drive, almost colliding with a powder blue Chevy and heads down St. Charles, only he takes the first U-turn, right in front of me.

I slip down in my seat as he motors past and look up just as he makes a left on Broadway.   I quickly start up the engine and move into traffic.   Thankfully, a truck makes a left on Broadway behind the Del Mar and in front of me.   I ease back in time to see the Del Mar make another U-turn through the narrow neutral ground at Benjamin Street and then pull up against the curb. Alb jumps out and heads for a gray, two-story house along the downtown side of Broadway. I drive by and pass Benjamin to hang a U-turn at the next street. I park on the same side of Broadway, beneath the overhanging branches of one of the oaks lining the street.

Alb hurries back to the Del Mar, accompanied by another young man, this one about five-four, with blond hair, and wearing a blazer over black slacks. They jump into the Del Mar and take off. I follow them, catching the address of the gray house as I pass – 521 Broadway.

They turn right at St. Charles. I try to keep up. Following someone in real life isn't like in the movies. Keeping up with them without being spotted is hard with New Orleans's mis-timed signal lights and stupid drivers. Lucky for me, they don't look over their shoulders.

We pass back in front of the Eindhovens and then in front of Audubon Park. The blond points to the park and I get that chill again. The Del Mar brakes and starts to turn into the park, only it doesn't turn. It accelerates and continues down the avenue. I fall back, hoping Alb hasn't spotted me in his rear-view mirror.

The Del Mar brakes and hangs a fast right on Calhoun Street. I slow down and follow them down the narrow street. Audubon Park is on our right now, a block away. I drop back and watch the Del Mar continue all the way to Magazine Street, where it turns right. I creep forward, and when I reach Magazine I look to my right. Alb and his buddy are walking away from the Del Mar, which is parked on Magazine. They walk into the park, heading straight for the gazebo next to the man-made lagoon. It's the gazebo closest to Magazine, the crime scene as described by coroner's investigator Nathan Stack. And I see it all now, like a curtain lifting.

I park directly behind the Del Mar, climb out and put on my coat. Then I remember something else Frenchy told me. Homicide work is ninety-five percent footwork and five percent brainwork. It's brainwork time now.

They don't see me coming. Alb reaches the gazebo first and starts looking around for something. The gazebo isn't white. It's made of thick wood and painted brown and green as it stands beneath the tall oaks. Alb's buddy stops just before the gazebo and brushes the grass with his feet as he looks. He finally hears me approach in time to look up as I arrive.

He blinks his blue eyes at me and retreats a step. His two button blazer is missing a button.

"Oh!" Alb notices me and steps out of the gazebo, his hands shoved in his pocket.

"Aren't you going to introduce us?" I ask.

"Uh, yeah. Mike. This is the P.I. I was telling you about." Alb points his chin at me. "Uh, Mr. Caye, this is Mike Fuller."

I reach over and touch the lapel of Mike's blazer. "How much does a coat like this cost?"

Mike looks at Alb, his lower lip trembling slightly.

"It's pretty expensive," Alb tells me.

I reach into my pocket and pull one of Mrs. E's fifties. "I want to buy it."

Mike gulps and starts to pull away.

"It's not for sale," he manages to say as I start to pull the blazer off.

"Yes it is," I tell him as I pull the coat off. I shove the fifty into the front pocket of Mike's short-sleeved dress shirt. I fold the blazer across my left arm. When I look down and finger the brass eagle button, Mike makes a squeaky sound like a frightened mouse.

I look at Alb and say, "I guess this makes him Leopold. Wasn't he the one who lost the pair of glasses at his murder scene? Or was it Loeb?"

Alb bounces on his feet. Mike retreats away from me toward the man-made lagoon behind the gazebo. He looks like he's about to rabbit. I move toward Alb who takes his hands out of his pockets and folds his arms in a typical defensive position.

"They found the other button," I tell them. "It got stuck in Sadie's clothes."

Alb stares at me, his face masked in a stiff grin.

When I reach him I say, "I strangled someone once."

His eyes widen. I tell him a story about how we stumbled on a German patrol outside Cassino and how it was man-to-man combat and I strangled a German. I describe the heart-stammering excitement, the way the man shivered as I squeezed the life from him. It's fiction, of course, but it works.

Alb opens his arms and tells Mike. "See. He understands!"

Mike's not convinced. He moves behind the gazebo and starts to walk around it.

I ask Alb, "What arm did she scratch?" I point to his long sleeves.

He smiles and says, "You are good. You figured the whole thing out, just like that." He snaps his fingers.

I point to his left arm and he nods excitedly. He unbuttons the sleeve and rolls it up and there are three deep scratches on his forearm. He looks at Mike again and says, "See, I told you P.I.s are smarter than cops."

Mike bolts toward Magazine.

"Whoa!" Alb calls out. "Don't worry. He works for my mom."

Mike is running flat out now.

"He doesn't care about Sadie. He's here to protect me." Alb looks at me and says, "Tell him."

I let my eyes answer. He shoves his hands in his pockets again and slowly loses the smile.

"Come on," I say.

"Where?" his voice is suddenly scratchy.

"Headquarters. I want to introduce you to a friend of mine. A lieutenant."

He folds his arms again. I reach over and grab his left arm and start to guide him back to Magazine. The Del Mar's engine roars to life and Mike looks back and yells for Alb to run. I squeeze Alb's arm and lead him back.

I push him around to the front of my car and lean him across the right front fender. I tell Mike to shut off the engine. He turns his terrified eyes to Alb who just grunts.

"Turn off the damn engine!" I take a step forward and Mike turns it off.

"Now throw me the keys."

He does, only they bounce off my hood and skid into the street.

I tell Alb not to move. I step out and pick up the keys. Then I open the Del Mar's trunk and pull out the paper bag. It contains a white shoe and a torn white stocking. I see something fly over my head and look back at Alb who has stepped away from my car.

He points to the bag and says, "Yeah. That's Sadie's all right."

I pull the trunk down and Alb jumps past me for the Del Mar. Its engine starts up and I realize what I'd seen flying over my head must have been Alb's set of keys. Alb dives into the car as Mike hits it and it burns rubber, leaving me with the bag.

He could have put it in reverse and squashed me between the two cars. Instead, Mike drives off with Alb down Magazine, as if they're getting away. I take a deep breath, get into the DeSoto, and make a U-turn to head downtown.

•

When the stenographer comes back with my statement, she hands it to Frenchy Capdeville, who hands it to me. She winks at me and leaves. It's not a flirty wink. She's married to one of my old partners.

I read my statement while Frenchy sucks on a Pall Mall. His feet are up on his desk. There's a hole in the sole of his left shoe. His brown suit needs pressing and his curly black hair needs a haircut. I finish reading and sign the statement. I sign the carbon, which is my copy.

Frenchy waits until I'm done to ask, "Okay, where's the coat and the stocking?"

"And the shoe," I complete the inventory. "At Seven Twenty-Two Union Street."

"What?" He pulls his feet off the desk.

"That's right." I smile. "It's at the *Item*. You know Paul Ordahl?"

Frenchy cringes. He knows Ordahl, ace reporter of the *New Orleans Item*. The man who works the crime-beat.

"Ordahl is having pictures taken of the evidence. I'm sure he'll surrender them to you as soon as you get over there."

Frenchy smashes his cigarette in one of the many ashtrays on his desk. He immediately fires up another Pall Mall.

"Ordahl had a stenographer take down my story first," I add.

"Yeah. Yeah."

"His editor's all excited."

Frenchy shakes his head at me. "I can't believe you did that."

"Hays was about to book Sadie's husband, wasn't he?"

Frenchy leans back and shakes his head. "Nope," he says. "I nixed that idea."

I would say good for you, but I know Frenchy wouldn't bum-rap a guy. Hays would, of course, in a New York minute. As if on cue, Hays opens the lieutenant's door and steps into Frenchy's office.

He glares at me. I stand and stretch. Hays leans against a file cabinet and says, "Why did you this?"

I shrug.

"You did it to be famous, huh?" Hays waves his right hand. "So you can be in the headlines. Private dick solves murder."

I stop next to him on my way out, shoot him a cold smile and tell him I did it so I could sleep tonight.

"Yeah," he says. "Right!"

•

The article is half-buried on page three of this evening's *Item* – 'Uptown Pair Implicated in Killing'. The word 'murder' doesn't appear in the article. Negroes aren't murdered. They're killed. Why am I surprised? Because the editor was excited?

The article doesn't even mention their names. It mentions a P.I., but Ordahl kept his promise. My name isn't there. It does mention, however, the names of a pair of hot-shot lawyers hired by the families. I'm not surprised.

I close the paper and look at my office windows at the rain slamming against them. I kick my feet up on my desk and tell myself I did my best. At least they didn't pin it on Sadie's husband. I think of Joe-Joe again and the nearly empty refrigerator. Tomorrow, when I bring the picture back to Loretta, I'll pick some groceries up on the way. For Joe-Joe. I have to do something.

I shut my eyes and listen to the rain. It's a hard, driving rain that slaps the windows in waves. A thunderclap shakes the building. I open my eyes and look at the rain as it washes the city.

"Wash it," I tell the rain. "Wash it good."

END of HARD RAIN

Hard Rain is for my friend, Harlan Ellison

Expect Consequences

"Once a man breaks a law, he can expect consequences.
Not just some of them. All of them."
from *Web of Murder* by Harry Whittington, 1958

As I carry Camille's casket through Lafayette Cemetery, on this bright, spring morning, it occurs to me, this is the first time I've helped bury a client. It's also the first time I bury a lover.

I'm pallbearer number six. Lucien Caye, thirty-one years old, private investigator. I'm in my black suit, dark sunglasses hiding my standard-issue, Mediterranean brown eyes, my face freshly shaved, my brown hair freshly cut.

We lay the casket on a roller next to the walled tomb where Camille will be sealed inside. I step back, through the strong scent of roses and stand next to a large, concrete sepulchre with small, concrete angels kneeling on top. Lafayette Cemetery, like all New Orleans cemeteries, is a little city of the dead, with crypts and sepulchres, its walls filled with oven vaults where we seal up our dead above ground. There are trees here too, magnolias with their dark green leaves and towering oaks with gnarled branches.

The priest begins praying as alter boys swing silver bowls back and forth, spreading the pungent odor of incense among the gathered and I think back to the first time I saw Camille Javal, nearly a year ago, May 22, 1949, a Monday.

•

I was reading the morning paper at my desk, feet propped up, coffee cup next to the small revolving fan on the corner of the desk. There was an article on the front page about former Secretary of Defense James Forrestal killing himself. He jumped from the sixteenth floor of Bethesda Hospital the day before. He was suffering something like battle fatigue. I'd been there, on that damn beach at Anzio, with long-range German artillery raining hell on us.

An article near the bottom of the page caught my attention, about a body found at one of my favorite hotels, the Jung. "The body of Texas sales executive Milton Hines was found – "

The outside door of my building opened and I looked at the smoky-glass door of my office as a shadow moved behind it. I pulled my feet down as the door opened and she stepped in. She wore a gray skirt-suit and black high heels, her wavy hair hanging to her shoulders, hair so dark it looked black until she stepped into the sunlight streaming through the Venetian blinds and I could see the brown highlights. A slim figure at five feet-five inches, Camille leveled those wide, blue-gray eyes at me and asked, "Are you the detective?"

Definitely a New Orleans accent with its flat *A* sound, as if Brooklyn had a southern variation. Her pouty lips were painted a deep crimson.

I stood, introduced myself and waved to one of the chairs in front of my desk. She sat and crossed her legs, propping her black purse in her lap.

"What can I do for you?"

She looked at the Venetian blinds. "I'm a little embarrassed to say this, but I think I've been taken advantage of."

Figured there was some lucky bastard out there.

"How?" I asked when she didn't continue. The fan blew a whiff of her perfume my way. Nice. Very nice.

"I need you to find someone for me." She turned back to me, her lower lip quivering. "His name is Byron Barr and he's been staying at the LaSalle Hotel. On Baronne Street."

I knew the place. Not much of a hotel.

"I think he took my broach." She pulled a photo from her purse and passed it to me. "I had it appraised last year. It's very valuable."

It looked it, a golden scarab with a large emerald in its center and a dozen diamonds dotting its legs. A piece like this would be hard to sell, unless he was smart enough to break it up, sell off the jewels.

"When did you last see it?"

"Day before yesterday. I had Byron over for lunch and I was wearing the broach." Her voice faltered for a moment. "When he left, I saw it wasn't on my jacket, so I searched the sofa." She looked at the blinds again, "Where we had been sitting. But it was gone. I searched my entire house."

She took in a deep breath. "We were supposed to have dinner yesterday, but he didn't show and doesn't answer his phone at the hotel." The creamy complexion of her face became red. "I want you to find him and see if he took my broach."

"Have you called the police?"

She shook her head and looked at the newspaper on my desk. Understandable. She gave me her address on Prytania Street and her phone number and a two hundred dollar retainer, which was too much, but I figured she could afford it with that ruby ring on her right hand and the diamond bracelet dangling from her left wrist.

"Do you have a picture of Barr?"

She shook her head and I asked for his description, which she gave me in detail – Thirty years old, six-feet tall, thin, with sandy-brown hair, blue eyes and 'brilliant' white teeth to go with an ever-present smile. He wore expensive clothes and smiled a lot.

Barr and I were the same age and height, that was the only similarity.

"When can you start on this?" The quiver was back on her lips.

"I'll walk out with you." Standing, I led the way out, grabbing the coat of my tan suit, opening the doors for her.

"Where's your hat?" she asked as we stepped out on the banquette.

"Never wear one. Messes up my hair."

She almost smiled, thanked me and stepped over to her car, a shiny blue, 1949 Tucker sedan. I watched her climb in and took a moment admiring the lines of her car, nearly as nice as her lines.

Climbing into my gray, pre-war 1940 DeSoto coach, I eased my way up to North Rampart and hung a left. The LaSalle was on South Rampart Street, just on the other side of Canal Street. I parked at a meter, dropped in a nickel, and went into the foyer of the three story, red brick hotel that had seen better days.

The day manager, a heavy-set ex-fireman told me Mr. Barr checked out the day before. A five-dollar tip got me inside Barr's room on the second floor. It was a small room, with a double bed, wash basin, a two-drawer dresser, one hardback chair and a narrow closet. The maid hadn't gotten to the room yet. She came every third day. So I rooted around and found two things in the wastebasket – a white linen shirt with a torn sleeve with the initials *A.J.* on the pocket and a wadded up piece of paper with a name and a number: Hines 337.

Hines?

It took a few seconds to click in. That was the name of the body at the Jung. I searched the room again, but couldn't come up with anything else. On my way out I asked the manager if he knew Barr.

"Never seen him."

•

I parked at another meter alongside the Jung Hotel, back on Canal Street. Ten stories tall, this brown brick building had one of the biggest ballrooms in the city, as well as a very fine café inside. I found the hotel detective, George Crane, drinking coffee in the corner table of the café. Crane had been my sergeant briefly, when I was at the Third Precinct, before the war. Retired from NOPD, he had a nice cush job now.

"Until something like this happens," he told me. In his late forties, with a lot less of his light brown hair, he was a couple inches taller than me, but much beefier now that he'd retired.

"At least we have a suspect," he added.

"You do?"

"We got witnesses." He grinned at me.

"That's good. Was Hines staying in Room 337?"

"How'd you know that?"

"Your suspect, is he a white male, thirty, six feet tall, thin, sandy hair? Smiled a lot."

"Bingo!" Crane was impressed.

I showed him the piece of paper I found in Barr's room.

"Let's call Homicide."

We went to the desk phone and he called Lieutenant Frenchy Capdeville.

"What's the name?" Frenchy asked when Crane put me on the line.

"Byron Barr." I described him and told Frenchy he might have stolen a broach. I described the broach.

"What's your client's name?"

"I'll give you that if we get the broach."

Frenchy hung up without thanking me.

Crane patted me on the back. "Now they have a name."

He invited me to join him for lunch so we went back into the café. He ordered two oyster loafs. As I sipped my coffee-and-chicory, Crane told me Hines was bludgeoned to death. The suspect was seen talking with Hines in the lobby the afternoon of the murder. Hines was killed during the night. Later that night, our suspect was seen taking the elevator down from the third floor. Flirted with the elevator operator, a new girl, pretty. He convinced the garage attendant that he was Hines' son and drove off with Hines' Cadillac. Hines was well known, staying at the

Jung every three months as he came through town. Even the garage attendant knew he had a son. And the suspect did have the car keys.

"Thank God criminals are stupid," Crane added as our oyster loafs arrived and we feasted on the deep fried oysters stuffed into a half-loaf of French bread.

No wonder he was getting fat.

•

My office, on the first floor of a two-story, gray building at the corner of Barracks and Dauphine Streets, was in the low-rent section of the French Quarter, away from Canal Street and the tourist attractions – Jackson Square and St. Louis Cathedral. My apartment, directly upstairs, gave me access to the lacework balcony that wrapped around the corner of the building.

Camille's Tucker was parked on Barracks, in front of the building. As I parked behind her, she climbed out and hurried to me, didn't even let me get out.

"Byron called," she said, leaning in my window. "From Mississippi. He wants to meet me."

It took several questions to get the entire story out. Barr said he was calling from a pay phone in Pass Christian, on the Gulf Coast. Asked her to meet him at the Jourdan Café on Highway 90 at a place called Henderson Point at six p.m.

"I don't know where that Point is." She said wringing her hands as she backed away to let me out of my car.

"I do. It's just the other side of Bay St. Louis."

"I need you to come with me." She bounced on her toes.

"Sure, but there's no hurry. It's not far."

I started for the building, figuring I'd called Frenchy Capdeville before leaving, but Camille was already climbing in her car. I went over and told her we didn't have to leave right away, but she started up the engine, so I took off my coat and climbed in. Even in the confines of the car, her perfume wasn't overpowering, but it was effective.

Readjusting the holster of my Smith and Wesson .38 snub nose, on my right hip, I sat back and let her take me away. Her skirt was up past her knees, giving me a good view of her sleek calves. A woman's legs in nylons always got my attention, especially legs as shapely as Camille's. I tried not to stare.

The Tucker's ride was smooth, like a much larger car. Camille pointed out its features as we made our way to Gentilly Boulevard to Chef Menteur, which became Highway 90 as we left town. She told me about the disc brakes, pop-out windshield, padded dash, all-round independent suspension, and a smooth-as-silk automatic transmission.

We caught the bridge at The Rigolets and watched a tug push a dozen barges from the gray-brown water of Lake Pontchartrain through the pass on the way to Lake Borgne and the Gulf of Mexico beyond.

I told her I had gone to Holy Cross and she said she'd gone to Sacred Heart High School. Figured, her being an uptown girl. She told me her parents were both dead now. So were mine, which turned those blue-gray eyes to me for a lingering moment.

"Any brothers or sisters?" she asked.

"Nope."

"Me either." Again a lingering look, followed by, "How old are you, Mr. Caye?"

"Lucien. Unless you want me to call you Miss Javal for the rest of our lives. I'm thirty-one."

A smile crossed her lips for the first time. "I'm twenty-six."

I wouldn't have asked, being a southern boy, but she volunteered.

"Are you a vet?" Her eyes were wide and searching.

"Regular Army. I was a Ranger in North Africa and Italy."

"My father was killed in Normandy. D-Day, plus three. He was a captain. Engineers."

Past The Rigolets, we moved from swampland on either side of the road through thick forest. Eventually, crossing into Mississippi, we drove though piney woods laced with scrub oak.

"How long have you known this Byron Barr?"

"Three weeks," she said with a hitch in her voice. "Met him at the Blue Room. Lena Horne was performing. We sort of bumped into one another and – one thing led to another."

The Blue Room at the Roosevelt Hotel brought in top-notch entertainers. I saw Martin and Lewis there last year. She told me Barr was an actor and a singer.

"He's been on Broadway," she added with some excitement. "Lately, he's been doing nightclubs throughout the south." After a while she said, "What he needs is a break. A real break. Hollywood maybe."

Or gullible females.

We made it to Henderson Point just before four. The Jourdan Café sat on the gulf side of Highway 90, in a long curve coming off the bridge across Bay St. Louis. A yellow, one-story brick building with a row of windows facing the highway, the café had an oyster shell parking lot with a lone black pick-up truck parked there. I spotted Barr through the windows, as he sat at the counter in an expensive navy blue suit. Camille didn't see him until we walked in. She let out a high-pitched noise and stopped in her tracks.

Barr was in the middle of signing 'Little Brown Jug' for the blonde waitress, who leaned across the counter, staring at him all googly-eyed. I hate that song, so I didn't mind tapping him on the shoulder, so he'd turn to see Camille behind me.

"Baby!" He jumped off the stool and scooped her in his arms, doing a little twirl with her. He was smooth, all right, even introduced Camille to the waitress, Miss Ruby Stevens, formerly of Miami Beach. Ruby looked about thirty-five, buxomly with tired blue eyes, but still a pretty woman. Grinning widely, Barr stuck his hand out to me and introduced himself.

"Lucien Caye," I said, shaking his hand firmly. He returned the firm grip, then let go and pointed us to a booth next to the windows. He slid in, patting the seat next to him for Camille, who slid in the other side. I sat next to Camille, pulling out my Smith and Wesson as I sat, holding it next to my right leg.

Camille noticed it and tensed a moment, her eyes bulging. I gave her a reassuring look as Barr ordered coffees for everyone, including the two men in coveralls in the back booth, obviously from the pick-up truck.

Barr reached across the table and took Camille's left hand in both of his. She was right, his teeth were brilliant white, his eyes as blue as the sky.

"I'm so glad you came," he told Camille.

She pulled her hand away. "What happened to you last night?"

He leaned back and raised his hands to show fresh bruises on both. "I got into a little scrape." Again with the big smile as Ruby put cups and saucers in front of us and filled our cups with coffee, leaving cream and sugar bowls. Barr scooped three heaping spoons of sugar in his and stirred.

Camille touched the side of my leg with her left hand as she told him, "Remember my broach. The scarab?"

Barr gave her an innocent-eyed look.

"It's missing."

"Did it fall off? You know. The sofa?" The big smile disappeared in a look of real concern. He was an actor, all right.

"That scrape you were in," I asked. "Was it at the Jung Hotel?"

"As a matter of fact, it was." He picked up his cup and took a sip, hand straight and steady. "What are you, some kind of cop?" The smile again, all joking.

I told him I was a private investigator and he put his cup down and leaned forward.

"Like Sam Spade or Philip Marlowe!" He sat up excitedly. "I'm intrigued."

"That scrape involve a Mr. Hines?" I asked. I could feel Camille staring at me.

Barr nodded slowly. "Ol' Milton." The smile was back, directed to Camille. "That's why I couldn't meet you for dinner. There was a problem."

Camille leaned back, out of my line of sight, and grabbed my pants leg and twisted. Ruby came back from helping the men other customers and sat on the nearest counter stool.

"What kind of problem?" I asked.

"It all got out of hand and I think I might have killed him." Barr smiled, shrugged his shoulders and took another drink of coffee, his eyes moving from mine to Camille's and back to mine. Ruby let out a gasp. I slid out of the booth and let him see the .38 in my right hand. Ruby tumbled from the stool. Barr just leaned back and shrugged again, smiling and looking from me to Camille.

"Keep your hands on the table," I told him, then asked Ruby to call the Sheriff's Department.

"Lucien," Camille's voice was deep and firm. "What's going on?"

I nodded to Barr. "You tell her."

He reached for her hands, but she pulled them away and slid out of the booth next to me.

"Can't we just talk this out?" Barr asked me. "Like in *The Maltese Falcon*. The gunsel. They talked it out."

I heard Ruby in the background telling the Sheriff's Department to hurry. Getting nowhere with me, Barr turned the charm on Camille, telling her it was all a bad mistake. He didn't mean to hurt Milton Hines, it just happened.

"And you can't bring him back, so I panicked and ran. But I called you, didn't I, Baby?"

A black Ford with a gold five-point star on the side and a red bubble-top police light skidded into the parking lot. I slid my revolver back into its holster and stepped between Barr and the front door. Two khaki-clad deputies stepped in, both bigger than me, both wearing straw cowboy hats and gold badges with Harrison County Sheriff on them.

"Ruby?" The nearest deputy said and Ruby pointed to me.

I pointed to Barr and told them he just admitted killing a man in New Orleans. The deputies looked confused, so I turned back to Barr and asked him what he'd done with Milton's Cadillac.

"It's around the corner at Summer's Motel."

I explained to the deputies how Milton Hines had been murdered and if they'd call Lieutenant Capdeville, NOPD Homicide, he'd confirm the story.

"Ain't nobody callin' nobody," the nearest deputy declared. "The high sheriff'll be any minute."

Ten minutes later, the high sheriff showed up, parking a gold Cadillac in the oyster shell lot and climbed out in his own khaki uniform and cowboy hat.

"Dis here," the nearest deputy announced as the sheriff entered, "is Joe Yule, High Sheriff 'a Harrison County."

Yule smelled of cheap aftershave and smiled as much as Barr, only his smile was more reptilian.

"Go on," the nearest deputy prodded me, "tell da' high sheriff 'bout dat murda."

I laid out the facts again, feeling Camille grabbing the back of my arm as I spoke. Sheriff Yule rubbed his abundant chin and leered at Barr, who rolled his eyes as if was I telling quite a yarn, and finished off his coffee. He lifted his cup to Ruby who promptly refilled it. I couldn't be sure, but it seemed Yule recognized Barr, or recognized his type. Yule stuck a hand out toward Barr and asked, "You got da' keys to da' dead man's Cadillac?"

Barr reached into his coat pocket. I guided Camille behind me and moved to my left, leaving the high sheriff in the line of fire, if Barr came out with a gun. He came out with a set of keys he deposited in the high sheriff's palm. Yule passed them to his deputies and told them to go search the Cadillac. Turning to me, he asked if I was carrying a weapon.

"Yes, sir," I opened my coat and turned my holster his way. He took out my .38 and stuck it in his pants pocket.

"And just who are you, anyway?"

I explained, making sure I put in how I was the ex-police.

"Y'all came here lookin' for trouble?"

"No, sir. I came with her. And I called you right away."

Ruby backed up my story, to which Sheriff Yule asked her for a piece of pecan pie to go with his coffee. He rested his butt against a stool by the counter and nodded for Camille and me to make ourselves comfortable. We took stools away from Barr, Camille keeping her hand on my shoulder.

Ruby slid a huge slice of pecan pie toward the sheriff, along with a cup of coffee. She put fresh cups out for Camille and me. I took a sip. Wasn't bad for pure coffee.

After downing two mouthfuls of pie, Sheriff Yule wiped his mouth with his shirt sleeve and told Barr, "You in a heap 'a trouble, boy."

"I know I am." Barr shrugged and smiled, like he just couldn't help what he did.

"You ever been 'round Biloxi?"

"Sure. How can anyone forget Biloxi?" Barr grinned at Camille and me.

"You ever been to da' Starlight Hotel?"

"Sure." Barr leaned back and nodded. "Starlight. Starbright. What star do I see tonight?" He sang it.

Yule took a hit of his coffee, then said, "A man who looked an awful lot like you left da' Starlight a month ago with the hotel owner, Art Jefferson. You have any idea what happen' to Mr. Jefferson?"

Barr nodded. "Yeah. I had to kill him." He fanned his coat. "This is his suit I'm wearing."

I had to catch Camille and move her to a booth, where she recovered slowly, batting her eyes at me, squeezing both my hands. I looked at Barr as he told the Sheriff and Ruby how Art Jefferson had let him audition for the Starlight, had him sing and dance.

"We were drinking Bourbon and I saw Art spiking my drinks, giving me twice as much Bourbon as he gave himself. He asked if I had a place to stay and offered to put me up for a night or two, so I went home with him.

"That's when he grabbed me and we fought and I had to kill him. He was a pervert, you know. But he had good taste in clothes." Barr fanned the coat again.

He looked at Camille and must have seen the expression on her face because Barr became suddenly serious. "I was desperate, Baby. For money. *For money,* Baby. That's all. That's the only trouble I've ever gotten into."

What about murder?

Camille covered her face with her hands and Barr shrugged. He looked up at the sheriff and said, "You see, I have a weakness for beautiful women." He nodded toward Camille and then at Ruby who snorted at the fool.

"I have da' same weakness," Yule said. "Only I ain't a moron."

Another deputy arrived and Yule told him to keep an eye on Barr. Yule called out to me, "What's the name of dat lieutenant back in N'Awlins?"

I gave him Frenchy's name and the direct number to the Detective Bureau and Yule went in the back to use the phone. He came out ten minutes later, while Camille was in the ladies room.

"I have something else for you sheriff," I said and Yule stepped over. I told him about the shirt I found in Barr's room at the LaSalle with the initials *A.J.* on the pocket.

"Sounds like more 'a Jefferson's good taste in clothes."

"I'll make sure you get it."

"Good. Now we're all goin' down to the office for some statements. Ruby, you gon' hav' ta' close up a spell."

•

It was almost midnight before Camille and I were finished. Yule gave me back my gun and asked if Camille was gon' be all right. She nodded.

Yule told us the shoes Barr was wearing belonged to the Jung Hotel victim. "This boy's bad news."

I had a question. "What exactly is a high sheriff? Is there a low sheriff?"

Yule chuckled. "Naw, da' boys just like to kid me, like I'm da' sheriff of Nottinum. You know, like in Robin Hood."

Sheriff of Nottingham? Jesus.

As Camille and I stepped into the dark Mississippi night, I asked why she hadn't mentioned the broach to the Sheriff.

She turned those big blue-gray eyes to me and said, "Can we spend the night here?" She moved her face up toward mine and turned her head and I met her lips half-way. It was a soft kiss, a very soft, gentle kiss that nearly rocked me on my heels. She pulled away and took my hand.

I drove the Tucker back into Bay St. Louis and found a stately-looking hotel, once a Victorian mansion, in the center of the small town. No, we didn't do it. We took separate rooms. Her idea. And I had a hard time falling asleep, thinking of her lying in the next room.

•

She looked just as beautiful the next morning, waiting for me out on the front veranda. She had another surprise for me. She wanted to see Barr, so we went back to the Sheriff's Department only the judge wouldn't allow any visitors. No bail. No visitors.

On our way out of town, we passed Frenchy Capdeville in his black prowl car, barreling along Highway 90 as if there was no speed limit in Mississippi. Camille said nothing the entire way home. It was a fast ride home in a car with a 'rear-mounted flat-six helicopter engine'. She kissed me again, before letting me out on Barracks Street. The same, soft kiss, no tongues, but it still rocked me.

She called me once a week after that until Byron Barr's trial. Sometimes we talked about Barr. I told her I thought he was such a show-off, he couldn't help bragging about what he'd done. The papers were full of his exploits and his picture. Camille agreed but I could tell it was reluctant. Sometimes we talked about world affairs.

In June, we talked about how Truman called the nation 'hysterical' over Reds, how the nation 'isn't going to hell, despite the wave of anti-communism hysteria'. She agreed with Truman speaking out against screening books taught in schools.

I had just finished reading in the paper how Jake La Motta knocked out Marcel Cerdan to capture the middleweight title. I mentioned it in passing and she jumped right on it, glad an American had retaken the title.

In July, when RCA announced the invention of a system to broadcast color television, she called all excited about it. I had to admit I didn't even have a black and white set yet. I told her I went to movies a lot, invited her to come along, but she declined. I asked her out a dozen times, but she always said no, but thanked me for asking.

In early August, we talked about the Ingrid Bergman scandal, how Hollywood's latest Joan of Arc left her husband for another man, Italian film director Roberto Rossellini. Later in August, she called to ask if I could take her to Byron Barr's trial. No problem. She stayed on the line, upset over the death of

Margaret Mitchell who was hit by a speeding car in Atlanta. She hoped they'd find a sequel to *Gone With The Wind* among her papers. I had to admit, it was a pretty good book and a great movie.

•

I had driven by her place enough times to recognize she'd had the camellia bushes removed from the side of her immaculately white, three-story, Greek Revival house. There was a front gallery along its second floor, supported by six Greek columns. Camille lived with an elderly aunt and uncle. I'd hadn't seen her since our foray into Mississippi.

I parked my new 1950 Ford four-door sedan in the crushed-rock driveway and watched her come down the wide staircase from the gallery. She'd cut her hair, but not too short, and wore another gray outfit. I recognized it as part of the new 'Dior' look (I've always liked looking at models in the advertising sections of the paper). She wore a light gray silk jacket with rounded corners and a neatly nipped waistline over a pleated skirt that was only about ten inches from the ground, too long. Not figure-hugging, but elegant on Camille, who'd look good in a burlap sack, especially a short burlap sack.

"Is this a new car?"

"Yep." I explained how I picked out a Ford because it's like every other car on the road. I needed to blend in. Can't imagine a PI riding around in a red sports car. Actually my black Ford served another purpose. It was identical to NOPD's unmarked prowl cars. Civilians wouldn't notice, but criminals might and leave me alone on stakeouts.

At first she didn't seem nervous, sitting next to me with her legs crossed, that same perfume stirring my pulse. When I parked on Tulane Avenue, just down from the courthouse, I noticed her hand shaking as she checked herself out in the mirror of her compact.

The Criminal Courts Building was a foreboding place, a gray concrete hulk at the corner of Tulane and Broad with the barbed wire Parish Prison attached to its rear. Built around 1930, the building had less charm than the German Reichstag.

Moving down the long, marble hall, the sound of Camille's high heels echoing off the high ceiling, I recognized George Crane in the crowd outside the courtroom. The hotel dick wore an ill-fitting, blue seersucker suit, his eyes lighting up at seeing Camille. Crane introduced me to David Meyer, a short man in a white suit and a reporter's notepad in hand. I introduced Camille, who grabbed my hand and held on, to fend off the leering men.

"I hear you're the man who put it all together," Meyer told me.

"Who told you that?"

He pointed to Crane who winked at me because he sicked the press on me. Helluva joke. I told Meyer he'd got it wrong, but I could see he wasn't convinced.

"The trial sure came around fast," Crane said.

"That's because Barr waived all pre-trial motions," Meyer explained, which I could see perked Camille's curiosity. "He could have stood trial in Mississippi first, but the high sheriff told me the D.A. wasn't keen on it. Afraid Barr would get a sympathetic jury, killing an alleged homosexual." Meyer's high-pitched voice grated on me and I tried to walk away, only Camille hung in place.

"Killing a prominent businessman in a swanky New Orleans hotel is another story." Meyer nodded to punctuate his statement. The Barr Case had generated a lot of publicity. I just hadn't read the bylines to realize, at the time, Meyer was the one milking the case.

"The wonderful Mr. Byron Barr has been holding press conferences in parish prison." Meyer checked out Camille again, from head to toe, causing her to move behind me. "Sings and dances for us and the other prisoners. The man's quite an exhibitionist. Claims this is all because he loves women." Meyer turned to Camille. "Did he know you?"

Camille pulled me closer.

"Guess not." Meyer nodded to me. "Sorry, pal. It's just Barr gave me the names of two women here in town and both thought they were engaged to him. He's quite a character."

Camille squeezed my hand so hard it hurt. As the trial started, we remained in the hall. In Louisiana, witnesses were sequestered and couldn't watch the proceedings. We were also not supposed to talk about the case in the hall. Camille and I sat on a bench across the wide hall, away from everyone. I spotted the Hines family, clumped together just outside the courtroom, the widow still in black and two grown sons, one with a pretty good looking red-headed wife.

Ruby Stevens came late and I almost didn't recognize her in a lavender skirt-suit that was a little too short. She really had nice legs. All made up, with her long blonde hair hanging free to her shoulders, she looked very nice. Smiling shyly, she came up and asked if she could sit with us. She sat on the other side of me from Camille and immediately announced she felt Byron Barr was insane. Camille leaned over me and agreed, saying she'd hired a doctor who would substantiate it.

When she turned those gray-blues to me, I asked, "You're working for the defense?"

"I don't want him to hang."

When I was called to testify that afternoon, I noticed Barr was wearing Jefferson's suit, or more-likely a pretty good copy. I wondered if he was wearing Hines' shoes as I took the witness stand. He smiled and waved at me as I was sworn in. He smiled through my entire testimony, leaning forward, listening intently as I explained how I'd put two and two together to come up with four. It didn't seem like much to me, although the D.A. played it up as if I'd solved the Jack the Ripper Murders.

Yes, I went to the LaSalle and then the Jung and called Homicide. Yes, I went to Mississippi and Barr confessed to me. I had to add that he actually confessed to Sheriff Yule and there were others present. Even Barr's defense attorney, the famed mob lawyer Robert Modini, acted as if he was in awe of what I'd done. I figured he was going to paint the police as being incompetent.

Camille wore a charcoal gray skirt-suit the following day. Ruby wore yellow and kept making eyes at me, you know, staring into my eyes for long seconds as we sat in the hall. I had a hard time reading the newspaper. David Meyer laid it on thick with a story he entitled: Private Cop Solves Murder. At least he spelled my name correctly, while making me look like a mix of Sherlock Holmes and Mike Hammer. He described me as having 'piercing brown eyes'.

Jesus.

Ruby testified the second day and like me, was asked to stay around until testimony was completed.

Camille wore a pale gray dress the third day, another 'Dior' type with a matching jacket. Ruby wore a different yellow dress that was almost transparent when she stood next to the large windows with the sun beaming through. Camille was upset, not because of what Ruby wore, but because she was never called to testify.

"I guess the D.A. doesn't want to muddy the water with too much redundant testimony." I told her. "Defense lawyers love to search for inconsistencies in witnesses' stories."

Camille couldn't understand why the *defense* didn't call her, although it did call the psychiatrist she hired. Meyer came out and told us her doctor testified that Byron Barr suffered from a neurological disorder, only the judge cut the testimony short because the state had produced two doctors who testified Barr was legal sane.

"He keeps humming," Meyer said. "He greets each juror, waving and winking. He even broke into a little tap dance after the jury filed out."

"Crazy," Ruby said.

"So this neurological disorder," Camille cut in. "That won't help him?"

Meyer shrugged. "He's been screwing up for too long. He got a dishonorable discharge from the army for sleeping with a colonel's wife."

I could feel Camille stiffen as she sat next to me. She was just as stiff the following evening when the jury returned with its verdict. We were allowed in and sat at the rear of the courtroom, Camille holding my left hand in both of hers. The judge had Barr rise and he bounced up and waved at the jury. The jury found Barr guilty of murder.

The words echoed through the room, accompanied by gasps and mumbling. Byron Barr just nodded, then shrugged, turned and smiled at the crowd – the place was packed with mostly women. The judge asked if Barr had anything to say.

"Yes." Barr opened his arms and addressed the jury. "Gentlemen, you have my best wishes."

Camille was so pale, I thought she was going to faint.

•

It rained that evening and I watched the black clouds over the rooftops of the lower Quarter, watched the rain pelt the roofs, bounce in the street below my apartment balcony, wash across my building in sheets.

My doorbell rang, so I buzzed the downstairs door and stepped out on the landing. She came up the stairs wearing a black raincoat and hat and I didn't realize it was Ruby until she took off the hat and shook out her long, blonde hair. I held my door open and she stepped in without a word. I don't think we said ten words that evening.

She started taking off her clothes on the way to my bedroom and I followed. Ruby wasn't the woman I wanted but she was the one I got. She was pretty athletic and nearly wore me out. Twice. There was nothing between us beyond the sex and the next morning Ruby returned to the piney woods of Mississippi. I returned to work and never saw her again.

•

Thanks to the publicity from David Meyer's articles, I had a lot of business all of a sudden. Camille called me every evening between the verdict and the day the judge sentenced Byron Barr, but she stayed away from the sentencing.

I sat next to Meyer in the same courtroom, even more crowded than before, women mostly. Byron Barr came in wearing the now-famous navy blue suit and a huge smile. He actually tap danced to the defense table. The judge asked if Barr had anything to say before sentence was pronounced.

"Not really, your Honor."

The judged sentenced him to death by hanging. Gasps echoed through the courtroom. Two women cried at either ends of the room.

Barr opened his arms once again and said, "Thank you, your Honor. I'll try not to make a fuss." He turned to his audience and said, "It was money. If it wasn't for *lack* of it, I'd have never gotten into trouble."

He pulled his arms down and stuffed his hand in his coat pockets. "I never intended to harm anyone." He looked up at the ceiling and in a deep voice, announced, "My only weakness is beautiful women."

Meyer wrote it down verbatim.

Outside the courtroom, he grabbed my arm and asked why Camille wasn't with me. "She's visited him in jail more than any of the others," he said, which sent a sickening feeling through my stomach. "She brings him a rose every time, a blood red rose."

I thanked him for keeping her name out of the paper. He said I owed him for that. "Don't forget," he reminded me as I walked away.

That evening, when Camille called I asked her about the broach.

"Oh, that's gone I guess," she said in her sad voice. "I heard about the sentence on the radio this afternoon. Are they really going to hang him?"

"They usually do."

She changed the subject, telling me how she was upset the Russians got the atom bomb. "It's the worst news I've heard, since the war."

I told her it was inevitable. Military advancements never remained secrets long.

"I guess you're right. Like gunpowder. The Chinese had it for centuries, just making fireworks with it until the Europeans found out about it and realized they could blow up things with it."

Boy was she ever right.

•

Camille didn't call the next evening, nor the next. I called and left a message with the maid, but our regular night talks had ended. Byron Barr stayed in the news. David Meyer kept my name in the news too, even reporting the results of my subsequent investigation of the internal thefts at D.H. Holmes Department Store. I expected the store to publicize how they caught two middle managers stealing from the registers, but didn't think they'd disclose they used a private investigator, much less mention my name. Of course, I gave Meyer some inside scoop, which dressed up his story.

I owed him, after all.

I was beginning to think I'd need a secretary or maybe a partner with all the business I got from the publicity. The busier I got, the more I thought about those sad, blue-gray eyes, and the elegant line of Camille's face, and those crimson lips and sleek calves.

Camille called later in the year, telling me she'd just read a book by a British writer about a grim future. The book was *Nineteen Eighty-Four.* She called in February when the same writer, George Orwell, suddenly died. I told her she was right about the book and how I thought it was the best book I'd read in a long time.

In March, she called, furious about Klaus Fuchs, who was sentenced to only fourteen years for giving the Russians the atom bomb. "And look at Barr's sentence," she complained. I let her go on, never telling her I thought Byron Barr was getting what he should have expected. The bastard sure garnered enough publicity, holding press conferences in jail, entertaining the newspapermen.

Byron Barr composed a song for his execution and, according to David Meyer's newspaper account of the hanging, sang it on the way to the gallows. It was called, 'I'm Fit as a Fiddle and Ready to Hang'. Barr's last words to the assembled was, "Don't forget me."

Camille called at eight o'clock that evening. "Can you come over?"

I was there in fifteen minutes.

She opened the large carved wooden door, stepping from behind in a white slip, a brandy snifter in her left hand, her hair loose around her face, those pouty lips painted cherry red. I closed the door and followed her swaying hips through the foyer into a study, where she sat on a dark green sofa and crossed her legs. She pulled her slip up over her knees.

"I'm sorry," she began. "Do you want a drink?"

I shook my head. "Are you drunk, little lady?"

"This is my first drink." She raised it and took a sip, making a face as the liquor went down. I sat in the love seat across an ornate wood and glass coffee table from her and told her I didn't think she drank.

"I don't. This is a special occasion."

"It is?"

"Yes. And you know why." She took another sip and put the snifter on the coffee table. "He's gone."

Uncrossing her legs, she leaned over toward an end table and picked up a white envelope. She tried to toss it to me, but it fell next to the coffee table. I picked it up. The envelope had Camille's name on it but no stamp. As I pulled the letter out, I figured he gave it to her in person. Yep, it was from Barr, all right.

Dearest Camille,

I hope you will miss me as I have missed you. I am sorry for putting you through all of this. Don't forget me, Byron

Camille blinked back tears, her lips trembling as she said, "He probably sent the same note to a dozen women." She tried to laugh, but it came out as a cry. I moved to the sofa and put my arm around her, pulling her to my chest as she cried. Just as I was thinking I'll never figure women, she stopped crying and asked, "Am I pretty?"

I let out a long breath. She pulled away and looked into my eyes, wiping hers with her fingers.

"Am I pretty?"

I nodded slowly. "My God, you are beautiful. Absolutely gorgeous." I cupped my hands around her face and drew her to me. She closed her eyes and pursed her lips and I kissed them ever so softly. I felt that kiss through my entire body. Our lips began to move against each others and the kiss intensified. Her mouth parted and our tongues touched and I moved her across my lap. I felt her arms around my shoulder as she hugged me closer.

She pulled back and kissed my lips again and again, in a frenzy, then sank her tongue into my mouth for another long, passionate French kiss. I felt my fingers creep up and pushed down her slip strap and bra strap. Camille pulled her mouth from mine, and pressed her forehead to mine and whispered, "I want you to come up to my room with me."

I nodded.

"I want you to make love to me on my bed."

She stood and pulled my hands up to her and led me through the house, turning off lights as we went to a spiral staircase and up to the second floor.

Camille's bedroom was pink lace and white furniture, her bed, old fashioned with a lace canopy atop, one of those beds you had to climb up into. She climbed on and I followed as she lay on her back. I hovered over her face and kissed her again and slowly undressed her. Camille Javal's body was like alabaster – creamy pink and soft-warm that sent rivets of fire-passion through my fingers as I caressed her. She was the most loving woman I'd ever touched. As our passion rose and I looked down into her eyes, I saw such emotion there, it surprised me.

"Oh, Lucien."

After – as our bodies struggled to return to normal she told me she had wanted to give me what Byron Barr never had. Then she gave it to me again.

•

It rained the next day and the next, nearly flooding the streets.

I called Camille three times, but the maid said she wasn't in, even late in the evening. I left messages.

The third morning, Frenchy Capdeville woke me with a phone call that left me sitting up in bed, my heart aching, my eyes burning. She'd left a note on her end table next to the empty bottle of barbiturates she used to leave this world. He gave me the note at the morgue.

My Dear Lucien,

Thanks for all your kindness.   Please don't forget me, Camille

It occurred to me, as I stood there with shaking hands, I should have expected this.

•

I look up at angry, gray rain clouds moving overhead as the graveyard workers hurry to seal up Camille's oven tomb with quick-drying mortar. They'll have to put her headstone on later. The rain comes and I stay, letting it slap my face, pepper me with heavy drops. I keep staring at the quick-drying mortar. I know she's lying in there in another gray dress, her arms crossed.

Don't know what I feel exactly as I stand here, except a terrible loss.

Don't know what I've learned from all this, except I'll never forget her.

How could I?

END OF EXPECT CONSEQUENCES and

THE END

of

NEW ORLEANS CONFIDENTIAL

ABOUT THE WRITER

O'Neil De Noux writes realistic crime fiction featuring the accurate dialogue of the street and strong settings, primarily New Orleans. He also writes breath-taking erotica and science fiction adventure stories in the vein of Edgar Rice Burroughs. His publishing credits include seven novels, five short story collections and over two hundred short stories published in multiple genres.

De Noux's published novels include *GRIM REAPER, THE BIG KISS, BLUE ORLEANS, CRESCENT CITY KILLS, THE BIG SHOW, MAFIA APHRODITE* and *SLICK TIME. THE BIG KISS* was translated into Swedish and published in Sweden in 2006, under the title *TVÅ HÅL I HUVDET* (*TWO HOLES IN THE HEAD*). His short story collections include *NEW ORLEANS MYSTERIES, HOLLOW POINT/THE MYSTERY OF ROCHELLE MARAIS, NEW ORLEANS NOCTURNAL* and *LASTANZA: NEW ORLEANS POLICE STORIES*, which received an "A" rating from *ENTERTAINMENT WEEKLY MAGAZINE.* De Noux adapted one of the *LASTANZA* stories "Waiting for Alaina" into a screenplay, which was filmed in New Orleans and broadcast on local TV in 2001.

In March 2006, the first edition of *NEW ORLEANS CONFIDENTIAL* was published by Point*Blank* Press. From *Publisher's Weekly*, 3/13/06: "Former homicide detective De Noux turns out an engaging, fast-paced collection of stories featuring private eye and womanizer extraordinaire Lucien Caye as he tracks philandering husbands, possible murderers and missing cats. Set predominantly against the rich backdrop of 1940s New Orleans, these stories-abounding with ample bosoms and willing women-are fun, and the author knows his stuff when it comes to the Big Easy."

In May 2006, *NEW ORLEANS IRRESISTIBLE*, a collection of erotic detective stories by O'Neil De Noux, was published by EAA Signature Series Books. *AMERICAN CASANOVA – The*

New Adventures of the Legendary Lover, A Collaboration of 15 Writers Directed by Maxim Jakubowski was also published in 2006 (Avalon Publishing, New York). A non-fiction book, *SPECIFIC INTENT*, was a lead title from Pinnacle Books and a main selection of the Doubleday Book Club. This true-crime book details the intricate police investigation of a murder case which shocked south Louisiana.

O'Neil De Noux's short stories have been published in the U.S., Canada, Denmark, England, France, Germany, Greece, Italy, Japan, Portugal, Scotland, Sweden and Ukraine. From 1993 to 2005, De Noux taught creative writing and mystery writing at Tulane University, University of New Orleans and Delgado Community College. After Hurricanes Katrina and Rita, De Noux taught creative writing at McNeese State University, Lake Charles, LA. He is the founding editor of two fiction magazines, *MYSTERY STREET* and *NEW ORLEANS STORIES*.

O'Neil De Noux has worked as a homicide detective and organized crime investigator. He has also been a private investigator, U.S. Army combat photographer, criminal intelligence analyst, newspaper writer, magazine editor, computer graphics designer. As a police officer, De Noux received seven commendations for solving difficult murder cases. In 1981, he was named 'Homicide Detective Of The Year' for the Jefferson Parish Sheriff's Office. In 1989, he was proclaimed an 'Expert Witness' on the homicide crime scene in Criminal District Court, New Orleans, LA. Mr. De Noux is a graduate of Archbishop Rummel High School in Metairie, LA, Alabama's Troy University, and The Southern Police Institute of the University of Louisville, KY (Homicide Investigation).

After his home was seriously damaged by Hurricane Katrina, O'Neil De Noux re-settled on the northshore of Lake Pontchartrain in 2006 and returned to law enforcement. He is currently a Police Investigator with the Southeastern Louisiana

University Police Department in Hammond, LA. In 2008, De Noux was awarded the department's highest decoration, the *Chief's Award of Excellence* for outstanding service.

In September 2009, O'Neil De Noux received an Artist Services ***Career Advancement Award for 2009-2010*** from the Louisiana Division of the Arts for work on his forthcoming historical novel set during The Battle of New Orleans.

•

ALSO BY THE AUTHOR
Novels
Grim Reaper
The Big Kiss
Blue Orleans
Crescent City Kills
The Big Show
Mafia Aphrodite
Slick Time

Short Story Collections
LaStanza: New Orleans Police Stories
Hollow Point & The Mystery of Rochelle Marais
New Orleans Irresistible
New Orleans Mysteries
New Orleans Nocturnal

Screenplay
Waiting for Alaina

Non-Fiction
Specific Intent
A Short Guide to Writing and Selling Fiction

•

"O'Neil De Noux ... No one writes New Orleans as well as he does." James Sallis

" ... the author knows his stuff when it comes to the Big Easy." *Publisher's Weekly*, 3/13/06

NEW BOOKS by De Noux
http://www.oneildenoux.net

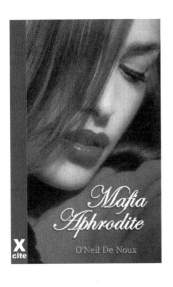

11467240R0015

Made in the USA
Lexington, KY
06 October 2011